"Oh."

Casey let out a breath. She didn't look fed up anymore, just resigned. That bothered Jack more than her stubbornness. "I guess it's time I accepted you the way you are," she said. "That's why we can't be together any longer."

Perversely, he wanted to argue, but to what end? He'd nursed the fantasy that he could win Casey back on his own terms, but her pregnancy made that impossible. Whatever fantasy she'd clung to about him, he'd apparently popped that balloon, as well.

"I guess we both need to accept each other," he conceded. "You're in a difficult situation and I'm doing my best to help. Now, would you like to come with me to interview your tenants?"

She dumped the crocheting on the coffee table. "Sure," she said. "Let me get my jacket."

It was a truce of sorts, Jack thought. He hoped it would last.

Dear Reader,

A special magic happens when a hero and heroine come to life. It's something that an author tries her best to engineer, but she can't count on it, no matter how carefully she plans their backgrounds, their motives and their personality quirks.

That's what happened the first time I wrote dialogue between Jack and Casey, in the second part of chapter one. Although their story is a serious one involving a pregnancy, a mystery and a town with secrets, I found myself chuckling at the way she torpedoed his attempts to stick to logic.

I guess an author isn't supposed to admit she laughs at her own jokes, but I have to be honest. It's fun to hear what these characters decide to say completely on their own. I feel privileged to be the first to witness their unexpected actions, too. And I'm grateful, because they give rise to plot twists a lot more rewarding than anything I could intentionally construct.

I enjoy hearing from readers, either at my mail address (P.O. Box 1315, Brea, CA 92822) or via e-mail, jdiamondfriends@aol.com. I do my best to answer all mail. As well, you can check on my upcoming releases at eHarlequin.com and at jacquelinediamond.com.

Thanks for reading!

Warmly,

Jacqueline Diamond

JACQUELINE DIAMOND

THE BABY'S BODYGUARD

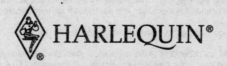

HARLEQUIN®

TORONTO • NEW YORK • LONDON
AMSTERDAM • PARIS • SYDNEY • HAMBURG
STOCKHOLM • ATHENS • TOKYO • MILAN • MADRID
PRAGUE • WARSAW • BUDAPEST • AUCKLAND

ISBN 0-373-75050-1

THE BABY'S BODYGUARD

Copyright © 2004 by Jackie Hyman.

www.eHarlequin.com

Printed in U.S.A.

ABOUT THE AUTHOR

A former Associated Press reporter, Jacqueline Diamond has written more than sixty novels and received a Career Achievement Award from *Romantic Times Book Club* magazine. Jackie lives in Southern California with her husband, two sons and two cats.

Books by Jacqueline Diamond

HARLEQUIN AMERICAN ROMANCE

913—THE IMPROPERLY PREGNANT PRINCESS
962—DIAGNOSIS: EXPECTING BOSS'S BABY
971—PRESCRIPTION: MARRY HER IMMEDIATELY
978—PROGNOSIS: A BABY? MAYBE

Chapter One

One stuffed bear in the crib atop the yellow-and-white comforter. Check.

One set of freshly painted walls stenciled with birds in flight. Check.

One changing table with drawers, one diaper stacker and one set of white shelves—the latest addition—screwed neatly into the wall. Check.

Something was missing.

How about a husband? Casey asked herself ruefully as she replaced the screwdriver in her tool kit.

Actually, she had a husband, although not for much longer. She'd expected him to sign their divorce papers weeks ago so they could finalize the split, but so far her lawyer reported no success.

Probably Jack was off to some exotic locale providing security services for a client. You could always count on him to be there when people needed him.

Except for his wife. And the daughter he hadn't wanted.

Tears pricked Casey's eyes as her hand cupped the bulge. It rippled in response. Less than a month to go until she could hold the little girl in her arms, count the fingers and gaze into her loving eyes.

Casey had already picked out a name: Diane. She'd always loved the sound and flow of it, like running water in the moonlight.

She hadn't hesitated when Dr. Smithson asked if she wanted to know the gender. There'd been enough surprises already, including this pregnancy.

Jack would be furious if he found out. He'd adamantly opposed having children. The issue had hardened into the wedge that drove them apart, although they'd had other, less obvious problems. But she believed they might have worked those out.

Toolbox in hand, Casey took one more fond look around the room before turning off the light, and that's when she realized what was missing. Books. She wanted her daughter to grow up smelling leather-bound volumes even before she could read.

That, at least, Jack would approve of.

She went into the living room to select a couple of classics from her collection. When the phone rang, she scooped the handset absentmindedly off an end table while trying to choose among such favorites as *Black Beauty*, *The Wind in the Willows* and *Little Women*.

"Arnett residence."

"Casey, it's Gail." Tension underscored the gravelly voice. "Remember the prowler? He's back."

Casey stiffened. Instinctively, she glanced through the living-room window into the darkness. But if someone lurked outside, she couldn't tell.

Ten months ago, when she'd moved back to Richfield Crossing, Tennessee, to manage the rustic property she'd inherited from her parents, she'd loved the rental cabins and the slightly larger main house. She'd considered the property charmingly rural, not isolated. These last few weeks had given her second thoughts.

A sixtyish nurse who worked for Dr. Smithson, Gail Fordham wasn't easily intimidated, but the prowler she and other tenants had spotted during the past month had rattled her as well as Casey.

"Did you call the police?" Unfortunately, the local constabulary consisted of one aging chief, a part-time rookie, a dispatcher shared with several other towns and a few clerks.

"Sure. They said they'd have someone swing by, but you know how much good that will do." Quickly, Gail added, "I'm not afraid for myself, Casey. I figure if it's Dean, he'll get bored after a while and go away or drink so heavily we'll find him snoozing in somebody's hayloft." Dean was Gail's alcoholic ex-husband who lived in Michigan. "I just wanted to warn you so you won't go outside and run into whoever it is."

"Thanks. I appreciate it."

"If you're worried, I could come over and sleep on your couch. It's not good for you to be alone this close to delivery," the nurse said.

"You shouldn't go outside while he's around," she warned.

"I've got a baseball bat. If I run into that jerk, it'll be the worse for him." The image of the middle-aged nurse clopping an intruder dispelled some of Casey's tension. "And I'll make sure you get the sleep you need."

For a flicker of an instant, Casey allowed herself to imagine how comforting it would feel to have someone watching over her. It wasn't Gail who came to mind, however, but Jack.

Why isn't my own husband here when I need him?

Resolutely, she yanked herself out of incipient self-pity. She owned the property. If anyone ought to take responsibility for the tenants' safety, it was Casey. Her parents had taught her never to pass the buck, and she didn't intend to start now.

"I've got my own baseball bat," she said. "I'll handle him, Gail."

"Now wait a minute! What if he's armed?"

She *would* have to mention that. "I'm just going to take a look around. At least we could settle once and for all whether it's Dean." Although she'd never met the man, she had Gail's description of him as balding and in his sixties.

"Think about the baby. You can't take any risks with her!"

"She'd be proud of her mom. Don't worry, Gail. I'll be careful."

Despite the fact that she'd taken self-defense classes while living in Los Angeles, Casey had no illusions about her own invincibility. But the situation brought home the fact that she was going to be raising a daughter by herself. Suppose this creep lived around here and got the idea that he could make Casey and her tenants—who included several retired people—cower in fear.

Not on her watch.

Okay, so she had sometimes acted on impulse. Like marrying Jack two months after she'd met him. And sleeping with him eight months ago when she went back to L.A. to hammer out the details of their divorce, resulting in a pregnancy that she hadn't told her husband about and hoped she wouldn't have to.

Sometimes her lack of foresight got her into hot water, Casey conceded. But this trespasser made her mad. And the last time she'd called the police, it had taken them forty-five minutes to show up.

The only problem, she realized, was that some gardening tools that might serve as weapons lay tucked in the storage shed behind the carport. They could only be accessed by going outside.

Why not take her camera? In the darkness, its flash might ferret out a suspect she couldn't see and it would certainly provide a means of identifying him. She wouldn't need to attack anyone or even get close.

Jack would hate the idea. If he were here, he'd warn her, as Gail had, that the man might be armed. But this wasn't L.A.; it was Richfield Crossing, a town of around five thousand people where crime consisted mostly of fistfights outside the Whiskey Flats pool hall. Most likely the prowler would turn out to be a mixed-up teenager or a transient looking for food.

Casey threw on a sweater against the April coolness and retrieved her digital camera along with a flashlight. She also took a key and locked the door, although normally she left it open.

On the porch, as her eyes adjusted to the moonlight, she breathed in the perfume of blooms mingled with the scent of newly plowed fields a short distance away. A cool, moist breeze reminded her of last night's fast-moving rainstorm.

Casey's heart swelled with love for this place. Six years ago, she and her best friend, Sandra Rawlins, had moved west, full of dreams and fantasies. It had taken many changes and the breakup of her marriage to make Casey realize that Tennessee was where she belonged. More than ever, she appreciated the fact that her parents had bought this property, the Pine Woods Court, for their retirement. She just wished they'd had more time to enjoy it.

Still, if only Jack had agreed to have a family together, she'd have stayed in L.A. with him. The more she'd pleaded, however, the more he'd withdrawn, until nothing remained between them but a strained civility. That, and the white-hot passion that had flamed at their last meeting.

Casey didn't regret what she'd done, because she loved her daughter even before birth. And she felt glad that at least she had a beautiful place to come home to, where Diane could grow up surrounded by old friends and lots of open space.

Unfortunately, right now that space had been compromised by someone who was obviously no friend. Someone about to be captured for posterity in all his digital ugliness.

As her vision adjusted, nearby dogwood trees came into focus, their pink blossoms appearing white in the dimness. Eager to catch the culprit before he escaped, Casey descended the steps in her rubber-soled shoes.

The four cabins, former motel units that her parents had remodeled into rentals, lay scattered about the wooded property behind the main house. To reach Gail's place, she followed a footpath along rising ground, leaving her flashlight off to avoid attracting attention.

As she walked, the muscles of her abdomen, perpetually sore these days, tugged from the weight of the baby. Ignoring them, Casey listened for the crack of a twig or the brush of leaves.

She was nearing Gail's place when she heard a creaking ahead, like that of a wheelbarrow or perhaps the hose storage reel. The trespasser might have bumped into something, or perhaps a raccoon was poking around with its dexterous little hands. The creatures abounded in the woods, along with possums, squirrels and deer.

"Gail?" Casey risked calling out, since she didn't want the tenant to attack her by mistake. "Is that you?"

No answer.

When she emerged from the tree-lined path, the illumination seeping through the cabin windows intensified the surrounding darkness. Now Casey remembered what else she should have brought—her cell phone—although the darn thing didn't always work up here, anyway.

She heard another squeak behind the cabin. Treading lightly, she angled closer.

In the shadows, a dark figure moved. Holding her breath, Casey lifted her camera and pushed the button.

As the flash ignited, a blast of icy water caught her full in the face. She staggered backward, dropping the camera and fighting a losing battle for balance. Her arms flailed as she tumbled, out of control.

Fear for the baby's safety stabbed through Casey, followed by the jolt of her rear end hitting the ground. Ahead, scurrying noises marked the prowler's flight into the woods.

He'd escaped. This time, he'd physically assaulted her and put her pregnancy at risk.

Although she'd avoided any real harm, hot fury dispelled Casey's shivers. She was going to catch this creep, no matter what it took. And no matter who she had to call on for assistance.

AS JACK SQUEEZED ALONG the aisle, a travel bag slung over his shoulder and his laptop tucked beneath one arm, the flight attendant favored him with a warm smile and her umpteenth once-over. Marianne had the healthy tan of a surfer, a bubbly personality and an obvious interest in getting better acquainted.

They'd found several occasions for idle conversation during the flight from Hawaii, where he'd changed planes after arriving from Malaysia. Marianne had made a discreet inquiry regarding the absence of a wedding ring and responded to his explanation about his pending divorce by slipping her phone number onto his tray.

As he returned her cheerful farewell, Jack felt the card inside his pocket. He ought to call her before she headed out of L.A. again on the Honolulu run.

His partner in the Men At Arms Security Agency had insisted he take a day or two off to recuperate from a month of fourteen-hour days spent setting up a security system for a textile company. He wouldn't mind spending his break with a willing companion.

Jack didn't want to bring her to his Palms-area home, though. During the past eight months, he'd discovered that having a guest around only made the place seem emptier. Besides, it struck him as disloyal to Casey to take a woman to the house they'd once shared, even though she was the one who'd chosen to leave.

As he headed for the baggage claim, his cell phone rang. Seven-fifteen on a Friday evening and somebody couldn't wait, Jack reflected wryly. Moving out of the stream of foot traffic, he flipped it open. "Arnett."

"Jack! It's me." The hint of a Tennessee accent carried him out of his surroundings and into a warm zone he'd discovered the day he met Casey.

"How're you doing?" Somehow, he managed a casual manner that gave no hint of the hot summer storm she aroused.

"I'm standing here dripping wet and my butt's sore."

The tantalizing image speeded his heart rate. He imagined his shapely wife with a T-shirt plastered against her lovely breasts, writhing eagerly against him as his hands cupped her bottom.

Put a lid on it, Arnett. She left you. Besides, she probably wants to know why you haven't signed those divorce papers yet. "I take it you didn't call to turn me on, right?"

"Jack!"

"So what's up?" He dodged a luggage cart that threatened to take a piece of his ankle with it.

"We've got a stalker," Casey said.

The word snapped him out of his sensuous frame of mind. "What do you mean? Are you all right?" Suddenly her description of her physical state took on ominous overtones.

"Some tenants have seen a prowler a few times, possibly one of the women's ex-husband. He showed up again tonight."

"He attacked you?" Jack's gut response was to go after the guy. Having grown up in foster homes, he'd seen his share of men bullying women and it enraged him. During his years at the LAPD, he'd had to work hard to rein in his anger when dealing with domestic abuse.

And this was Casey. Maddening, alluring, a little bossy and sexy enough to melt him with one flash of her blue eyes. He'd kill anyone who hurt her.

"He squirted me with the hose and knocked me down. I didn't even get a picture of him," she grumbled.

"A picture?"

"I had my camera aimed right at him," she said.

"But you can describe him to the police, can't you?" Jack pressed.

"Well, no," she admitted. "It's dark."

He knew Casey liked to handle situations her own way but he was having trouble putting the pieces together. "Walk me through this. Did you see the prowler or not?"

"I heard him poking around behind Gail's place," she replied impatiently. "So I tried to take his picture."

"You went out alone at night, unarmed, to confront a stalker?" He barely suppressed a groan. "Did he say anything?"

"What would he say? 'Hey, that's not my good side, wait till I turn around'?" she demanded.

Jack gritted his teeth. He didn't want to argue, he wanted to get the facts straight. "You heard someone or something rummaging but you didn't actually see it. So for all you know it could have been a bear."

"A bear shot me with a hose?"

She had a point. Nevertheless, he realized, he should take nothing for granted. "You aren't standing out there soaking wet hoping he'll show up again, are you?"

"I'm not stupid!" Casey flared. "Gail heard the commotion and came out. She checked me over…I mean, she's a nurse…you know, to make sure I wasn't hurt."

"I assume you'd know if you were hurt." Judging by her outspokenness, Casey's physical condition sounded just fine. "Where are you?"

"At home. Gail left a few minutes ago. Now listen. The cops still haven't arrived. I'll be lucky if they get here by midnight." Given the time difference, that was three hours away, he noted. "I wondered if you could refer me to a security agency in Nashville. I'm not sure who to call."

He supposed he or his partner, Mike, could dig up a name, but he knew how much companies charged. "It won't be cheap. I'll help with the cost, of course."

"No, you won't." Casey had refused to accept alimony, a fact that made it even harder to explain why Jack hadn't signed the papers yet. Fortunately, she wasn't asking about those right now. "I'm the one who owns this property. I'll see to it."

Once his wife made up her mind, you either caved in or took matters into your own hands. "I'll need to do some research."

"When can you get back to me?"

"Is tomorrow soon enough?"

"That would be great." She hesitated, and for a moment Jack hoped she had something to tell him.

Maybe she regretted their split the way he did. Maybe she'd decided she loved him enough that she didn't need children to make their family complete. Maybe the separation and loneliness had given her time to think.

Jack would have done almost anything to win his wife back. But every time he looked at a child, the misery of the past nearly overwhelmed him. At eleven, with his father in prison for robbery and his mother dead of cancer, he'd gone from a home in turmoil to a series of foster placements where he'd been at best an outsider and at worst a nuisance.

The memories remained raw and the wounds barely scabbed over. The one thing he couldn't do, even for Casey, was relive them by having a child.

She broke the silence at last. "The sooner we catch this slob, the better. Several of my tenants are elderly and I don't want them to have to worry about this."

Jack tried not to register disappointment that she had nothing further to say. It almost made him angry, though, that Casey cared more about her tenants than her husband.

Well, she'd just handed him a golden opportunity to give their marriage one more try. To nab the prowler, he planned to dispatch the best-qualified security agent at his disposal. Himself.

"I'll take care of it." To forestall any protests, he added, "I'll be in touch tomorrow."

"I really appreciate it. Thanks, Jack."

"No problem." After a brisk goodbye, he clicked off.

Although he'd have preferred to get right back on a plane, Jack knew he needed to swing by his house, catch up on the mail and repack. Guiltily, he remembered the African violet he'd bought to make the place seem homier. It must have perished weeks ago, completely forgotten.

Nobody in her right mind would consider a guy like him a suitable father. Surely a little in-person persuasion would make Casey see reason. And if not, well, at least Jack would have tried. In the process, he'd take care of that prowler, too.

Readjusting the bag on his shoulder, he dropped the flight attendant's card into a trash bin with a silent apology. Then, rejoining the stream of pedestrians, he made his way toward the ticket counter.

Chapter Two

When Casey strolled into Ledbetter's Garage on Saturday, she found that Royce had dived inside the truck he was repairing. All she could see of her former high-school boyfriend was his jean-clad rear end, somewhat expanded since his football days, sticking into the air in all its glory.

"Nice view," she commented.

The clanking noises he'd been making halted abruptly. A moment later, an oil-smeared face emerged.

"Well, hi." Royce grinned flirtatiously, not at all daunted by his greasy condition. "Your car's ready to go. Tuned up, oil changed, brakes checked."

"Great." Although it galled Casey to have someone else work on her car, she couldn't perform the maintenance due to her expanded waistline. "What do I owe you?"

"Let's call it even." He shook his head, which set his light-brown ponytail waggling.

"Let's not." Casey might be short on funds, but she didn't want to owe Royce any favors. She hadn't fallen in love with him in high school and it certainly wasn't going to happen now. "I prefer to pay my debts up front."

Since her condition had become obvious, Royce had mentioned several times how much he loved kids. Too bad she couldn't picture waking up beside him every morning. Or, to be honest, any morning.

"Whatever." The mechanic ambled into his office, where an oil-smudged computer blinked below a bikini pinup calendar. Posters of football heroes covered the other walls. "A hundred and twenty-three eighty-eight, if you insist. How's your camera?"

She'd told him earlier that she planned to stop by Lanihan's Department Store to find out whether the gush of water had damaged it. "It's fine. Apparently the case protected it."

"You mean you got the guy? You know who it is?"

"Uh, no," Casey admitted. "There's this big blur where his face ought to be."

"Too bad. At least you have your camera back for the party tonight, though." Accepting her credit card, Royce swiped it through a machine.

"You bet."

Two of her tenants, Enid Purdue and Rita Rogers, were throwing her a shower. Half a dozen friends and neighbors planned to attend the event, which, due to the small size of the cabins, would take place at Casey's house.

She hadn't realized she'd mentioned it to Royce earlier when she dropped off the car, but she must have. Or else word had spread. Nothing stayed private for long in Richfield Crossing.

"So this stalker or whatever he is, you think you scared him off?" Royce asked as he waited for the computer to finish processing her bill.

"I doubt it. Seeing a pregnant lady take a tumble isn't likely to intimidate him."

"I heard the police came out." He certainly *had* been paying attention.

"Larry Malloy wouldn't scare a cockroach. And he isn't likely to find one, either, even if it's six feet tall." Although the town's young, part-time police officer had arrived half an hour after she'd called Jack, he'd taken only a cursory glance around the property. She doubted she'd ever see an arrest unless her attacker marched into the police station and confessed to the chief.

Royce handed her the charge slip. She tried not to wince as she signed it, knowing what a hole the amount would make in her bank account.

The tenants' rents had sounded like sufficient income when she decided to move here, but she hadn't realized how big a bite maintenance and taxes took out of that. Once the baby got old enough to leave with a sitter, she'd have to look for a part-time waitress job.

Royce tore off her copy and handed it over. "Casey, everybody admires your guts, but you don't have to go through this alone."

She flashed him a smile. "I'm not. I have friends."

He might have said more had a lean man in his late forties not strolled into view through the open door. "Got my truck done yet?" asked Al Rawlins, who owned the town's movie theater and video store. "Oh, hello, Casey." He clamped his mouth shut, obviously not thrilled to see her.

"Hi." She wished she didn't feel so awkward around Al and his wife Mary, who had once been like a second set of parents. "How's it going?"

"All right." Al looked meaningfully from Royce to the truck sitting with its hood open. "I'm in a hurry."

"Almost done." He headed off to finish the repairs.

Casey stood there wondering what to say, although she doubted she could patch this relationship no matter how hard she tried. She and Al's daughter Sandra had been her best friend for years. When they moved to L.A. together, she knew the Rawlinses had seen her as an anchor for their high-spirited child, but she hadn't been able to stop the aspiring actress from getting mixed up with drugs. Finally she'd had to move out for her own safety.

"Well, I'll see you around," she said at last and went out to the car. Al didn't answer.

In L.A., she'd hated the sense of letting Sandra down. A week after leaving, she'd gone back to their old apartment hoping to persuade her friend to give up drugs. She'd discovered that a couple of new people had moved in. Not only were they obviously high, but Sandra had joined them in making sarcastic remarks about do-gooders.

Although Casey had attempted a few more times to maintain the friendship, Sandra had bridled at any suggestion of what she termed pushiness. Since the conflict between them didn't help her friend, Casey had finally stopped calling.

A short time later, she'd met Jack at the restaurant where she worked as assistant manager. He'd stopped in for lunch with his partner, flirted with her and returned that evening to ask Casey on a date.

She'd been struck by how different he was from Sandra's fast-living friends and the other, rather superficial men she'd met in California. At first, she'd been drawn to his quiet strength. Later, her admiration had grown as she'd discovered both his intelligence and how hard he'd worked to overcome his lack of family support.

They'd married a few months later and spent two years together. Two years of finding out that she couldn't fill the void left inside Jack by his miserable childhood. Two years of loving a guy who spent most of his time working and who didn't know how to meet her halfway emotionally.

Casey had hoped a baby would bring them together, but he'd adamantly refused to have one. The stronger her longing grew, the more her husband had withdrawn.

Matters had come to a head a year earlier when she visited Tennessee to help her widowed mother recover from a heart attack. Being back in Richfield Crossing had made Casey realize how lonely and isolated she'd become.

On her return, she'd told Jack she was willing to stay in L.A. only if he would change his mind about children. When he refused, she'd filed for divorce.

Casey still missed him, especially at times such as last night when she'd yearned for his reassuring steadiness. But in the long run, she was better off standing on her own two feet. Besides, she had baby Diane to take care of now and to love.

Still, she couldn't pretend she preferred it this way. Or maybe the overcast sky was weighing on her spirits, she conceded as she drove along Old Richfield Road. Living in California, she'd grown accustomed to almost constant sunshine.

Casey shook her head. No use blaming the weather. The memory of last night's close encounter had heightened her sense of vulnerability and this feeling was compounded by her approaching delivery date. But she refused to yield to negative thoughts.

So what if she encountered a few obstacles? She'd never believed life was meant to be easy. And she had much to be grateful for.

Her mood lightened when she caught sight of the freshly painted green-and-white sign advertising the Pine Woods Court. Turning into the driveway past the compartmentalized community mailbox, she rounded some trees and basked in the lights shining from her house into the gray afternoon.

Casey parked in the carport. As soon as she opened the front door, the scents of vanilla and cinnamon engulfed her. She could hear pans rattling in the kitchen.

Enid and Rita must have spent hours decorating. They'd draped the walls with pink honeycomb bells and had floated bunches of baby-shaped balloons up to the ceiling. A stork centerpiece dominated the paper-covered table, with candies strewn about. On the coffee table, bowls of nuts circled a pair of candles in the form of baby bottles.

"This is fabulous." Casey hurried into the kitchen. "Whatever you're baking, it smells great."

Two flushed faces regarded her, one at the oven, where the owner was removing a tray of sweet rolls, and the other from the counter. At seventy-one, Enid Purdue still carried herself with the authority of a high-school math teacher. She wore her champagne-blond hair fluffed, with a flowered dress softening her figure. As Casey entered, she finished propping two cards on which her bold handwriting labeled one coffeepot "leaded" and the other "unleaded."

Shorter and rounder, Rita Rogers, who was about half Enid's age, manipulated the hot pan onto the stovetop. Rita might be mentally handicapped but she worked hard in the cafeteria of the Benson Glass Company and never missed a chance to help a friend. She also knew her way around an oven.

A wave of gratitude flooded through Casey. "You guys are amazing."

"Thanks." Rita glowed with pleasure.

"How's the camera?" Enid asked. "I brought mine in case we need it, but it isn't digital."

"It's fine." As she produced it from her purse, Casey no longer worried about how it had come to be damaged. A prowler now seemed a minor problem and, for all she knew, he'd already decided to make himself scarce.

The Pine Woods had been built for happiness. How could anyone ask for a better home to bring a baby into?

As she'd told Royce, she didn't need a guy. She had her friends.

JACK REALIZED as he swung through Richfield Crossing that he'd expected something different. Munching on dried jerky he'd bought at a convenience store, he checked out the mismatched structures.

Although he'd never been here before, he'd imagined he knew the place from Casey's tales about growing up, but he could see now that he'd filled in the blanks wrong. He'd pictured quaint stores packed tightly along the streets, their facades painted in coordinated pastel colors with artsy brickwork in the streets and signs that blazed with neon. Just what he might expect in a California beach community.

Instead, the stores occupied odd-sized lots, dispersed between community buildings, a church, a doctor's clinic and a seedy-looking bar, plus the occasional house converted into an accounting firm or a law office. In the early evening, most of them lay dark.

Although the town appeared clean and well tended, it would give an urban planner fits. Nothing wrong with that; sometimes Jack thought the urban planners in California got drunk on their own sense of omnipotence. Yet the irregular spacing and the jumbled styles made him feel off balance.

Since renting a car in Nashville, Jack had driven for mile after mile past open fields and vast stretches of dense pine. In the L.A. area, one urban area blended into the next without a break.

He tried, and failed, to imagine living in the middle of nowhere, without a shopping mall or a tall building in sight. Perhaps he'd never get used to a place like this—but then, he didn't have to.

Following the directions he'd printed from the Internet, he cut through the downtown—if you could call it that—and, a short distance farther, turned right on Pine Woods Avenue. Although he hadn't traveled more than a few miles from town, farmland occupied one side and, on the other, trees studded the rising ground.

Man, this really was the boonies. How could Casey love it so much?

In L.A., she'd enjoyed browsing through bookstores and curio shops, attending the theater and people-watching at the Santa Monica Pier, none of which she could do in this backwater. Surely once Jack reminded her of the comforts she'd left behind, she'd reconsider.

Besides, he'd come ready to bargain.

He'd worked it out in his mind last night as he visualized the trip ahead. Jack was prepared to reduce his travel for work, although it wouldn't be easy with Mike eager to expand the company they'd founded because they preferred working for themselves. They'd discussed bringing in a third partner and hiring more operatives, but even then, some travel couldn't be avoided. Still, he'd find a way to cut back if Casey were willing to give up her preoccupation with a baby.

If she didn't love him enough to meet him halfway, he'd have to respect that. Have to back off, even though he'd never craved anything as much as her presence in his life. But he didn't intend to lose.

Besides, Casey had asked him to fix this business with the prowler. And no matter what else happened, he intended to do that.

When he spotted the sign reading Pine Woods Court, Jack veered into the driveway. It curved to the left, so heavily landscaped that, through the leaves, he could barely make out the one-story brick house that he guessed belonged to her.

Next to it, he spotted half a dozen cars parked in a small lot rimmed by trees. Since the driveway continued, he assumed the renters kept their cars at their cabins farther inside the property. So who did all those vehicles belong to?

From the green-and-white house came a burst of laughter. Oh, great. Casey must be giving a party.

Jack pulled into the lot and sat considering the situation. He hadn't planned on making a grand entrance. Maybe he should drive back into town and find some place to eat dinner, and hope this party didn't last all evening.

On the other hand, what if the prowler turned out to be someone Casey knew? If so, he might be sitting in her living room right now, enjoying her hospitality and sizing up his opportunity to burglarize the place.

In Jack's experience, catching people off guard helped to foil them. No one was expecting him. And with his trained eye, he might note incriminating details other people missed.

Okay, he'd just invited himself to the party. With luck, Casey would be too polite to throw him out in front of her friends.

Jack's shoes crunched on gravel as he headed for the porch. In the dusky light, he identified plenty of vantage points from which a stalker could watch figures moving behind the translucent curtains, although he saw no one lurking in the area at the moment. Still, with overgrown trees providing heavy cover, this place posed a security headache.

Another burst of laughter. All the voices sounded feminine. Could this be a Tupperware party? he wondered. That seemed like the kind of domestic thing Casey would go for.

Jack experienced a pang of nostalgia. He'd never lived in a house with cut flowers in vases until he got married. He'd never known a woman could smell so good, either, or what a difference it made when she put up curtains and even, to his amazement, baked her own bread. He'd more or less thought the stuff grew inside plastic bags.

As he mounted the steps, it occurred to him that the prowler wasn't likely to be attending a Tupperware party. He also didn't relish bursting into the middle of a ladies-only event.

He stopped. Better to double back to town. If he couldn't find a decent restaurant, at least there must be a grocery store.

Inside, a female voice grew louder, calling her goodbyes. Before he could retreat, the door opened and the chatter of voices seemed to blow a maroon-haired young woman onto the porch.

Her gaze swept Jack's tailored business suit and short, reddish-brown hair. "Now don't tell me you're that fellow who's been sneaking around!" she announced loudly enough to be heard in the next county. "If you are, you can sneak around my house any time. I'm Mimi."

She thrust out her hand. He shook it, too astonished by her remarks and overt friendliness to reply.

"Who's out there?" A young woman with long dark hair joined the first one. "My gosh, Casey, there's a hunk on your porch! Where'd you come from, mister? Don't tell me! My dreams!"

Jack had never been greeted with quite this degree of welcome by strangers. Did these women talk this way to any man who showed up, or were they that desperate for male companionship?

"Let me see, Bonnie." A large-boned woman with steely hair loomed in the doorway. "Well, if he's the prowler, he's making a fool out of me, because I figured it was my ex-husband. If you've come to sell us something, mister, better speak up before these ladies auction you off to the highest bidder."

"Actually, I was looking for my wife," Jack explained.

Mimi groaned. The other two stared at him. Suddenly he didn't feel so welcome.

"You *would* have to be married," said the one he thought was Bonnie. "Who's your wife?"

"I think I can guess," Mimi told her.

"What is going on out there on my porch?" It was Casey's voice, at last. "Gail, I can't see who—"

The guests parted to let her by. Shock registering on her face, she broke off in midsentence.

Jack felt a sweet familiar ache at the sight of his wife. Those bright blue eyes, those curving cheeks with a sprinkling of freckles. He wanted to cup Casey's chin and kiss her, to run his fingers through the light-brown hair curling around her shoulders and pull her tightly against him.

There was something funny about her denim jumper, though. It didn't fit her right, or had she gained weight? It was hard to tell at this angle, and he didn't want to stare.

"Jack," she said flatly. He couldn't read her mood.

More faces appeared behind her, wearing various degrees of curiosity and, in a few cases, disapproval. "Do you want us to stick around, Casey?" someone asked, to which another woman answered, "Are you crazy? They've got plenty to talk about. Hand me my jacket, would you?"

The noise of the departing guests made conversation impossible. Jack eased inside and let his wife say her farewells while he tried to make sense of the decorations.

Pink ribbons and balloons shaped like babies. Bits of wrapping paper with infants on them, and open boxes revealing a folded playpen and a car seat. It couldn't be anything else but a baby shower.

Whose baby?

He turned to survey his wife. She was hugging an older woman—hugging this person at arm's length, because her stomach intervened.

He couldn't believe it. He'd known how much Casey wanted a baby, but he'd never figured she'd try it alone. What had she done, gone to a clinic? She hadn't mentioned another man—if she had, Jack would have finalized the divorce in a hurry—and surely she hadn't jumped into bed with a guy just to get pregnant.

He kept thinking he must be imagining this. That he'd arrived at the wrong house, which happened to belong to a woman named Casey who was a dead ringer for his wife. Or that she'd held the party for a friend and he'd missed some new fashion that required wearing dresses that stuck out in front.

Jack sucked in a deep breath. What a mess. He'd flown all this way to help her, and he still planned to do that, but she'd obviously decided to rule him out of her life. She'd made this decision on her own, precluding any chance of reconciliation.

It felt like the time a suspect had whirled around and sprayed him with Mace. The agony had been so intense that, even though he knew it caused no permanent harm, he'd feared for a moment he couldn't bear it.

The last of the women trailed out the door, casting inquisitive glances his way. Jack forced his features into the expressionless mask he'd perfected as a teenager, when he'd frequently moved to a new foster home and a new high school. Never show weakness. Never show any feeling at all, no matter how hard your gut screamed for relief.

At last Casey closed the door. When she swung around to face him, he got an unobstructed view of her abdomen in profile. If he'd had any lingering hope that he might be mistaken, the sight dispelled all doubt.

He tried not to focus on how full her breasts looked or how lustrous her skin had become. If anything, pregnancy made her more beautiful, but if he mentioned it, she'd never believe him. Defiance glinted in her gaze and he knew that if he weren't careful, she'd give him a tongue-lashing.

He'd probably get one, anyway. She appeared to be in that kind of mood.

"I didn't know," he said.

"Obviously not." Casey crossed her arms protectively. "I suppose I should have said something but you'd have thought I was trying to trap you."

"Trap me?" He'd assumed it was the opposite. She'd clearly rejected him.

"Well, you didn't want a baby."

"That much we agree on." Jack hoped she'd start making sense soon.

"I figured you might see it as a betrayal." Her lips quivered, and she pressed them tightly together.

"How else could I see it?"

"As a…well, not a mistake." She lifted her chin. "As a blessing."

"Congratulations." He surveyed the room filled with torn wrapping paper, balloons, toys and stuffed bears. "Looks like you've got everything you need."

Despite his attempt to make conversation, she glared as if he'd just insulted her. "Is that all you have to say?"

He must have missed some clue, one of those feminine things that always eluded Jack. "Nice place," he ventured.

Utter silence. Disbelief writ large on her face.

Too bad she didn't appreciate his attempts at diplomacy. "So I guess you want to talk about it," he ventured.

"About 'it'?" Fury vibrated in her voice. Jack wished she didn't look so sensuous, with her hair mussed and her eyes even larger than usual.

"The, uh, fact that you're pregnant," he managed to say.

Finally, a nod. "Some kind of reaction would be appropriate."

How was a man supposed to respond when the woman he'd married did something to split them apart forever? He didn't see how anything he could say would help, but he'd better try or Casey was going to lacerate him. "I guess I'm pleased for you."

"Jack! I want to know how you feel!"

"How should I feel?"

"I don't know! You tell me."

He gave up searching for the right words. It was no use, anyway. "How do I feel? Like I got sucker punched. We aren't even divorced yet and you went out and did this. I guess it's none of my business whether you picked some clinic or some guy, even though technically you're still my wife. How do I feel? Lousy. Ticked off. Like an idiot for flying here from California because I was worried about you and figured you needed a bodyguard. Okay? How'd I do?"

As he spoke, his legs carried him around the room like a tiger pacing its cage. All these fripperies and cutesy-pie decorations made him want to rip them down so he could breathe.

"Oh, my gosh." Casey's jaw dropped.

"'Oh, my gosh' what?" Jack demanded, annoyed at receiving a reaction he couldn't interpret, although at least she wasn't throwing things at him.

"You don't get it," she said wonderingly.

"Get what?" He wished he knew how his wife managed to speak what sounded like English without making one bit of sense.

"It's yours," Casey answered.

Chapter Three

"My—?" Jack didn't finish the question, because, finally, he did get it.

Last August, when his wife had showed up in L.A. to go over their settlement, he couldn't keep his hands off her. Although she'd felt the same way, the passion wasn't enough to persuade her to stay.

"I thought you were on the pill," he added numbly. The truth was, he hadn't given any thought to a pregnancy, although he could see now that he should have.

"I'd just gone off it," Casey said. "I didn't think I could get pregnant yet. I was wrong."

Having had plenty of experience with people who manipulated and lied, Jack knew she might have done it on purpose. But he didn't believe that. For one thing, he respected Casey too much to think so poorly of her. Also, had her goal been to maneuver him into agreeing to start a family or to pressure him to pay child support, she wouldn't have waited eight months for him to stumble onto the truth.

"You weren't going to tell me?" he demanded, not so much from outrage as because he'd learned that asking questions was a good way to mask difficult emotions. And right now his emotions were about as confused as they'd ever been.

Casey clasped her hands in front. "I knew you didn't want a baby and I never meant to force you."

"Some things are hard to hide," he pointed out. "Don't you think I'd have learned the truth eventually?"

"In nearly three years, this is the first time you've come to Tennessee." Restlessly, she began tossing the party detritus into a paper bag.

A woman in her condition shouldn't have to clean up by herself. Guiltily, Jack realized Casey's friends probably would have stayed to help if he hadn't arrived.

He began collecting paper plates bearing the remains of cake and ice cream. The smell of food reminded him he hadn't eaten anything since breakfast except the beef jerky. Fortunately, he was used to missing meals.

"So when is it due?" He couldn't say the words "the baby" yet. That made the whole thing seem too real.

"In a few weeks."

"I'll pay the doctor bills." It was the least he could do.

"They're taken care of." Pulling down a banner, she stuffed it into her sack. "Around here, the doctor lets you pay on an installment plan."

How typical of Casey to insist on handling everything herself. Jack wished she'd let him help. He knew better than to insist, though.

They worked in silence for a few minutes before she added, "You're not mad?"

"I'm too buffaloed to be mad," he admitted.

"Does that mean you might get angry after you've had time to absorb it?" she probed.

Seeking a reasonable response, he said, "I don't suppose this is your fault any more than it is mine."

Sadness and resignation mingled in her expression. "No," Casey replied tiredly, "I don't suppose it is." Hauling her sack, she went into the kitchen. Jack suppressed the urge to carry it himself, because he could tell she wanted a few minutes alone.

He'd said the wrong thing again. Under his breath, he cursed his ineptness as he collected more wrappings.

The problem was, he had no idea what remark had set her off. He didn't understand how she felt or how he felt, either. As for how to deal with Casey, he might as well have stepped out of an airplane to discover himself on an alien planet where a two-headed, gibberish-speaking native was expecting him to say and do the right things.

He didn't know where to start.

I DON'T SUPPOSE this is your fault.

Well, there was an enthusiastic response, Casey reflected grumpily. She dropped the sack near the back door, since she didn't feel up to carting it outside and wrestling with the heavy, locking trash can lid that kept animals at bay.

In spite of everything she knew about Jack, her heart had leaped at seeing him in the doorway. When he'd given her that baffled, little-boy look and run his fingers through his hair in consternation, she might have gathered him into her arms if the guests hadn't been standing around.

And if her abdomen wouldn't have gotten in the way.

What had she expected, that he'd take one look at her bulge and turn into an ecstatic daddy-to-be? Jack had made his position clear, so she shouldn't be surprised that one glance at her advanced condition hadn't changed his mind. But it was heartbreaking.

Anxious to keep busy, Casey began unloading the dishwasher Enid had run earlier. As she stowed cake pans and trays in the cabinets, she calmed at the memory of how much fun she'd had, playing silly games and eating too much at the party.

Her friends had been more than generous. She really appreciated the way they'd chipped in for a playpen and car seat, which meant a big savings to her budget. She made a mental note to begin writing thank-yous as soon as she found a spare moment.

Why did Jack have to show up and make everyone go

home early? Why did he have to make her heart beat faster and remind her of how much she missed him?

She wished seeing him didn't have this effect. Also that he would at least pretend to be excited about the baby. Instead, he acted as if this were an irksome inconvenience, like a car that had broken down and couldn't be fixed.

It would have been better if he hadn't found out. They could have led their separate lives peacefully, as if they'd never met.

Oh, right. As if she could forget him when every time she looked at her daughter she was likely to see his eyes or his grin. Diane's very existence reminded her of the unforgettable night when they'd created her.

Standing motionless on the linoleum, Casey forced herself to be honest. She'd longed for Jack to find out. She'd wanted him to grin and admit what a huge mistake he'd made by foolishly rejecting fatherhood. Then, no doubt, they could have strolled off into the sunset, pushing a baby carriage and feeding each other bonbons.

Well, that wasn't going to happen. So he ought to leave, and the sooner the better.

Of course, she had to be practical if she wanted him to accept the heave-ho. He *had* come an awfully long way with good motives and, being a guy, he must want food, Casey reasoned.

Retrieving some of the finger sandwiches Enid had stored in the fridge, she tucked them and a cupcake inside a lunch bag. At least he couldn't say she sent him away hungry.

Then she heard the one noise a woman never, ever expects to emanate from a room in which she has left an unaccompanied male.

He was running the vacuum cleaner.

Astonished, Casey went to watch. Not that she imagined sprites had sneaked in to do the cleanup, but some things had to be witnessed to be accepted.

The first thing she saw in the living room was Jack's dark

suit coat draped over a chair. The second was the tantalizing way his button-down shirt emphasized the contours of his chest as he navigated the vacuum around the table legs.

He stopped to move a chair aside and pick up a bit of ribbon that had fallen beneath it. The attention to detail tickled her. She'd always admired her husband's thoroughness, although she'd never seen him vacuum a carpet before. Whatever he did, he did well.

A moment later, he switched off the machine. When the noise died, he glanced up sheepishly. "I thought I'd help."

"Thank you." Casey pointed to the lunch sack. "I packed some food for you to take to wherever you're staying."

"I appreciate the offer." He wound the cord into place. "But I'm staying here."

She decided to pretend she hadn't heard. "There's a motel about three miles away, just past Lake Avenue." Casey saw no reason to mention that her parents used to manage it. She'd grown up on the premises before they bought the Pine Woods.

He replaced the vacuum in a closet. "The couch will suit me fine."

"You don't honestly believe…" She halted the flow of words, remembering why he'd come. "Maybe you should explain exactly what I can expect while you're here."

"How many choices do I have?"

"You get to do A: Catch the bad guy. Go on, give me your sales pitch. How do you plan to do it?"

One eyebrow quirked but he kept a straight face. "Assess weaknesses and recommend improvements. Interview witnesses. Implement safety procedures. Catch the creep by whatever means necessary. I guess that sums it up."

It sounded as if it could take a while. She hoped the investigation wouldn't take weeks. Hours would be better. Minutes, even. If she let herself get dependent on Jack, she would feel all the more hurt when he left. "What kind of time frame are we talking about?"

Jack assumed a commanding stance with legs apart and head cocked. "I can make my evaluation in a day or two, but I'd rather…"

"A day or two is an absolute maximum."

He took a deep breath. Calming himself, probably. "Let's concentrate on the facts. How often does he show up?"

"This is the fourth time in a month," Casey said. "That works out to about once a week."

"How many people have seen him?"

"Gail and me. And Enid, or at least she heard somebody rustling around in her bushes one night. Enid and Gail live in the two closest cabins." After a moment's thought, Casey added, "Our mailbox got damaged, too, about three weeks ago, but it looked like a car scraped it. It's right by the road."

He took a notepad from his pocket and scribbled on it. "Always at night?"

"So far."

"Has anything been stolen?" He spoke with the impersonal tone of a police officer.

Casey shook her head. "Not that I know of."

"Any threats? Anonymous letters or e-mails? Hang-ups on the telephone?"

"No," she replied.

"Besides the woman who thinks it might be her ex, does anyone else have reason to believe they're being stalked?"

She responded in the negative.

Jack made another note and then seemed to remember who he was talking to. "Shouldn't you be sitting down?"

"I'm fine." Stubbornly, she held her ground, trying to ignore the way her abdomen tugged on her overstrained muscles.

He turned a chair backwards and sat down facing her. "Casey, when you told me someone sprayed you with a hose, I wasn't aware you were carrying a child. It sounded bad enough before, but this is worse. That was a vicious thing to do."

"He might not have been able to see in the dark," she protested. "He might not have realized I'm pregnant."

"Unless it's someone who knows you."

Maybe that possibility should have occurred to her before; however, she found it hard to accept. "I guess it's your job to suspect everyone, but that's ridiculous."

"Why?"

Because this was Richfield Crossing, not L.A., she thought in annoyance. But she already knew he wouldn't buy that argument. "Nobody has a motive." Since she gained no ground by continuing to stand, she yielded to common sense at last and sank onto the sofa.

"Don't be so sure," Jack retorted. "A predator doesn't need the kind of motive you or I might recognize. And there are other motives that might not be obvious. A grudge, for instance. What about former tenants? Did your mother report any problems?"

"No. Everybody's lived here for at least two years."

"Are any of them unstable? I presume your mom ran a credit check, right?"

She nodded. "I hope you're not planning to give them the third degree! They're not just renters, they're friends."

"I'd like a list of their names," he said calmly. "I'll start interviewing them first thing tomorrow. Trust me, I know how to debrief witnesses without antagonizing them."

"Tomorrow's Sunday." Casey supposed she shouldn't be throwing roadblocks in his path, but Jack's hard-nosed attitude put her back up. Besides, her attacker had to be a stranger.

"Tomorrow afternoon then," he countered. "Don't tell me they spend the entire day in prayer and seclusion."

"This isn't a monastery!"

"That much would be obvious to anyone looking at you." Grinning crookedly, he reached out and took her hands. Casey saw his gaze fall on the wedding ring she wore.

Did he think she still considered herself married? She only wore the ring because of her condition, but let him think whatever he liked.

Besides, a glow was spreading through her as his thumbs stroked the backs of her hands. He smelled of masculine aftershave lotion, which reminded Casey of how she used to enjoy burying her face in his thick hair and trailing her mouth down to the corner of his jaw. It had always made him catch his breath and lean toward her…

…Just as he was doing now, so close their foreheads nearly touched. She ought to draw back. She didn't want to give him the wrong impression. She didn't want to give herself the wrong impression, either.

Her shift of position must have put pressure on her abdomen, because Diane kicked. Startled, Casey pulled back. "Ow!"

Worry deepened the faint lines around Jack's mouth. "Is something wrong?"

She shook her head. "The baby let me know she doesn't like being squeezed. It didn't hurt. She just startled me."

He frowned. "You said 'she.' Does that mean you had one of those tests?"

Casey nodded. "It's a girl. I'm naming her Diane."

"That's a nice name." Releasing her hands, he flexed his shoulders. "I think I'll eat that food now. Then I'll take a stroll around the premises. I'd like to see how things look in the dark."

She decided not to argue, although the question of whether Jack was staying here and for how long remained unresolved. Right now, she felt too relaxed.

After he went out, instructing her to lock the door behind him, Casey remembered what he'd said about this possibly being someone she knew. She preferred to speculate that it might be a transient camping out on vacant land in the area. If so, she hoped Jack would find him soon.

Maybe this visit hadn't been such a bad idea, as long as

they kept it short. Like it or not, he was Diane's biological father. Someday their daughter would want to meet him and establish a relationship.

When that day came, maybe he'd remember sitting here learning about her for the first time. It might make him a little more welcoming.

For their daughter's sake, Casey hoped so.

JACK'S PATROL DIDN'T turn up anything suspicious. It did reveal how exposed the cabins were, however.

The few exterior lighting fixtures left plenty of shadows, and no lampposts brightened the twilit footpaths. Prowling through the darkness, he could see right into most of the four units through their flimsy curtains. They didn't even have fences to stop someone from crossing through the yards.

If it weren't so expensive, he'd recommend installing surveillance cameras. But that, he admitted silently, might be overkill.

While he tried to keep his mind on the job, his impressions from the past hour kept drifting back. He still couldn't fully grasp the fact that he'd gotten Casey pregnant eight months ago. All this time, his child had been growing inside her, and he'd had no clue.

His child. A little girl. Diane.

He couldn't figure out how to integrate the idea of her into his worldview. Certainly he bore the tyke no hard feelings, even though she'd sprung into being against his wishes. And he knew he had moral and legal obligations to her. But what exactly was he supposed to do?

It wasn't as if he had any role models to draw on. His own father had loved only one thing: alcohol.

He'd lost job after job because of it, and beaten his wife and little boy in a rage when he was drunk. Jack had learned early how to stay out of Pop's way. He hadn't been big enough to defend his mom and she'd never mustered the strength to stand up for herself. When she became sick, Pop had disappeared. Later, he'd landed in prison.

The last time Jack had heard from his father, while he was in college, it had been with a request for cash. Knowing what the money would be spent on, he'd refused. A few years later, his father had died from alcohol poisoning.

Maybe he should have suffered regrets. The only thing he'd regretted had been his father's complete failure in relation to his family.

Jack knew he wasn't like his old man. He rarely drank, and he would die before he'd hurt Casey or her child. Just thinking about how defenseless they were made his fists clench in a protective gesture.

The problem was, although he knew theoretically what a father was supposed to be like, he didn't have it in him. Maybe the instincts lay buried, but the prospect of digging them out got him tangled up with frustration and pain, old emotions he tried hard to put behind him.

He could still hear the sarcasm darkening Pop's voice when his irritation level began to rise. He remembered the explosions and his mother's fear, along with his own terror and misplaced sense of guilt. The old wounds had never fully healed. Jack didn't intend to rip them open again.

Grimly, he finished tracing the perimeter of the cleared part of Casey's property and turned back. From the rental car, he collected his suitcase and laptop and let himself inside with a key he'd borrowed from Casey.

When he entered, the living room lay quiet. Instead of loud music or the blare of a TV, only a soft humming from the direction of the bedrooms broke the peace.

"Casey?" he called.

"In here."

Pushing past his reluctance, Jack walked through a short hall and entered the nursery. Casey stood ratcheting a teddy-bear mobile onto the crib. When she saw him, she pushed a button on the device, setting off a music-box version of "The Teddy Bears' Picnic."

His wife smiled as tinkling music filled the room. Tiny teddy bears revolved, their furry paws outstretched as if eager for Diane's arrival. You couldn't have shot a better commercial for home and happiness, Jack thought with an ache.

At the first foster home he'd gone to, when he was eleven, he'd walked into a nursery where the parents' own six-month-old sat cooing and playing with a clown mobile. He didn't remember the tune, but it had made him long for his mother.

The foster parents had rushed in and ordered him out as if he posed a threat to their precious offspring. He was never to go in there again, the man had snapped. They'd set up a cot for him in the sewing room; that was his place.

He'd learned later that that couple had never cared for foster children before and had taken him in because they needed money. They hadn't been prepared for the moodiness of a pre-adolescent, for his flashes of anger or even for his poor table manners.

Jack knew many foster parents provided loving care, sometimes adopting the children. He hadn't been so lucky. The six months he'd spent in that first house had made it agonizingly clear he didn't belong.

Every time he'd heard music from the nursery, the sound had underscored the fact that he no longer had a home and probably never would. He'd had to harden himself to hold back the tears, as he was doing now.

Casey misread his reaction. "You don't have to glare at me! Anyone else would be glad I'd set up such a nice welcome for the baby."

"You've done a great job," he muttered.

"You might try to sound as if you mean it."

He could see that she'd put in a lot of work. She'd painted the place and probably stenciled those birds on the wall herself. The yellow-and-white color scheme, the shelves holding a couple of leather-bound classics—who could ask for more?

Not Jack. What he'd asked for was less. "I can't change how I feel, so let's not argue about it," he told her. "Do you want to hear my preliminary observations about the property?"

"Sure." She closed her tool kit. Some of his strain eased as they exited through the hall.

After stowing her tools in her office, Casey led the way into the old-fashioned kitchen, where the lingering scent of baking soothed Jack's spirit. He'd loved spending time in the kitchen while they were living together.

Without asking, she poured them both decaf coffee. He would have preferred the regular version but didn't want to impose.

"Shoot," she said.

No need to consult his notes. "To start, you need better lighting. Also, I'd recommend you consider fencing the yards."

"Unless I put up barbed wire, a prowler could go over it or through the gate." She dosed her cup with cream and sugar and served his black, the way he liked it. "I don't see that it would do much good."

"It's partly psychological," Jack explained. "It provides a sense of containment. It also gives an intruder pause because it can slow down his escape." He found the brew more flavorful than expected. Or maybe he simply enjoyed it because this was Casey's house.

"I can't afford to build fences, anyway," she said. "That's not a request for money. It's a statement of fact."

He knew better than to argue. "I don't suppose you can afford to put up lighting along the footpaths, either."

"You got that right." She still seemed remote and almost combative. Apparently his attitude toward the nursery had set her off.

Jack refused to apologize. He'd warned her how he would

likely react to a baby, although he hadn't been specific. "If you can't afford lighting and fences, you certainly can't afford guards."

"I suppose not." She propped her elbows on the table. "I don't know what I was thinking when I called you for a recommendation. I felt so mad about getting sprayed, I couldn't think straight."

Maybe, he thought, she'd subconsciously hoped he would come. But he knew better than to count on it. "My next suggestion is to organize your tenants into patrols. Two-person teams carrying cell phones. Not twenty-four hours a day, obviously, but during the evening when this guy's most likely to show up."

"One guy's in his eighties and Enid's in her seventies. I don't want them trying to play super cop," Casey said. "Plus even my more able-bodied tenants could break an ankle trying to patrol these woods in the dark."

"There's one more choice."

"And it is?"

"You're going to have to put up with me until I find this guy."

She shook her head. "I appreciate the offer, but, as I said before, I think you should leave as soon as possible."

"Last night, you were ready to do whatever it took to nail this louse. You felt desperate enough to call on your almost-ex-husband, and we both know that's pretty desperate." Jack hoped a little humor might soften her resistance, but he saw no change in her attitude. "Now I find out you're pregnant and more vulnerable than ever, but you're backing off. Let me run this guy down."

It seemed the least he could do. A man didn't abandon his wife when she needed him, even if she'd abandoned him first.

Casey rested her chin on her fist. It took all his self-control not to reach out and touch her cheek.

"Let's be honest," she said.

"I've never been anything else."

"You don't want to stay," she said. "You feel obligated. You hate being here, hate being around anything that reminds you of babies. I can read you like a book, Jack. You're going to make us both miserable."

He couldn't claim otherwise, so he ignored her point. "Pretend I'm some hired hand who's here to do a job. Then you won't care whether I go gaga over nursery stuff."

"No."

"That's it? Just plain no?"

"Try this: nyet, nein, no way. Is that clear enough?"

He could be just as stubborn as she. "I'm not leaving until we wrap this up."

"I'll get a restraining order." Casey folded her arms. "Well?"

Jack didn't think she'd do it but he knew better than to push her. "Is that what you really want? You're so eager to get rid of me you're willing to risk having this guy keep bugging you?"

Her lips formed a thin, stubborn line. Finally she said, "I don't even think it's a good idea for you to stay a day or two."

"Casey!" She was so stubborn, she made mules look compliant. Jack came very close to saying so.

"I'll let you stay tonight because it's getting late, but that's all. Really, the more I think about it, the more I believe it's probably just a neighbor's kid," she told him. "Nothing's been stolen or damaged except for that mailbox, which might not even be connected. It's not that serious. I overreacted."

An assault on a pregnant woman seemed serious enough to Jack, but he'd run out of arguments. Before he could decide how to proceed, his cell phone rang.

Excusing himself, he answered. "Arnett."

"Jack? It's Mike." His partner sounded frazzled. "I've got to run up to San Francisco for a couple of days." He mentioned a client there who needed a security upgrade. "The problem is, I've got an appointment Monday with Paul Mendez. You remember him?"

"Sure." Paul planned to retire in another month from the Denver police department. He'd expressed interest in joining Men at Arms as a partner, and they could certainly use one.

They had a growing staff of guards assigned to various clients, and added other employees as needed, sometimes on a temporary basis. A manager, an administrative assistant and an accountant handled the paperwork. The partners themselves planned and supervised all major operations, as well as trouble-shooting to keep their clients happy.

"Well, he's going to be in town and wants to go over the financial details. Since you're back, I was hoping you could take care of it."

"I'm not exactly back," Jack admitted. Casey, who'd carried their empty cups to the sink, glanced at him wryly.

"Where are you?"

"Tennessee. A prowler assaulted Casey on her property." He saw no point in mentioning the pregnancy.

"I see." He probably didn't, though. A twice-divorced workaholic, Mike always put business ahead of family. "We really ought to attend to this. We both like Paul and it helps that he's bilingual." An increasing amount of their business involved Spanish-speaking clients.

Jack's gut instinct told him to fight harder to resolve this case, but he did have an obligation to his company. Also, Casey was standing right there mouthing the word, "Go!"

He shook his head.

"Restraining order!" she hissed.

For heaven's sake, why fight her? If she didn't want him, he had no business forcing his company on her.

"Okay," he said into the phone. "I'll catch a plane tomorrow."

"Thanks. I knew I…." The phone went dead.

Jack frowned. "It cut off."

"Happens all the time around here," Casey replied. "My service provider claims I live in a dead spot."

His gut urged Jack to stay to protect this woman. And this

baby, even though he hadn't asked for it. But he'd be kidding himself if he imagined that sticking around would make any difference to their future.

Maybe she was right that she'd overreacted. After all, she hadn't received any threats. Most likely some bum seeking shelter had panicked when she aimed a camera at him.

"All right," he conceded grimly. "Tomorrow morning, I'm out of here."

"We'll both be a lot happier," Casey said.

Jack seriously doubted it.

Chapter Four

Casey went to bed early and slept deeply, lulled by maternal hormones. About 3:00 a.m., she awoke with an urgent need to use the bathroom.

She slipped out into the hallway in her cotton sleep shirt. After using the facilities, she couldn't resist peeking into the living room, where Jack slept on the opened couch.

Moonlight through the window highlighted the length of his body beneath the quilt and played across his ruffled hair. The room filled with his subtle presence and the murmur of his breathing.

Her body burned with the memory of sleeping beside him, feeling his legs tangle with hers and his arm brush across her breasts. Sometimes they'd awakened, not even knowing what hour it was, and sleepily caressed each other until passion flamed.

Yet, despite their years together, he seemed exotic, as if she'd discovered a lion dozing in the living room. Jack came from a different world, one that she'd never fully understood. Although she knew his parents had died and that he'd spent his adolescence in foster homes, he disliked discussing the past.

Why should the sight of a nursery or the sound of a music box make a man glower? To Casey, those things spoke of happiness and innocence. They took her back to a simpler time when she'd been loved without reserve and when the future held unlimited possibilities.

It saddened her to realize the two of them lacked common ground. She'd loved Jack more than she would have believed possible, and she'd longed for their marriage to work. But it was no use hanging onto something that couldn't be fixed.

As she headed back to bed, she realized her mind was racing with memories. She needed to calm herself before falling asleep.

If she'd been alone, she might have played a soothing CD, but that would disturb Jack. Instead, she went into the nursery and turned on a table lamp.

The cheerful radiance surrounded Casey like a hug. She glanced up at the books she'd chosen for the shelf and picked an old favorite, the original *The Hundred and One Dalmatians* by Dodie Smith.

From a toy chest that her father had polished lovingly, she removed the fuzzy Dalmatian dogs she'd accumulated as a child and arranged them on the carpet. The worn fur only made them more appealing, reminding her of hours spent cuddling them as she invented stories.

"Hey, you guys," she said softly. It seemed to her that Pongo cocked his head and that Perdita's tail stirred as if trying to wag. "There's going to be someone new in your room soon. She won't able to play with you at first, and I don't want you to disturb her by barking all night, okay?"

She explained to them about Diane, how small she'd be and how she might chew on them before she was old enough to understand who they were. "But one day her little brain will click into gear and she'll figure out that you have feelings and that you love her."

Missis gave a knowing bark. As she warned the stuffed dog not to wake their guest, Casey felt a draft from the doorway.

Glancing up, she peered through a wing of unbrushed hair. Jack, a black kimono-style robe belted over pajama bottoms, stood watching her with a bemused expression. Maybe he thought she'd gone nuts, but at least he wasn't scowling.

"I couldn't sleep," she said.

He regarded the circle of dogs. "I don't recall meeting these guys before."

"My parents saved them for me," Casey explained.

"They saved your toys?" He seemed to find the idea puzzling.

"I guess they were hoping someday the grandchildren would play with them. Or maybe having them around reminded Mom of when I was small." Impulsively, she added, "She wanted more kids but she couldn't have them. I wish she'd lived long enough to meet Diane."

"I don't even remember having toys, although I must have," he said. "We moved a lot, sometimes without warning. Stuff got left behind."

"You don't remember any of them?" Casey couldn't imagine it.

He thought for a moment. "Some books, I guess. I don't know what happened to them." As he studied the array of stuffed animals, she thought she saw regret flicker in his eyes. Then he crossed his arms and shifted his attention to the window, where ribbons tied back the yellow-dotted white curtains. "You ought to get opaque shades. Anyone could see inside."

"Nobody around here…" She stopped, remembering the prowler. "I'm not used to thinking that way."

"It's my job to think that way." He cast one more glance at the stuffed animals with a veiled longing that touched Casey more deeply than words.

He'd lost so much along the way to becoming a man. He always shrugged it off when she asked about the past, as if it couldn't touch him, but she knew it affected him in countless ways.

"I wish you'd tell me more," she said.

"About what?"

"Your parents. Your life in foster homes. How can I understand if you won't share it with me?"

He edged away. "Sorry to disturb you. I came in because I heard someone talking."

"Just me and the pooches." Casey watched him go with a sense of loss. For an instant, she'd hoped he might open up, but she could see it was useless.

Nostalgically, she tucked the dogs back into the chest. She'd always taken it for granted that parents saved their children's favorite toys. How did it feel to be stripped of those memories?

Jack might as well have come from a distant planet. For a long stretch, she'd wished he would agree to visit Tennessee with her and that it would help their worlds to blend. But he'd never found the time. And now that he'd come, it was too late.

She couldn't reach him. Even the prospect of becoming parents wasn't going to bridge the gap between them.

Reluctantly, she made her way back to bed.

SITTING ALONE in the kitchen while Casey dressed for church, Jack ate toast and coffee and fought down a sense of unease. The view of seemingly endless trees, with the nearest cabin barely visible and no other buildings in sight, disturbed him with its emptiness.

One of his foster families had taken him and their other charges to a regional park on a few occasions, but the place had been filled with visitors. Here, he found the vast amount of space almost threatening. It reminded him of a recurring dream in which he searched through a devastated landscape for a woman in a white dress, or perhaps it was a nightgown.

Long ago, the woman must have been his mother. During the past year, he'd known it was Casey even though he couldn't see her face.

He tried to force himself to relax. After such a dysfunctional childhood, Jack knew his gut reactions weren't a reliable warning of real danger. Besides, he didn't have to search for Casey. He could hear her moving around in the bathroom.

Through the window came the sounds of birds twittering and leaves rustling in the breeze. Seeking a positive association, he decided the sounds reminded him of a book about pioneers he used to enjoy as a kid.

Come to think of it, he had many happy memories of stories. In some ways, he *had* taken his toys with him. All he'd had to do was venture into any library and he could visit them all over again.

Storybook figures obviously meant a lot to Casey, too. Last night, she'd looked adorable, sitting on the carpet talking earnestly to her toys as if she were still a child herself. He'd overheard quite a bit before she noticed him.

One day her little brain will click into gear. Until Casey said that, he hadn't thought about Diane as anything beyond a helpless infant. It was disconcerting to consider the bulge inside his wife as a person who would someday have ideas and relationships of her own.

He imagined a tot with tangled brown hair and blue eyes like her mother's, sitting on that same carpet solemnly communing with the Dalmatians. His daughter.

Yearning twisted through Jack. He'd always felt protective toward children and moved by their instinctive trust. Once, as a police officer, he'd unstrapped a baby from a car seat after a crash and barely managed to carry her to safety before the car caught fire. He would never forget the delicate feel of the girl's arms clasping his neck as he delivered her to her mother.

But he'd had no desire to stick around beyond that moment of connection. For heaven's sake, he was too impatient and moody to live with a little girl. He'd probably lose his temper and yell the way his father used to. The image of tears spilling down a child's face made his coffee taste bitter.

From the living room, Casey popped into the doorway. She'd

tamed her hair and donned a pink smock dress with an embroidered yoke. "You're welcome to come to church with me."

"No, thanks." He never set foot in one except to attend a wedding or a funeral, and not many of those. He and Casey had tied the knot at a chapel in a Las Vegas hotel, with her parents, his partner Mike and Mike's then-wife in attendance. "Besides, I have to leave by noon to make my flight."

Although he'd secured a midafternoon reservation out of Nashville, he had to allow for the hour and a half drive, plus returning the rental car and clearing security. Thanks to the two-hour time difference, that would put him in L.A. by dinner.

"I'm sorry I can't stick around to see you off but I'm teaching Sunday school," she said.

Could things get any cozier? Stuffed animals, baby showers and Sunday school. Suddenly Jack felt suffocated. At work tomorrow, he looked forward to taking command of the situation instead of gasping like a fish out of water.

"What?" his wife demanded.

"I'm sorry?"

"Your nose wrinkled as if something smelled bad," she challenged.

"Do you always have to try to read my mind?"

"I hope you weren't disapproving of my teaching Sunday school. Maybe you should join the class," Casey returned. "We learn valuable lessons from the Bible."

"I know a valuable lesson. Mind thy own business." He shook his head apologetically. "I don't mean that. Casey, I think it's great that you teach Bible school, okay?"

She nodded. "I'm sorry. I should respect your right to keep your thoughts private. It's just that you're so closemouthed and I care what you think."

"Have a good time," he said.

Casey sighed, gave a little wave and went out through the living room. A short time later, Jack heard her key turn in the front lock.

Gone. His hand tightened on the coffee cup.

He had to let her go, even though it was tearing him apart. She'd made her choice to send him away. His ability and desire to protect were all he had to offer, and she didn't want them.

He wished things could be different, but her pregnancy had wiped out any chance of the two of them returning to their old life in LA. Maybe they should have spent more time discussing the implications of having a child—financial and otherwise—but he had a feeling Casey would shut him out as she'd done when he offered to pay the doctor's bills.

He wasn't the only one who kept his most complicated feelings to himself. Sometimes she did, too.

It was time to put useless hopes behind him. In a few days, he'd call and inform her that he was signing the divorce papers. If she refused to accept money to help support their daughter, he'd open a trust fund for the little girl's college expenses. Just because he couldn't be a real father didn't mean he intended to abandon his responsibilities.

From the carport attached to the house, he heard a car start. His ear marked Casey's progress as she backed out and headed down the driveway.

The motor stopped just beyond the house, still humming. What was she waiting for?

He didn't know her routine. Maybe she gave one of the tenants a ride. Curious, Jack got up and went to the porch.

From the front, he saw that she'd stopped next to the parking area and exited the car. A cloud of dogwood blossoms obscured his view of the lot.

"Casey?" he called, and stepped down from the porch. Receiving no answer, he shouted louder. Still nothing.

Jack hurried down the driveway. The car sat idling, with the driver's door ajar. No sign of Casey.

He shouldn't have let her go out until he'd checked the premises. Why did he let himself get distracted? If some guy was stalking her, the arrival of another male might have roused him to further action.

Surveying the surroundings for suspicious movement, Jack noticed a squirrel dart across some sunny rocks but nothing more troubling. "Casey?" he called again. The name echoed faintly.

The crunch of footsteps straight ahead brought him up short. From behind a screen of branches, his wife appeared on the blacktop.

"Jack!" She hurried forward.

"I've been calling you." That wasn't the issue, of course. "What's going on?"

"You'd better take a look."

He moved closer, keeping a lookout all the while. These unfenced, heavily wooded premises provided too much cover for his taste.

His attention turned to the parking area. The other vehicles from last night had vanished, leaving his blue rental sedan sitting isolated. Isolated, but not undisturbed.

A large, leafy tree limb half obscured the windshield, where it had apparently fallen. Then he noticed a broken side window.

The damage also included a bent antenna and windshield wiper, both possibly attributable to the fallen branch. The broken window and the scratches on the hood, however, didn't correlate, and neither did the angle of the branch compared to the locations of nearby trees.

There'd been no storm last night and no winds to carry tree limbs any distance. This had to be intentional.

Jack circled the car without touching it. When Casey reached for the branch, he waved her away. "Don't disturb anything. I need to get the whole picture."

She withdrew her hand. "These trees are kind of overgrown. I've been meaning to have them trimmed."

He noted a rock on the pavement below the broken window. Dried soil clung to one side as if it had been wrenched from the ground. On the hood, the depth and straightness of the score marks reminded him of key scrapes.

"I don't think the branch fell by itself," he said. "I don't think it caused all this damage, either."

"That's what I was trying to figure out," she admitted. "It seemed accidental but it doesn't look right."

It ticked him off to see the vandalism. Jack didn't doubt for a minute that he'd been personally targeted. What outraged him even more was the sense that someone felt possessive toward his wife. "This is definitely vandalism, and I don't believe it's a coincidence that my car was chosen."

"Wait a minute." Casey peered through the window. "You left food inside."

He followed her gaze to the empty wrapper from his beef jerky, lying on the passenger seat where he'd tossed it. "So?"

"An animal might have tried to get in," she pointed out.

"Would that be the same bear that squirted you with the hose?"

She wrinkled her nose. "I was thinking of a raccoon. They can do amazing things with their hands."

"Ever see one throw a rock?"

She admitted she hadn't.

Jack returned to his line of thought. "Whoever did this was lashing out at me. He probably acted first on impulse, breaking the window and scratching my hood, then decided to try to make it appear like an accident. He either pulled the branch down or found it in the woods and arranged it to try to fool us."

"Jack, I'm sorry," she said. "I didn't mean for you to become a target. This could be expensive."

He shrugged. "I've got insurance. It'll just cost me the deductible, and the car's still drivable."

Those were deep scratches, though. And the rock had been thrown with force. Whoever had done this carried a lot of anger.

Yet until now, he reminded himself, there'd been no indication that Casey was the stalker's primary concern. He'd been heard or seen near two tenants' cabins, not her house.

Usually, perpetrators stuck to a pattern. This guy's unpredictability and his hostility made the hairs stand up on Jack's neck.

He checked his watch. A quarter to nine. "I'll tell you what," he said. "Let me come to church with you. If whoever did this is fixated on you, he knows you'll be there and he may show up. I might get a gut feeling about somebody." People revealed more than they realized through their body language.

Casey released a long breath. "What about your flight?"

"I can still make it. Just let me pack my bag. I'll caravan behind you to town, and afterwards I can head directly for Nashville." He'd have to push the speed limit, but he hadn't seen a sign of any state troopers on his way north.

She hugged herself. "I guess that makes sense."

Don't overwhelm me with enthusiasm. Well, what had he expected? "We might be a few minutes late. I'll need to photograph the car before we leave, so don't touch anything." He always packed a couple of disposable cameras. In his line of work, they came in handy.

"You're treating it like a crime scene."

"You got that right."

Casey regarded the car unhappily. "I wish this guy would just leave us alone. We'd be so much happier."

"If only bad guys thought that way!" Jack teased.

She gave him a reluctant smile. "You'd better get started. I can pack your gear for you, if you like."

"That would help."

After he finished snapping shots, stowing his suitcase and collecting the rock in a plastic bag as a precaution, it was clear they would be late for church. Too bad. Jack would have liked to watch people arriving. It might have helped him spot the guilty party, if he were there.

As he followed Casey's car into town, he realized that for once he belonged in a church, because he had a very appropriate assignment: to catch a sinner.

Chapter Five

Casey didn't know which upset her more: the possibility that the prowler was becoming violent, or the fact that he'd forced Jack to stay, even for a few hours, out of what was obviously a sense of obligation.

All the same, gratitude for her husband's presence helped to ease her delayed shock. When she first spotted the damage to the car, she'd instinctively reached for some reassuring explanation, but the more she stared, the more unavoidable Jack's conclusion seemed. This couldn't have happened by chance.

Maybe she'd made a mistake when she ordered him to leave. Still, sooner or later, he had to go. Maybe they'd get lucky and he'd spot the likely culprit right away.

The Richfield Community Church lay on the far side of town, a small white clapboard building with a picturesque steeple. Cars and trucks spilled over onto an adjacent lot.

As she and Jack walked across the pavement, Casey noticed him straightening and realized he must be focusing on the task ahead. He probably had no idea what a stir the arrival of her previously unseen husband was likely to create among the congregation.

When they entered the foyer, she could hear the deep voice of the pastor, Joshua Norris, issuing from the sanctuary, although the doors had been closed. Jack hesitated. "What's the etiquette?" he murmured. "I hate to just barge in."

"Let's wait till they start singing." The noise should cover the disturbance caused by their entry.

A few minutes later, Casey heard the piano—which she knew was played by the minister's wife, Bernadette—launch into a popular hymn. As the congregation swelled with song, she opened the door and led the way inside.

Brilliance poured through the stained-glass window above the pulpit and the arching side windows. To her, the whole place seemed to shine.

As always, the hymn lifted her spirits. Nothing seemed quite so unmanageable or threatening as it had before.

The congregants faced away from them. Only a few people appeared to notice their arrival, although she could already see them whispering to their neighbors.

When she pointed out two seats in a nearby pew, Jack gave a jerk of the head, indicating that she should sit. He, however, clearly intended to stand in the back where he could view the proceedings.

Although she'd have liked to stay with him, Casey couldn't stand for the whole service. She slid into place and picked up a prayer book.

Once the song finished, more heads turned. Her friend Bonnie smiled, her interest obviously perking when she caught sight of Jack. Royce studied the new arrival with something less than enthusiasm.

Casey remembered Jack's suspicions about him. She had to admit her ex-boyfriend didn't even try to disguise his mistrust of the newcomer, but she couldn't imagine him sneaking around the Pine Woods. And if he'd wanted to harm Jack, as a mechanic he could have done something far more deadly and hard to spot than scratching the paint.

The possibilities that came to mind alarmed her. Thank goodness Royce was no criminal.

Casey forced herself to look to the pulpit, even though her mind continued to buzz. Usually she enjoyed the service and tried to apply the sermon to her personal life. Today, she kept glancing around, wondering if one of these folks had become her enemy.

Not everybody in town attended, of course. Enid was the only one of the tenants in view, which didn't surprise her, since she knew the others liked to sleep late. There were also some people she didn't immediately recognize from this angle, including a woman in a scarf who sat with the Rawlinses.

Nearly an hour later, when the service ended, Casey rose stiffly. She'd never noticed how hard the pews were until she began carrying a baby.

Her friend Mimi approached. "I'll teach your class, honey," she volunteered. "You'd better keep your eye on that sexy guy of yours or somebody's likely to make off with him."

"Thanks." Casey had to chuckle at Mimi's cheerful manner. "That would help a lot."

"Did you see who's here?" Bonnie arrived with her younger sister, Angie, in tow. "They say a bad penny always turns up. I'm willing to give a person a second chance, but this one's got enough attitude to fill a barn."

"Who?" As she spoke, Casey noticed that the woman in the scarf was frowning in her direction. Good heavens, it was Sandra, her old friend, but much gaunter than the last time they'd met. She wore dark glasses, which seemed like an affectation even if she had been living in California, and had some kind of mark on her cheek. "What happened to her?"

"I heard she was in a car crash high on drugs," Angie said. "Rumor has it she's on probation."

Her older sister made a face. "If you heard all that, how come you didn't tell me? We could have told Casey last night."

"I heard it this morning. I think she just got back to town yesterday."

The young women stopped chattering as Jack approached. After greeting them briefly, he asked Casey, "Who's that man?"

She followed his gaze. "Al Rawlins." She explained about her connection to his daughter Sandra. "Why do you ask?"

"From the way he glared at you, I got the impression you're not one of his favorite people."

"I know. He blames me for Sandra's problems." Casey had familiarized him with her friend's situation long ago.

"Is something wrong?" Mimi asked. "The way Jack inspected the crowd, I figured we must have at least an FBI's Most Wanted hanging around."

"Somebody bashed his car last night," Casey explained. "We're trying to figure out who might have had a motive."

"That stinks," Mimi said. "It's not much of a welcome, is it? Well, I'd like to stay but I'd better go teach that class."

Casey thanked her again. Bonnie and Angie excused themselves also.

As soon as they were gone, Jack queried Casey about some of the other attendees. She identified Royce and Larry Malloy, the rookie cop who'd investigated Friday night's assault.

"I don't think either of them is the possessive type, and I've certainly given them no reason to be," she added.

"Men who fixate on women aren't necessarily connected to reality," he told her. "They invent scenarios in which the woman plays hard to get but secretly loves them. They can be very difficult to dissuade."

"What does it take to convince them she's serious?"

"Getting a restraining order or marrying someone else usually does the trick. Unfortunately, it may also flip the guy off the deep end. That's when stalkers become most dangerous."

As he spoke, Jack made notes on a small pad. Compiling a list of suspects, Casey supposed.

It troubled her to view old acquaintances as potential predators. Many of them were folks she wouldn't hesitate to call on if she needed help. Yet *someone* had knocked her down with a hose and scraped Jack's car.

"You said body language might give him away," she recalled. "What kind of behavior are you looking for?"

"People avoiding my gaze," he replied promptly. "Inappropriate or contradictory actions that indicate the person's putting on a pretense of normalcy. Restlessness, such as an adult who can't stop wiggling."

"I figure an adult who can't stop wiggling during a church service probably needs to use the bathroom." Casey had to admit that, as a pregnant woman, she had a rather biased perspective in that regard.

Jack didn't crack a smile. He'd gone into his no-nonsense security-agent mode. "Are any of your neighbors here?" he asked. "I don't mean tenants, but anyone who lives on an adjacent property?"

She pointed out Owen and Jean Godwin, Mimi's parents. In their sixties, they owned a nearby farm and rented some fields from her. Usually they sat with their good friends the Lanihans—Rafe, the town's mayor, and his wife, Louise. Today, however, the couples sat far apart, and she noticed Louise and Jean exchanging rueful glances.

"Would they have any reason to hold a grudge against you? Any family quarrels or disputes?"

She hadn't thought in those terms. "No, not really. The Godwins wanted to buy the Lone Pine before my parents acquired it but they couldn't work out a deal with the former owners. Still, that's hardly what I'd call a dispute. Plus there's no reason to hold it against me."

"They never asked you to sell to them?"

"Owen mentioned that if I ever considered selling, he hoped I'd give them first crack, and I said I would," she said.

"When was that?"

"Soon after Mom died."

"Any other neighbors?" Jack asked.

"The land to the west of me has an absentee owner. I've never met him, and I wish he'd sell the place, because sometimes people camp there until the police send them packing."

Chief Roundtree and his wife, Gladys, moved past them. Although the chief seemed preoccupied, Gladys examined Jack as if trying to memorize every detail of his appearance.

"What was that about?" he queried as the Roundtrees vanished into the foyer.

Casey explained who they were. "Gladys is a terrible gossip. I've heard she even questioned whether I was really married, as if my parents had been lying all these years!"

"Why would she think that?"

"Because she's bored and needs to feel important. She's been wanting to move to Virginia to live near their daughter." Casey had heard that from Enid.

"She's a bit portly to go wandering around your property at night," Jack conceded. "It doesn't seem like her style, either. She strikes me as more the arsenic-and-old-lace type."

How could he think that way about a harmless if annoying old lady? "You're getting the wrong impression of Richfield Crossing," she said. "These people aren't harboring hatred and malice. Sure, we don't always get along, but even if they dislike somebody, they don't turn to violence."

"Somebody did," he said doggedly. "I just haven't figured out who yet."

The sanctuary had nearly emptied except for the Rawlinses, who'd stopped to talk to the pastor. "Look, I don't have to teach the class after all, and I'm not in the mood for Bible study," Casey said. "We can leave now if you want. That'll give you plenty of time to make your flight."

"I'm not so sure I'm ready to go. After what we found this morning, I'm worried the prowler may be upping the stakes."

She was about to reply that the man might back off after Jack left, when she saw Sandra heading toward them. The changes in her friend were startling.

A deep gash marred what had once been a flawless complexion. The wisps of blond hair straggling from beneath the scarf had lost their luster, and the sunglasses couldn't completely obscure the dark circles beneath her eyes.

Sandra halted in front of her. "Go ahead, gloat," she said. "You knew I'd turn out like this, didn't you?"

Casey had no idea where this anger sprang from. "I hear you were in an accident. I'm sorry."

Her response did nothing to appease the other woman. "I suppose I should congratulate you on your impending motherhood. Sorry I forgot to bake an apple pie."

Casey refused to rise to the bait. "I didn't know you were in town. I'd have contacted you sooner."

"Don't worry, I'll be around for a while." Sandra's voice hadn't lost the throaty quality that had won her voice-over acting jobs in L.A. "Terms of my probation."

Realizing she and Jack hadn't met, Casey made a quick introduction. Her friend unbent as far as to shake hands. Then her parents joined them.

"So this is your husband," Al said. "Funny thing about the two of you girls having been best friends for so many years. It kind of surprised me when you didn't even invite her to your wedding. I guess when you turn your back on someone, you go all the way."

Casey felt as if he'd slapped her. Al had never been so outspoken before, and she hadn't suspected the depths of his resentment. Sandra's truculence was bad enough, but she knew it would pass. Her father's attitude seemed more threatening.

"Dad," Sandra warned, "I can handle this."

Jack caught Casey's arm. "You look pale."

"I'm fine." Despite her words, she realized her head was swimming. Pregnancy made her highly sensitive to emotional vibrations, and Al's hostility had caught her off guard. So had Sandra's.

"I didn't really mean—" Sandra began.

Mary Rawlins, her expression sour, spoke for the first time. "You don't need to apologize for anything."

"That's the truth," Al said.

The way they closed ranks made Casey suddenly and painfully aware of her own lack of family. Friends couldn't replace parents who put you first and stuck by you no matter what.

Jack's hand tightened on her elbow. "Well, there's nothing like reminiscing with old friends to brighten your day," he quipped. "I'm sure Casey would love to stay and chat, but she'll just have to tear herself away. Nice meeting you all."

She wanted to hug him. As soon as they reached the parking lot, she said, "Thank you. It felt good to have somebody on my side."

He cast an irritated glance back at the church. "From what you've told me about Sandra, she brought her problems on herself. If you hadn't moved out, she'd have dragged you down with her."

"She's obviously having a hard time." Casey couldn't help sympathizing.

"And taking it out on a pregnant woman? Her parents ought to be ashamed." Jack paused next to their cars. "I don't think you should drive. You still look under the weather."

"I'm feeling better." The sunshine restored some of her energy.

"I'll follow you home and make sure you're all right." He folded his arms. "Then I'm going to stay for a few more days till we figure out who's doing this. I don't necessarily think it's the Rawlinses. However, I'm adding them to my list."

Casey suspected she ought to protest, but the truth was, that moment of vulnerability had made her face a truth she'd been avoiding: no matter how self-sufficient she might be, the prowler had struck at the one time in her life when she was least able to defend herself.

If ever a woman needed a bodyguard, she did. And so did her baby.

Still, she didn't want to be selfish. Jack had other responsibilities. "What about your partner?"

"I'll deal with him," he said firmly. "There's no way I'm forcing my presence on you, Casey, but I think I should stick around."

"I'd appreciate that," she heard herself reply. A surge of relief confirmed that she'd made the right decision.

He helped her into her car. "Nobody's going to push you around while I'm here," he said.

"I'm sure the Rawlinses got the message loud and clear."

So had she, Casey reflected. It felt good to have Jack watching over her, even though she knew it couldn't last.

Chapter Six

Dark bitterness had surfaced in Jack when the Rawlins family arrayed themselves against Casey. He'd flashed back to a time in junior high school when he'd thrashed the class bully in a fair fight after school.

The next day in the principal's office, the bully's self-righteous parents had presented a united front, defending their jerk offspring despite the testimony of other students. Somehow they'd found out Jack's father was in prison, and they twisted this information to portray him as a criminal in the making.

His foster mother had objected, but she didn't know him well enough to match their passionate attack. The other boy got a few days' suspension, more of a holiday than a punishment. Jack was forced to transfer to another school. Away from his friends, with a blot on his record.

He knew the Rawlinses didn't have that kind of power over Casey, but seeing her harassed until she turned white had infuriated him. He'd barely held onto his temper and hadn't even tried to rein in his sarcasm.

When he called his partner, Mike must have heard the emotion underlying his tone, because he agreed immediately to postpone the meeting with their potential partner. "I'll ask if he can stay in L.A. until Tuesday. I think I can make it back by then," Mike said.

"Thanks." Jack paced around Casey's office, where he'd

retreated to use her land-based phone. As she'd warned, the cellular reception had proved inadequate. "Things around here are trickier than I expected."

"I'm glad to cut you some slack when I can." He could picture Mike running his hand through his short blond hair. A Marine before he'd become a cop, he had a build like a wrestler and a Semper Fi tattoo on one bicep. "I know you'll keep your priorities straight."

"You got that right," Jack said.

No need to go into detail. They both liked being their own bosses, building a company where they didn't have to suck up to anybody or worry about getting called on the carpet if they offended someone's delicate sensibilities. The flip side, of course, was working long hours, putting up with unpredictable clients and taking physical and financial risks.

"We've got another prospect next weekend." Mike named a Greek company for which they'd done some consulting in the past. "They're trying to put together a meeting in Athens with representatives from companies in Scandinavia and Vietnam to arrange a multinational manufacturing and trade agreement."

"Surely they've been planning this for quite a while!" Jack hated when clients added security as an afterthought. It made their job that much tougher.

"Apparently they weren't sure of the timing. Also, I think they're worried about the news leaking out to people who fear their jobs may be exported," Mike explained. "With it being so last-minute, we can't do our usual prepping. They don't even know which hotel they're going to use or, if they do, they're not telling us."

"That ought to be fun," Jack said ironically. "Especially in Greece." Its location close to the Middle East made its facilities difficult to secure.

"This conference may not happen at all," Mike assured him. "Or it may be postponed. I've got Nicos—" a European associate they sometimes worked with "—putting together a flexible preliminary plan and finding out what local guards are available, but if it comes together, we'll need to have someone from Men At Arms on site."

"I should be clear by then." Jack doubted Casey's patience with him would stretch more than a few days.

"Great."

Knowing he might have a deadline increased the pressure to catch the prowler. As soon as they hung up, he reviewed his short list of suspects.

Jack didn't believe the Rawlinses had sprayed Casey or vandalized his car, but he wasn't ready to clear them, either. The Godwins' desire to buy some of her land seemed like a better motive, but it had been the former owner who'd turned them down, not Casey. The auto mechanic seemed a better bet. He'd take a closer look at him later, along with the tenants.

The locals might not appreciate having an outsider stick his nose into their business. Still, he meant to serve warning. Anyone who messed with Casey had better be prepared to deal with him, now or in the future, as long as she or their child needed him.

The ring of the bell and the click of the door opening snapped Jack from his thoughts. He emerged to find Casey talking to a tall woman with salt-and-pepper hair whom he remembered meeting last night. She set a square case atop the coffee table.

"Gail's teaching me baby care and preparation for childbirth," Casey explained. "She's an obstetrical nurse."

He remembered that she was the tenant who believed the prowler might be her ex-husband. He needed to talk to her, but he didn't want to interfere with something so important. "Don't let me stop you."

"You're welcome to participate." The woman retrieved a life-size baby doll from the case, along with a diaper. Her movements had the calm efficiency of long experience "This is a rather informal way of teaching, but we don't have enough pregnant women right now to hold a formal childbirth class."

"Gail's offered to coach me during labor, too. I want to try to have Diane naturally, so I won't miss any of the experience."

Casey's cheeks had regained their color since this morning, Jack noted. She seemed to be looking forward to this childbirth business.

To him, it sounded painful and messy. He doubted any guy he knew would choose to go through an experience like that wide awake if he could help it. Even talking about it gave him the willies.

"Thanks for the invite, but I think I'll talk to the other tenants," he said. "I'm sure you ladies are way ahead of me on this baby business, anyway."

"Don't you want to ask Gail about her ex-husband?" Casey put in.

"I can do that later." The smell of talcum powder reminded Jack of his first foster home, although this time the association wasn't entirely unpleasant. Despite the initial rebuke, he'd peeked into the nursery occasionally because the baby always looked so glad to see him. The memory of that little face brought back the bittersweet emotions he'd felt, torn between wanting to fit in and knowing he never could.

"I think we have a squeamish father here." Gail's cool, professional manner took any sting out of the words.

"No way!" Casey said. "Jack was a policeman. He's probably delivered babies, right?"

"We had to learn the basics, but mostly we relied on the paramedics." Jack didn't retain much from his Police Academy days, anyway, although he and Mike made a point of keeping up their CPR certification.

Casey's shoulders drooped. He hated disappointing her. "I suppose it wouldn't hurt to learn how to change a diaper," he muttered.

Her smile encouraged him. It occurred to Jack that he

probably should visit his daughter when he had to fly cross-country anyway. Maybe she'd give him one of those big, toothless grins and let him pick her up. At least this time nobody would order him out of the nursery, and he wouldn't have to worry about his parenting skills if he only stayed for a little while.

"Okay. I was planning to start with breathing exercises, but we can do those later." Gail reached for the doll. "The first thing to remember about a newborn is that you want to support the head and neck." She demonstrated with firm, smooth motions. "Never, ever shake a child. I'm sure you know that, officer."

"Call me Jack. And yes, I'm aware it can cause brain damage." Despite himself, he listened with interest. This wasn't any baby they were talking about but Diane, the little girl who would resemble her beautiful mother.

She might also look a bit like Jack. He pitied her already.

As Casey paid attention to the nurse, her hand rested on her enlarged abdomen. She didn't seem to notice the way she stroked it.

When it came time to diaper the doll, Jack figured that part would be easy, since this infant couldn't squirm. Sure enough, he had no trouble positioning the diaper and attaching the tapes. It came as a distinct surprise, though, when the whole production fell down around the doll's ankles the moment he lifted her.

"Well, let's hope our little precious hasn't done a number in there," Gail remarked.

Casey laughed.

"What did I do wrong?" Jack stared at his failure in disbelief.

"You need to pull everything tighter," the nurse advised. "Let's try it again."

He did a better job the second time. To his satisfaction, Casey took a while to master the procedure as well.

The nurse lifted the doll when they'd finished, cradling it for a moment almost as if it were a real child. "Sweet, isn't she?" she said wistfully. "I can't wait until we hold the real one! Okay, I did things backwards today because I figured child care would interest your husband, but now let's talk about labor and delivery."

This topic made Jack a bit queasy, and his lungs ached when he tried the breathing exercises. As he listened to the nurse describe something called dilation, he could almost smell the hospital the times his mother had fled there after beatings and, later, while undergoing treatment for cancer. Jack had huddled next to her in an endless series of waiting rooms, frightened by the sick people around them and repulsed by the odor of antiseptics.

Suddenly he found the air chokingly stale. Blurting an excuse, Jack strode from the house, down the porch steps and into the clearing across the driveway. Amid the pine odor and the open vista, his sense of entrapment abated.

Whatever fatherhood called for, Jack didn't have it in him. Although it bothered him that he wouldn't be there for Diane, she didn't need a man pretending to be her daddy only because he missed her mother.

He needed to work. To have a role, to focus on what must be done. Right now, that meant investigating the prowler.

Mentally, he tried to piece together the clues. Nothing fit a pattern or formed a larger picture. Whoever this guy was, he had a peculiar way of making his presence known and possibly mixed motives.

A short time later, someone came out of the house. When he glanced over, he saw the nurse's sturdy figure in crisp pink trousers and a flowered blouse.

"Casey asked me to talk to you." The woman addressed him matter-of-factly. "We like to joke in obstetrics that we haven't lost a father yet."

"I'm fine." Jack didn't want anyone trying to soothe him

with platitudes or to psychoanalyze him, either. "I'd like to pose a few questions about the prowler, if you don't mind."

"Be my guest." She leaned on the porch railing, rubbing her fingers together restlessly. He'd be willing to bet she used to smoke at some point and still missed it.

"Tell me about your ex-husband." From his pocket, he retrieved his notebook. It felt good to have something concrete to do.

"Dean? He's two years older than me, so that would make him sixty-three," Gail said. "He's tall and solid but not fat. He works as a plumber and his clients think he's a good-natured guy, always telling jokes and making nice with the customers. That's because he doesn't drink much during the day."

"He gets drunk regularly?"

She nodded. "Mostly at night. That's when the nasty side comes out. I don't think I need to paint you a picture."

"You certainly don't." Her ex-husband sounded like Jack's own father and far too many domestic abusers he'd encountered as a police officer. As long as they earned a living, they figured they had the right to mess up their families' lives to their hearts' content. "Any kids?"

"No." Her expression soured, as if she'd bitten into a lemon. It was obviously a sore subject.

That must be tough on a woman who worked with expectant moms all day, but some people channeled their misfortunes into caring for others. In a way, that's what Jack had done when he became a police officer.

"Has Dean ever stalked you?" he asked.

"Not that I'm aware of. Usually he keeps everything bottled up and then explodes. I've got the scars to prove it."

He didn't see any on her face, but the guy might have made a point of battering where it wouldn't show. "How long were you married?"

Nearly thirty years, Gail said, although during the first twenty Dean had served in the military so he'd been absent for long periods. After mustering out, he'd spent a few years on the wagon.

A layoff from his civilian job had sent him over the edge by forcing him to face the aging process and confront financial difficulties. For whatever reason, he'd sunk into a cycle of depression and abuse that continued even after he was rehired. About five years ago, Gail had left.

Although he made some threats when she sued for divorce, Dean had never attempted to carry them out. Gail only heard from him about financial matters, and not very often then, since they'd reached a settlement that didn't involve alimony. As far as she knew, he still lived in Michigan.

"Has he visited you here?"

She shook her head. "I get Christmas cards from him, though, so I know he has the address."

"Has he met Casey or any of the other tenants?"

"No."

Jack took down the man's phone number, address and last name. Using an on-line database he subscribed to, he could check out Dean's arrest record and credit rating, which should give a clue as to whether the guy was at risk of becoming violent.

A thirty-year marriage might not be set aside as easily as Gail implied, Jack mused. The fact that she hadn't completely cut off contact might look like encouragement to her ex. Still, the man's behavior pattern didn't fit a typical stalker.

As he was pulling together his thoughts, Gail asked, "Do you carry a gun?"

"No, why?"

"I don't see how you can protect Casey without one."

"There are practical and legal reasons why I don't," Jack told her. "It's not easy to get a license in California, and even if I had one, I couldn't take a weapon on an airplane or carry it out of state. Also, if you keep a firearm, there's the risk of an accidental discharge or of a criminal getting his hands on it."

"You'd better hope this prowler isn't armed," Gail said tartly.

"Does your ex have a gun?"

She reflected a moment. "I never saw one. But in case it isn't him, you should know that plenty of people have them around here. For hunting and so forth."

That didn't surprise him. Keeping a gun in one's own home was legal in most places, although not necessarily safe. "Any of the tenants, as far as you know?"

"Bo has one." She waited as he flipped to a clean page in his notebook. "That's Bo Rogers. He and his wife Rita live in the cabin behind Enid's. He's mentally challenged, a very nice young man. In his midthirties, I'd say."

"Handgun or rifle?"

"Rifle, for hunting rabbits. He offered to bring me one, but I couldn't bear to eat a cute little thing like that," she said.

"There's another male tenant, isn't there? What about him?"

"Matt Dorning. He lives in the cabin behind me." She spelled the last name without being asked. "I don't know about a gun but he has plenty of knives."

"What kind of knives?"

"Mostly for whittling, I guess," Gail replied. "He sells animal figures to shops around the region. He's got a whole display of them in a case. The knives, I mean."

Jack asked a few more questions without learning anything significant. "Thanks." He closed the notebook. "You've been a big help." He paused in case she wanted to add anything. People sometimes revealed vital clues as an afterthought.

Not Gail. All she said was, "Casey could use your support, but I'm not going to tell you your business. I was sorry to hear about your car."

"Thanks."

She said a brief farewell, collected her supplies and departed, taking the footpath toward her cabin. Jack went inside.

In the living room, Casey sat on the couch, her head bent

over some yarn she was working with a hooked needle. Crocheting, Jack thought it was called. He had no idea what the floppy little circle in her hands was supposed to be.

"I'm going to go talk to a couple of your tenants," he told her. "You're welcome to come with me."

She didn't answer.

When Casey clammed up, that never boded well. "Something the matter?" he inquired.

Still no answer.

"Did Gail say something about me?"

She gave a headshake.

Seeking a way to break the ice, Jack asked, "What are you making?"

"Sweater." She stared at it far more intently than seemed necessary.

"Kind of a small sweater." He realized what a stupid comment that was. "For Diane, right?"

Her head bobbed. It marked progress, of a sort.

He sat on the couch beside her. During their marriage, Jack hadn't known how to respond when Casey ignored him, so he'd gone about his business. She always got over her sulks eventually, but the two of them never went back and discussed what had been bothering her.

It seemed to him, in retrospect, that issues had to be addressed or they piled up like trash in a corner. Besides, it didn't take a genius to figure out what had set her off. "You're upset because I walked out."

"You always do that." She lowered the crocheting. "Whenever I try to bring you inside my life, to include you in things that matter, you freak out."

"I'm sorry."

"I thought you might change." She blinked away tears. The sight of her distress made Jack's fists clench, as if he could fight off the villain who'd done this to her. However, that would be himself.

"Believe me, I wish I knew how to fix this," he said.

"You never tell me what you're thinking."

"It isn't worth repeating." He had no idea how to express thoughts that seemed jumbled and irrelevant. And painful.

"I almost wish you hadn't come back." Casey's blue eyes glittered. "I know it's stupid, but I started to hope you might begin to care about Diane. Fat chance, huh?"

"I do care. Anything you need, just ask. I'm not going to abandon either of you."

"Did Gail talk you into saying that?" she demanded.

"I'm not a complete jerk!" he snapped, annoyed at the implication. "Gail didn't have to talk me into anything. As a matter fact, she hardly mentioned the baby. We discussed her ex-husband."

"Oh." Casey let out a long breath. She didn't look fed up any more, just resigned. That bothered Jack even more than her stubbornness. "I guess it's time I accepted you the way you are. That's why we can't be together any more, and I regret it, but there it is."

Perversely, he wanted to argue, only to what end? Although he'd nursed the fantasy that he could win Casey back on his own terms, her pregnancy made that impossible. Whatever fantasy she'd clung to about him, he'd apparently popped that balloon as well.

"I guess we both need to accept each other," he conceded. "You're in a difficult situation and I'm doing my best to help. Now, would you like to come with me to interview the tenants?"

She dumped the crocheting on the coffee table. "Sure," she said. "Let me get my jacket."

It was a truce of sorts, Jack thought. He hoped it would last.

Chapter Seven

At least he'd tried to open up, Casey told herself as they strolled through the crisp afternoon toward Enid's cabin. She had to admit that she didn't always have an easy time expressing her own feelings, and it must be infinitely harder for Jack.

In her family, people had usually got along. When problems cropped up, they'd resolved themselves naturally because her parents shared the same values and dreams. As a result, they hadn't needed to work on their communications skills.

She couldn't imagine what Jack's life had been like. Although she realized he'd lost his parents and grown up in foster homes, she didn't understand his antagonism toward parenthood. To her, having a baby meant establishing one's own warm, safe home.

Once in a while, an uncharacteristic vulnerability would shine in his face, reinforcing her belief that, deep inside, Jack had a tender heart. If only he'd try to see things her way!

She could have sworn he'd shown real interest when he tried to diaper the doll. Surely he could learn to love his daughter, if he only let himself.

Fiercely, Casey jammed her hands into her pockets and picked up the pace. Believing in the impossible had landed her in the middle of a divorce, where she faced life as a single mom. She supposed she'd better rein in her fantasies before she got hurt all over again.

The curving lower driveway at Pine Woods Court formed a backwards S, with her house at the lower bulge and Enid's at the upper one. Above that point, the driveway split into the shape of an H lying on its side, with each of the four units occupying one endpoint. Until her parents bought the place, the cabins, shielded from view by swelling land and abundant trees, had rented by the week or month. They'd been popular among hunters, hikers and fishermen

As they walked, Jack gazed from side to side, taking stock. She saw him scan a rock outcropping and study an old, fallen tree that Casey had left in place because animals nested in it. Even though he probably viewed all of it as cover for criminals, she hoped he might start to enjoy the intrinsic beauty as well.

At her suggestion, he'd exchanged his suit for a corduroy jacket, jeans and suede work shoes that fit the surroundings and emphasized his natural masculinity. She liked his self-possessed stride, with no wasted motion or swagger.

Impulsively, she wondered how he'd react if she tugged him behind the outcropping, unzipped his jacket and pulled him onto the grass. She certainly knew how *she* would react as she imagined the warmth of his body sheltering hers from the spring breeze.

"Tell me about Enid." Jack's words yanked her to reality. "What's her background?"

"She was my high-school math teacher." When Casey flew back here after her mother's heart attack, she'd been pleased to find Miss Purdue in residence. "I wasn't exactly one of her more brilliant students and sometimes she made it tough on me, but eventually I earned her respect." After a moment, she added, "She's the one who organized the baby shower last night."

"Does she have any ex-husbands who might be lurking around?"

"She never married." Richfield Crossing didn't offer many romantic opportunities, particularly to a woman who worked with youngsters all day. "She told me once she wished they'd had the Internet back then, because she might have found someone."

"Any chance she's been looking for love on the web recently?" The technology had spawned a lot of good relationships and also some tragedies. A sheltered woman such as Enid Purdue might unwittingly draw the interest of a disturbed individual.

"She doesn't have an Internet account," Casey explained. "She goes to the library or borrows my computer when she wants to order something she can't find locally. So I doubt she's Internet dating. Besides, although she heard somebody rummaging around outside once, it doesn't appear that anybody's targeting her."

"You never know," Jack said.

Casey supposed that was part of the reason why people hired security consultants: because they always looked on the negative side. However, anyone who listened to Jack long enough risked becoming paranoid.

Trees obscured their view of Enid's cabin until they entered the small yard. Trying to see it from Jack's viewpoint, she noticed the elderly but well-maintained sedan in the carport, newly planted spring flowers along the front of the modest wood-sided home and a bird-feeder hanging outside the kitchen window.

At their knock, Enid opened the door. Her face lit up when she saw them. "Come on in!"

"Sorry to arrive unannounced." Until that moment, it hadn't occurred to Casey to call ahead. She and her tenants often dropped in on each other when they went out for walks.

"That's perfectly all right."

They stepped into the cozy interior. Upholstered chairs, ruffled curtains and a few too many end tables crowded the place. However, despite a wealth of figurines in several china cabinets, she didn't see a speck of dust.

Jack lowered himself carefully onto the sofa as if afraid the old-fashioned furniture might break. The place certainly hadn't been designed with men in mind, Casey mused.

"Hold on. I'm sure you'd enjoy refreshments." As if eager for the opportunity to entertain, Enid vanished into the kitchen. Jack didn't protest, perhaps because they hadn't eaten lunch. Although Casey hadn't felt hungry earlier, she quickly discovered she was starving. Since becoming pregnant, she'd had a hard time not devouring everything in sight.

Soon they were sitting around the claw-legged table, enjoying a large plate of tea sandwiches and cupcakes. Enid must have made the food yesterday in case they needed extra at the party, Casey realized, and felt touched by her neighbor's concern.

"Moms-to-be need to keep up their energy," her friend informed them. "Did you know that in Japan, mothers eat heartily just before giving birth? Here, they're supposed to keep their stomachs empty because we medicate women during childbirth, while they don't. The Japanese have the lowest infant mortality rate in the world, so they must be doing something right."

"I had no idea you took such an interest in the subject," Casey said. "Did you learn that when you went to Japan?" Enid enjoyed taking tours, usually to sites of historic interest.

Their hostess shook her head. "Gail loaned me a documentary about childbirth around the world. I think it's fascinating how different cultures approach such a fundamental process, don't you?"

"I've been more involved with preparing myself for the real thing," she admitted. "It's all uncharted territory to me."

Jack came up for air after downing a ham sandwich. "Casey just had a lesson, all those breathing exercises. I should think that would make it harder."

"Aren't you supposed to practice them too?" Enid asked. "I imagine you're going to be her coach."

"I can't stay that long." He helped himself to a chicken sandwich. "These are great."

"Thank you." She fixed Casey with a penetrating stare, the way she used to do when her less-than-star pupil forgot a math theorem. "I know Gail offered to help, but the doctor will need her assistance. If your husband can't be here, one of your friends ought to step in. What about Sandra, now that she's back?"

Casey cringed at the memory of their recent encounter. "When I ran into her at church, she didn't have anything nice to say about my impending motherhood. In fact, she seemed unhappy to see me."

"Displaced anger," Enid announced promptly. "Bunch of nonsense! It would do her good to stop blaming her problems on others. Well, never mind that. If you'd like a volunteer with absolutely no experience, I'd be more than happy to help. I hesitated to mention it before because I didn't want to intrude."

"What a sweet offer," Casey said. "You know, I'd like that. You're so calm, it might help keep me centered." Jack was tapping his fingers on the table. The subject must make him uncomfortable. "Maybe later we can set up a time to practice with Gail."

The retired teacher beamed as if she'd received a wonderful gift. "I'd enjoy that tremendously."

Jack produced his notebook, clearly eager to steer the conversation to his investigation. After explaining about the damage to his car, he said, "Do you have any idea who might have done this?"

"No, but if I were you, I'd ask Chief Roundtree to look into it himself," she advised. "I couldn't believe it when Casey told me he sent Larry Malloy the other night."

The pencil poised over the paper. "Why do you say that?"

"He's unlikely material for a police officer." Enid refilled Jack's coffee cup without being asked. "I'm sure he's matured since high school, but—well, never mind. That was several years ago."

"If you have concerns, I'd like to hear them." He waited expectantly.

"Larry used to goof off a lot in Algebra II," she said. "After I flunked him, his parents made him postpone getting his driver's license until he'd passed the class in summer school. He told some other kids he'd make me regret it, and one morning I came out to find that someone had let the air out of my tires."

"Did you confront Malloy about this?"

"No. I couldn't prove anything," Enid replied. "And of course it was no monetary damage, just the inconvenience. Now, though, I wonder if he'll put his heart into catching a vandal when he did the same kind of thing himself only seven or eight years ago."

"You don't know for sure that he did it," Casey felt obliged to point out.

"No one else had a motive," she said.

"The man we're seeking squirted a pregnant woman with a hose and caused several hundred dollars' worth of damage to my car," Jack said.

"Objectively speaking, the events are different in many ways," Enid agreed. "But they all sound like impulsive acts. Besides, I didn't mean to imply that Larry was some kind of criminal, only that I'm not sure he's the right man to handle the investigation."

Jack tapped his pen against the pad. "Thanks for the information about Malloy. You never can tell when this kind of insight will prove useful."

While he and Enid continued talking, Casey's thoughts drifted to the young officer. She hadn't known him well in school, since he'd been four years behind her. Still, it wasn't reassuring to think that someone barely past the age of defiance had been entrusted with investigating her assault. More then ever, she appreciated Jack's coming to the rescue.

Well, she'd better make good use of his talents while she

had the chance. "I need to introduce Jack to the other tenants," she told Enid. "I hope you don't mind."

"Not at all." Their hostess prepared a bag of cupcakes to go before showing them out. "I'm delighted you stopped in."

They thanked her again for the food and her offer to coach Casey. Outside, as they headed toward the Rogers' unit, she asked, "You don't suspect Larry, do you?"

"No more than a number of other people. Still, if he *was* the prowler, it must have given him a perverse satisfaction to pretend to investigate his own crime." Jack shortened his stride to allow for her more leisurely gait. "It didn't sound as if he did a thorough job."

"He spent maybe ten minutes looking around," Casey said. "He asked a few questions and wrote down what I said, but he didn't even come back the next day to look for evidence in the light. I don't think he fingerprinted the hose, either."

"And he could easily have picked it up while poking around, which gives him an alibi if his prints turn up."

It was the kind of detail Casey would never have thought of. "Was that dereliction of duty, not to take prints?"

Jack ducked his head. "Actually, no. Upsetting as it is, what happened to you doesn't fit the definition of a major crime. Collecting prints isn't hard; however, matching them to a perpetrator takes a lot of time, even assuming the guy's prints are on record."

They turned right onto the connecting lane. Ahead, on a gentle slope, a couple of deer lifted their heads from grazing.

Jack regarded them in amazement. "They act as if they're tame. Don't people hunt them?"

"Not on my property," Casey said. "I let my tenants fish in the creek, but if they want to shoot, they have to go elsewhere."

"I haven't heard any gunshots, so I guess your neighbors don't allow it either."

"As I mentioned, nobody keeps an eye on the property west of mine. But hunting season's restricted to fall and winter."

The deer continued to observe them. Although the animals remained motionless, Casey knew that, if frightened, they would vanish in seconds like a wheel of birds.

"I'm a decent shot on the target range, but I've never understood the appeal of sport hunting," Jack admitted.

He'd told her once that he'd never shot anyone on duty, though he'd had to draw his gun several times. He'd disliked doing it, he'd said, because aiming a gun at someone increased the risk of overreacting and pulling the trigger in error.

The Rogers' bungalow lay directly behind Enid's. As Casey approached with Jack, she noted that they hadn't yet planted their vegetable garden, which was surrounded by a high fence to keep out deer and rabbits. In April, with a cold snap still possible, it remained a patch of straggling weeds.

"Who lives here?" Jack asked as they came within sight of a freshly painted blue-and-white house. With the cutout shutters and rose trellises erected by the residents, it resembled a cottage from a fairy tale.

"Bo and Rita," Casey said. "They're…"

Before she could finish, he grabbed her arm and half lifted, half dragged her into a clump of pines. "Down!"

Automatically, she obeyed. The pungent smell of pine surrounded her as she crouched. "What is it?"

"A man. Aiming a rifle at us." Jack's arms encircled her protectively. Despite the troublesome circumstances, Casey relished the contact.

"Bo's never threatened anyone." He worked as a custodian at the glass factory, and had received several certificates for reliability and dedication. "He and Rita may be mentally challenged, but they have exceptional common sense."

"He might have gone ballistic. That can happen to anybody." Jack indicated a faint trail through the trees. "I'll distract him while you head for Enid's place. Keep to the curve of the land and stay as close to the trees as possible."

Casey peeked out. She could see Bo now, a rifle cradled in his arms as he scanned the area with a worried expression. "I don't think he means any harm. They're not used to strangers coming around, and Rita frightens easily. With all this talk about a prowler, Bo might simply be taking precautions."

"Drawing a gun on someone isn't a very wise precaution," Jack replied tensely. "People have been known to fire back."

"We're not in L.A.," Casey said. "Anyway, Bo doesn't know you. I'm going to call him by name."

"Wait!"

If she didn't act now, this situation could escalate to the point where someone might get hurt. "Bo!" she shouted. "It's me, Casey!"

"Don't you ever follow directions?" Jack's eyes narrowed.

"Not on my property," she shot back. "I respect your expertise, but you ought to trust my instincts."

"I'm your bodyguard," he growled. "Let me do my job, all right?" Another glance toward the house and he shook his head. "Too late. He's coming. Casey, get down."

Her heart rate speeded. She knew Jack expected compliance, but hiding would simply make Bo even more nervous. "Bo!" she repeated. "I brought my husband to meet you. We just came from Enid's house."

"How do I know it's really you?" he responded.

"Don't you recognize my voice?"

"It could be a recording," he said.

Jack clamped his hand on her arm. "Stay here. He's not thinking straight."

"Yes, he is." She shook off his grip. "It's going to make him suspicious if I don't come out."

"He's already too suspicious for my taste," her husband muttered.

Casey didn't have time to explain what she understood instinctively, that Bo was doing his best to navigate a dazzlingly complex world where movies made the impossible seem real.

To him, the notion of bad guys faking a recording of his land-lady's voice must seem perfectly credible.

"I'm going to come out now!" she called. "Bo, put your gun down. You don't want to shoot me by accident!"

"I wish you wouldn't do this." Jack quivered with suppressed tension. But to his credit, he didn't force the issue.

Pushing aside a pine branch, Casey stepped slowly into view. In front of her, Bo Rogers had lowered the muzzle of his rifle and stood staring intently. Of medium height, with thick, sandy hair, he wore the belligerent expression he assumed when he believed someone might be trying to trick him.

As a youngster, Casey's mother had told her, cruel children had often made him the butt of their jokes. His essentially sweet nature and his good luck in meeting Rita at a special school had saved him. Still, he'd made up his mind never to let anyone push him around again. She respected him for it.

When he recognized her, he broke into a smile. "It *is* you!"

"I should have phoned ahead," Casey apologized. "Would you like to meet Jack?"

"Sure!" Embarrassed, he poked the rifle into the ground. When her husband came out and she introduced them, Bo wiped his hand on his coveralls before shaking firmly. "Sorry if I scared you."

"It's not a good idea to point guns at people," Jack told him. "A police officer might fire if he feels threatened."

"Oh, they all know me around here." Bo gestured toward the house. "Come on in."

Rita, who'd met Jack at the party, ushered them inside. Always tidy and freshly painted, the cabin sported posters from animated films including *Shrek* and *Finding Nemo*. The entertainment center held a large assortment of fantasy and animated films.

Jack listened politely as their hosts enthused about the latest DVD releases. Patiently, he kept asking about anyone unusual they'd seen in the area, repeating the question when their attention strayed. The courteous way he treated the couple impressed Casey.

She suspected his manner hadn't come easily. Jack had had a rough time in school, she'd gathered from what little he'd said about his early life. Showing kindness and patience spoke for the depth of his character and, perhaps, for compassion he'd learned from his own experience.

"The only person I've seen around is the movie man," Bo said at last.

"The movie man?" Jack inquired.

"From the Roxy."

"That's the theater. Sandra's parents own it," Casey told her husband. To Bo, she said, "You mean Al Rawlins?"

He nodded. "I see him by the creek sometimes."

Jack made a note. "What time of day?"

"I don't know," Bo replied.

Realizing he might be taking the question literally and meant he hadn't checked his watch, Casey asked, "Was it at night?"

"Early morning," Bo said. "On Saturdays when I go fishing."

"What was he doing?" Jack queried.

"He was fishing, too."

That didn't make sense to Casey. "The Rawlinses live about a mile from here. The creek runs within a quarter-mile of their property, so I don't know why he'd come all this way."

"Did he tell you why he likes to fish here?" Jack inquired of Bo.

"He just waved," the tenant told him.

"We'd better talk to Al ourselves, although we'll have to be circumspect about it." He asked Bo a few more questions, but the couple had nothing else to report. Jack thanked them earnestly.

That left one more tenant for him to meet, elderly Matt Dorning, but as they stepped into the mild afternoon, Casey's stomach muscles tightened. Not wanting to alarm the Rogerses, she said nothing until they'd cleared the porch.

When her hand flew to her abdomen, Jack registered concern. "Is the baby kicking again or are you going into labor?"

"Neither one—at least, I don't think so." Since she'd come within three weeks of her due date, Casey couldn't dismiss the possibility of labor, but this had happened before. "There's something called Braxton Hicks contractions that occur sometimes, preparing me to have the baby."

"How can you tell they're not labor pains?" he asked as they walked slowly.

"I can't be sure. I'll have to see whether they intensify." Although the tightening had passed, Casey didn't feel like paying any more visits. "Let's call it a day."

"Agreed." Jack rested one hand on the small of her back. "Gail's your nurse, right?"

"I'll phone her when we get home." But Casey didn't feel in any hurry, now that the contraction had ended.

The sunshine on her face and Jack's touch sent her spirits soaring. She loved the Tennessee landscape bursting with spring scents and colors, but it meant even more with her husband close by.

"I've missed you," she blurted.

"Let's get you inside." He steered Casey along the path.

She realized her comment must have made him uncomfortable. "I'm not trying to make you feel guilty."

"About what?" He sounded genuinely at sea.

"About not having been here."

"Casey, I'm not that touchy," Jack said. "I'll feel better after you talk to the nurse, that's all."

"I'm perfectly healthy. Walking is good for me."

"It might not be good for Diane."

He was acting as nervous as any father-to-be. Casey wanted to throw her arms around him, but her judgment warned her not to make too much of his reaction.

She'd always known he had a deep capacity to care about others, which was part of what made him such a good protector. That didn't mean his attitude toward the baby had changed.

Still, she couldn't avoid feeling a glimmer of hope. It lasted for a few more steps…until a second contraction turned her belly hard as a rock.

"Uh-oh," she said.

This time, she didn't quibble when Jack hurried her inside.

Chapter Eight

Jack paced through the living room, trying to make sense of Casey's one-sided conversation on the phone. From what he gathered, the nurse seemed remarkably calm about the whole thing. Far from reassuring him, her reaction made him wonder if his wife was receiving the best possible care.

During his mother's long battle with cancer when he was eleven, his helplessness had frightened and angered him. Now he wanted to take action.

His restless strides carried him into the kitchen. Shouldn't he boil water or something? He vaguely recalled that people did that in old movies, although he'd never figured out what they did with the water once they heated it.

Pregnancies could go dangerously wrong. Why didn't Gail insist she check into the hospital until her condition stabilized?

"Well?" he demanded as soon as Casey hung up.

"She said to call her back if I have any more contractions. Two in a row might mean something or it might not."

"That's it?" Jack couldn't believe this cavalier approach. "Shouldn't they run some tests?"

"She could examine me to see if I'm dilated, but if I'm really in labor, it's going to become obvious within the next hour. Besides, I have a regular checkup scheduled tomorrow with the doctor." Casey took Enid's cupcakes out of the bag and set them on a plate. "Since my waters haven't broken and I'm not in pain, she thinks there's no cause for alarm."

"That's all?"

"I mentioned that Enid volunteered to coach me, but she didn't recommend it unless she gets a chance to prepare." Casey ran water into a kettle. "If she doesn't know what to do, she could be more hindrance than help."

"You're not telling me everything, are you?" Jack said.

"About what?"

He indicated the kettle. "You're boiling water."

"So?"

"That's what women do when they're giving birth." He folded his arms decisively.

"I'm making herbal tea." She looked as if she were fighting a smile. "Would you like a cup?"

Okay, so he'd overreacted. Still, someone had to watch over Casey. She'd admitted this might be labor, in which case perhaps she shouldn't be eating or drinking. "Did Gail recommend drinking tea?"

"She did," Casey conceded. "Along with a relaxing bath." Mischievously, she added, "Care to join me?"

"I doubt we'd both fit in the tub." All the same, a scene from the early days of their marriage flashed into Jack's mind. They'd celebrated moving into their new rental home by taking a sensuous shower together, starting with champagne and ending with memorable lovemaking on a fluffy rug.

His body ached to repeat the experience. As if his wife could even consider making love this close to childbirth!

Casey waved one hand for his attention. "The expressions on your face! Jack, I was kidding."

"I know that." And yet… "You said you missed me," he reminded her. "Don't you ever miss me that way, too? That is, leaving aside the physical impossibility right now."

A blush brightened her cheeks. "Sure, I miss you that way. Jack, I never said I didn't love you. I said I couldn't go on living the way we were. I wanted you and this baby. Why can't I have both?"

He let the question hang in the air, almost afraid to answer. "Because you hate the way I live," he ventured at last.

"You could move here," Casey suggested.

He didn't belong in Richfield Crossing. And what would he do for a living, drive a tractor and pitch hay for the cows? "Do you realize how hard I've worked building up this business? It means a lot to me."

"You have so many talents, you could fit in anywhere!"

"If you wanted a local boy, you should have married Royce." He regretted the remark as soon as he saw her lower lip tremble. "I didn't mean that."

Turning away, Casey poured hot water over her tea bag. With her back to him, she said, "Sorry I brought it up."

He knew he should back off now, but he couldn't bear it. "I'm just sorry you care more about this place than about your husband."

"And the baby?" she asked. "Where would she fit into this picture?"

He couldn't answer that. "It seems like no matter what picture we paint, one of us doesn't have a place in it."

"I'm afraid I have to agree with you."

Leaving her to enjoy her tea in privacy, Jack went through the living room into the office, where he'd set up his laptop. The best way he knew to settle his thoughts was to work.

Flipping open his pad, he busied himself typing in notes, adding a few observations as he went. All the while, he searched for a pattern that might point to a suspect.

First, he summarized the facts. During the past month, several tenants had seen or heard a prowler. The only person attacked had been Casey, apparently to stop her from taking a photo. There'd also been vandalism against his car, indicating that the perpetrator might have known who he was.

In addition, Casey had mentioned earlier damage to the

mailbox. Although she'd said it appeared to be accidental, the perp had tried to make the attack on Jack's car look like an accident, too.

None of it fit a clear model. If someone held a grudge, who was the target and where did the motive lie? Jack turned to his list of names.

Al Rawlins appeared to blame Casey for his daughter's problems, and he'd been spotted on the property. Also, although Larry Malloy's grudge against Enid Purdue dated to high school, the rookie cop's involvement in investigating was suggestive. Just as arsonists loved to watch their fires burn, criminals often gloried in the attention given to their misdeeds.

Jack hadn't forgotten about Mimi's parents, the Godwins, who'd once wanted to buy the property. In addition, Casey's ex-boyfriend naturally fell under suspicion. Most attacks on women came from men they'd been close to.

That brought him to Gail's ex-husband. Unlike the others, he might be ruled out or brought to the fore by information available on the Internet. Jack typed in the address of a data service to which his company subscribed.

Within half an hour, after widening his search to include other Web sites, he'd discovered several significant facts about Dean Fordham. He'd maintained a spotless credit report for the past three years, although prior to that he'd had his ups and downs. Also, according to a group that built housing for the homeless, he'd received a volunteer award nine months earlier for installing free plumbing.

Most significantly, a personal Web site contained photos of his recent wedding, along with shots of the couple's new home in Hawaii. The two had moved there to be near his wife's grown children.

That didn't sound like a man obsessed with his ex-wife or keen on flying to Tennessee to conduct petty harassment. Jack downloaded a photo of Dean to show around in case anyone recognized him, but he put a question mark next to the name in his file.

Despite Gail's suspicions, they could probably rule out her ex-husband. That didn't bring Jack any closer to figuring out who *was* behind the attacks.

Tomorrow, he'd conduct more interviews. In the meantime, he hoped the prowler didn't plan further mischief that might put Casey or anyone else at risk.

WHETHER IT WAS the effect of the hot tea and warm bath or simply nature taking its time, the muscle spasms disappeared. Casey half wished they'd return so Jack could be here to welcome Diane into the world. Still, given his obvious discomfort at discussions of childbirth, he wasn't likely to relish being present amid all that mess.

What a contrary man he was! Inhaling the rose scent of her soap, she luxuriated in the tub and let her thoughts wander back to the concern in Jack's green eyes as she reported what Gail had advised.

What a fuss he'd made about her boiling water! His comment had been so cute that she might almost have convinced herself he wanted to be a daddy. But when she'd mentioned taking Diane back to L.A., he'd clammed up as always.

No, not quite as always. Resting one hand on the bulge, Casey acknowledged that Jack had been more open about his feelings today than she'd ever seen him. He'd tried, at least a little, to reach out to her.

Not far enough, though. It seemed as if they stood on opposite sides of a bridge that he refused to cross. The fact that the bridge would transport him to a world they could share wasn't enough to make him leave his familiar surroundings.

Her heart squeezed. Strolling and talking together reminded her of the early days of their relationship when they'd delighted in each other's company. She kept wanting to nestle into Jack and find a way to make a home together.

Quit torturing yourself. It isn't going to work. Deal with it.

Heat suffused Casey. She realized her temperature must be rising from the bath and from her pregnancy-fueled internal furnace. Letting herself overheat wasn't good for the baby.

Struggling into a straighter position, she gripped the edge of the tub and tried to rise. Push as she might, however, she couldn't lever herself up without risking a fall. It felt as if she'd gained five hundred pounds.

Only one possibility came to mind, embarrassing as it might be. She had to call Jack in to help.

For modesty's sake, Casey tried to reach the towel rack, but that didn't work either. She'd underestimated her weight gain at five hundred pounds, she reflected ruefully. A ton would be more accurate.

Oh, well, she wasn't baring anything her husband hadn't seen plenty of times.

"Jack!" Receiving no answer, she called his name louder and added, "I need your help!"

Footsteps shook the house and he flung open the door. "Are you bleeding? What happened?"

The near panic on his face sent guilt flooding through Casey. Blushing, she said, "I can't get up. I'm afraid I'll slip."

He frowned. "No more contractions?"

She shook her head. "Just clumsiness. I'm sorry if I worried you."

"I'm glad it's nothing more serious." In his relief, he finally took a good look at her and blinked, visibly startled at the sight of her enlarged and uncovered body.

It was the first time anyone except her nurse or the doctor had seen her pregnancy in all its glory. In a way, Casey had been glad that nobody else had to see her whalelike proportions.

She didn't consider herself ugly, exactly, yet now she became acutely aware not only of her enlarged tummy but of other changes, from her darkened nipples to her thunder thighs. It certainly wasn't the stuff of fashion magazines.

Jack continued staring as he reached for a towel. Casey sighed. "I know I look funny."

"You look amazing." He drew the oversize terry cloth from the rack. Kneeling beside the tub, Jack brushed a damp strand from her temple. "You remind me of a fertility symbol."

Casey's nipples tightened beneath his gaze and an ache bloomed lower down. He'd asked if she missed him that way. The answer was an emphatic yes, now more than ever.

In the misty air, his sweater clung to his torso. She wished Jack were naked too.

It seemed only natural when he leaned over the tub and kissed her. Casey's tongue met his and her hand came up, damply, to caress his shoulder.

The way his mouth played over hers stirred a longing she hadn't experienced in eight lonely months, to feel his bare skin brushing hers and his hard masculine body merging into her soft, feminine one. If only they could share another wonderful night like the one when they'd created their baby.

Breathing hard, Jack lifted his head. "We have to stop. You're in too vulnerable a condition."

"We could work around it."

He choked back a laugh. "Casey, you're outrageous!"

Her gaze trailed down to the telltale distension in his jeans. The evidence of his arousal inspired her to make this strong man yield completely.

"Let me stroke you all over and drive you wild," she said.

"You've always been brash." His breath came faster, she noticed. "But we can't."

"Let me try." She unsnapped the front of his jeans and cupped him with her hand. Jack groaned. "I love it when you get big and hard."

"I can't believe you're doing this." His lips moved across hers again.

Casey took that as encouragement. She'd never tried to bring her husband to climax this way before, but it thrilled her to see his eyelids lower and feel his pelvis shift in an instinctive rhythm.

His excitement told her how desirable he found her. And it brought them close in a way neither of them could express with words.

Enjoying every moment, Casey fondled him. When his hands claimed her breasts, intense pleasure nearly overwhelmed her. Although she had to assume an awkward position on her knees and at an angle in order to reach him, the indulgence of her long-suppressed sensuality more than made up for it.

The pressure of Jack's hardness against her palm encouraged her to rub him in a spiraling cadence. She could tell he was trying to control his excitement, and prolong the ardor, yet his body defied him. She reveled in the arching of his back and the waves of release until at last he brought the towel into play.

Leaning against the tub with his head close to hers, he murmured, "That was incredible. It's been a long time."

She hadn't considered the possibility that he might have taken other lovers since their separation. It was gratifying to realize that, apparently, he hadn't, and that her pregnancy hadn't diminished his response to her. "We've never been able to resist each other, have we?"

"That's for sure," he said ruefully.

"Good." Casey didn't want to lose the special exhilaration they awakened in each other, even if they couldn't live together any more. She doubted she'd ever feel so close to another man.

"It's your turn." Tossing the towel aside, Jack reached for a fresh one. "First, let's get you dry."

She let him help her out, but drew back when he tried to stroke her. "It could bring on contractions."

"Would that be so terrible at this stage?" Jack asked.

"I suppose not," Casey admitted.

He draped her with the towel but left the front open, studying at leisure. "Someone ought to sculpt you like this."

"I doubt they could find a big enough piece of marble," she shot back.

He chuckled. "If I mention your alabaster skin, will you slap me?"

What a delicious man, Casey thought, and wished he could still be hers. Well, for the moment he was, and she intended to enjoy herself. "I've always thought actions speak louder than words."

"Then let's go." He guided her toward the bedroom.

From the front of the house, the doorbell sounded. "Ignore that," she said.

Jack hesitated. "You don't think it could be important?"

That was the problem with being a landlady. You never knew when someone might need you. "I suppose so. Okay. Would you mind answering it?" She adjusted the towel. However, it still failed to cover her completely.

"I certainly don't expect you to, not in that condition." After one more appreciative glance, he buckled his belt and went out.

In the bedroom, Casey pulled on a loose top and stretch jeans, and brushed out the hair she'd piled atop her head. From the front, she heard a familiar female voice that brought her sharply to attention.

"I can come back later," Sandra was saying. "I know I should have called. I went out for a drive and dropped in on impulse."

So much for her and Jack's intentions, Casey mused. But she wanted very much to reestablish a good relationship with her old friend.

She hurried out. "You're not going anywhere! Don't even think about leaving!"

A shaky smile greeted her. "Are you sure?"

"Absolutely." She debated whether to give Sandra a hug, but the moment passed. "What can I get you to drink?"

Jack, to his credit, chimed in, "I was about to make coffee. How about it?"

"I'd love some," Sandra said. "It's getting cold out. I hear it might rain."

They went into the kitchen, which stirred happy memories. Although Casey's parents hadn't bought this place until she was in community college, Sandra had occasionally come for dinner. Other times, she and Casey had baked fudge or cookies and shared confidences across this table.

The woman who edged onto her chair now bore little resemblance to the cheerful, healthy young woman from years ago. Without the sunglasses and scarf she'd worn at church, Casey got a daunting view of hollowed eyes, overbleached hair and a scarred cheekbone.

"I'm sorry about the things I said this morning." Her voice, while still recognizable, had become raspier. She'd also lost most of her Tennessee accent. "I just arrived home yesterday and my parents didn't tell you'd moved back. It came as a shock."

"Sorry it was so unpleasant." When Casey extended the plate of cupcakes, Sandra took one hesitantly. Jack discreetly kept busy measuring coffee and water into the drip machine.

"I'm going to be real honest here, because there's no point in hiding things." Sandra laced her fingers on the table. "While I was using drugs, I had a miscarriage. Messed up as I was, I still wanted that baby. Nobody told me you were pregnant. I…I just wasn't expecting it."

Now Casey understood the pain that had prompted her friend's cutting remark about motherhood. "I can see why you'd be taken aback."

"I didn't know about that you and Jack having had problems, either. When I saw you so happy with everything perfect, it was like a slap on the face." Sandra's edginess and the pallor of her complexion spoke volumes about what she must be enduring. "I know I shouldn't stoop to being jealous, but right now I have a hard time keeping my emotions in line."

"It took a lot of courage to come here this afternoon." Casey's heart went out to the woman she'd loved as a child and a teenager. "I'm glad you did."

Coffee dripped noisily into the pot. Leaning on the counter as he waited for it to finish, Jack regarded Sandra coolly. "Are you undergoing treatment while you're here?"

Casey feared she might take offense, but she gave no sign of it. "I finished five weeks of rehab in L.A. One of the points they emphasized was that you need to get away from the people and circumstances that encourage you to use drugs. That's why I came back. Dad offered me a job working for him."

"So you're planning to stay." Casey indulged in another cupcake. "That's going to be a big change."

"Yeah, I had a lot of stupid dreams, didn't I?" Sandra rested her chin on one palm. "The boys around here thought I was so darn beautiful, I figured those Hollywood producers couldn't resist me. Was I an idiot or what?"

"You gave it a try," she said. "Otherwise you'd have spent your whole life wondering about what might have been."

Tears brightened her friend's gaze. "You always know how to make me feel better."

"She's good at that." Jack brought two mugs of coffee, along with milk, sugar and an extra glass for Casey.

Sandra spooned sugar into her drink. "If you don't mind me changing the subject, people at church were talking about some prowler around here. Larry Malloy says the guy squirted you with a hose. I hope you weren't hurt."

"Only my pride. I was madder than a wet hen." As she filled the glass with milk, she couldn't resist adding, "And probably wetter, too."

"Officer Malloy brought it up?" Jack pulled back a chair and joined them. "How did you happen to be talking to him?"

"He used to work for Dad after school, so he came over to speak to us at church." Sandra pushed a wedge of lank hair behind one ear. "I asked him how his job was going and that's when he told me."

"He didn't exactly turn the place upside down trying to figure out who did it," Casey said. "That's why I called Jack."

"You're some kind of cop, aren't you?"

"I used to be. I do private security now," he explained. "I'm conducting my own investigation at my wife's request."

"Any suspects?" As Sandra took a sip, the mug shook slightly.

The drugs, or her need for them, must still exert a strong influence, Casey thought sympathetically. She wished she could go back in time and warn her friend—but then, she *had* warned her. Sandra had chosen not to listen.

"A few names have come up. Larry Malloy's, for example." Jack watched her closely.

"Larry? That's silly." She wrinkled her nose. "I'll bet I know who you've been talking to—Prune-face Purdue." The unkind nickname had been muttered behind Enid's back for years by some of her less-motivated students.

"You don't like her?" he asked.

"She always favored the really smart kids. And Casey, because she worked so hard. But Prune-face thinks she's above us ordinary mortals. Did you see her this morning? She looked down her nose at me like I smelled bad." Sandra shrugged. "Oh, who cares?"

"Did Officer Malloy say anything about her?" Jack probed.

"No. But she tells people he let the air out of her tires one time, even though it could have been any of the kids who flunked her class," she replied dismissively. "Anyway, when would Larry have time to prowl around here? He's busy working two jobs."

"Two?" Casey queried.

"He's a part-time watchman at the glass factory." She rose to pour herself more coffee. "He'd prefer to be full-time at the police department, but Dad says the town's budget won't stretch that far."

"Has your father mentioned anyone he suspects of being the prowler?" Jack spoke offhandedly.

"Why do you mention Dad?"

"I thought he might have seen the intruder. Doesn't he like to fish around here?"

"I have no idea," Sandra said. "You're the one who's investigating. Who do you think it might be, aside from Larry?"

Jack made a vague remark about checking possibilities. He also cited Gail's ex-husband, although he explained that the man had remarried and moved to Hawaii, which was news to Casey.

He showed them both a printout photo of the man. Neither had seen him.

After downing one more cupcake, Sandra excused herself to go help her mother with dinner. "I didn't want to leave things on such an unpleasant note between us," she told Casey. "I'll be seeing you around. Jack, are you staying long?"

"A few days. I can't spare any more time away from work."

"Too bad." She didn't sound sorry, though. "I'd better hurry before it pours. It's getting pretty dark out there."

They said brief goodbyes. Casey wished they'd had more of a chance to talk about things that really mattered, such as how Sandra felt about the past and what lay ahead for her. But perhaps her old friend wasn't ready to have such an intimate discussion, especially not in front of a man she hardly knew.

"She took a lot of interest in the prowler," Jack observed as they cleared away the cups.

"I figured it was just idle curiosity."

"Maybe so." Jack waved her back to a seat. "Is there any place to order pizza around here?"

"No, but I've got one in the freezer." She'd bought the kind with extra cheese, for the calcium.

He set about preheating the oven and preparing a salad. Casey loved the way he pitched in and fixed dinner. Jack had always taken the initiative with meals. He'd once explained that he'd had to do that while growing up or go hungry.

As she watched, her mind replayed the conversation with

Sandra. "I didn't like the way she talked about Enid. I know Sandra's struggling, but she seems so agitated and negative, even resentful. She never used to be like that."

Jack tore up lettuce for a salad. "She isn't the person you used to know. Don't trust her." He spoke the last sentence with emphasis. "You'll never know whether it's her talking or the drugs."

"But she's clean!"

"It hasn't been long enough for her to be sure from one hour to the next whether she can stay off them," he said. "Maybe she came here to apologize. Or maybe her father sent her to find out if we're on his trail."

"He wouldn't do that and neither would she!" Casey flared. "I grew up around these people."

"I've more or less ruled out Dean Fordham," Jack said. "All the others on my list are people you know and most of whom you grew up with."

"It might be a transient," she insisted.

"And if it isn't?" When she didn't answer, he said, "If I can't catch this guy before I leave, you're going to have to stay on guard. I have to prepare you to protect yourself. Just remember, you've got the baby to think about now."

Casey didn't want to be suspicious of everyone around her. Although she'd always understood that she and Jack viewed the world differently, she'd believed that in time he would come around to a more optimistic attitude.

It saddened her to realize that, right now, his point of view had to take precedence. "I'll be careful," she promised.

"Even with Sandra?" he pressed.

"Sandra would never..." She halted, the words *hurt me* dying in her throat as she remembered the angry words thrown at her earlier.

"Her first loyalty is to her parents." Jack rummaged through the cabinets until he found a cookie sheet for the pizza. "Never forget that. If it comes to a choice between you and her family, they'll close ranks against you."

"Are you speaking from experience?" she asked.

"Very long and very painful experience." Removing the wrappings, he plopped the pizza on the metal sheet and thrust it into the oven.

More than ever, Casey wished she could take Jack into her arms and make the bad feelings go away. But it wasn't in her power to do that. And maybe it never had been.

Chapter Nine

Thunder and lightning bolts that lit up the living room woke Jack during the night. Electrical storms being rare in Southern California, he found this one both fascinating and awe-inspiring.

Rain hammered the roof, adding to the din. Surely by now Casey must have awakened, he thought, but when he went in to check, he found her sleeping.

As he stood in the doorway, a flash illuminated the figure beneath the quilt. She lay on one side, curled to accommodate her shape. The mounds and valleys of the covers and the spill of long hair brought back vividly the sight of her in the bathtub that afternoon.

He'd been struck by Casey's natural vibrancy and the silky texture of her skin. His entire body had responded to the realization that it was their lovemaking that had filled her belly with a child. To his surprise, the sensations had stimulated him beyond restraint.

Taking a deep breath as he studied his wife in the darkness, Jack recalled the intense pleasure of her stroking. He felt himself coming alive again.

He wanted to share with her the same wild exhilaration. Bringing each other to climax without being able to consummate their passion the traditional way seemed intensely intimate, a shared enterprise. Except that they hadn't fully shared it.

Jack wished Sandra hadn't barged in. Although he admired Casey's desire to help her old buddy, he not only didn't appreciate the interruption, he disliked the woman at a personal level.

As a police officer, he'd come to detest druggies. They lied, betrayed their friends, stole and tried to pull everyone around them down to their level. Sure, he knew some people recovered, but he didn't want Sandra around his wife.

He didn't trust Sandra not to take advantage of Casey's loyalty. The fact that he might be powerless to prevent it only made him resent the woman more. Once he returned to California, who was going to protect Casey, not only from her assailant but from herself?

Outside, lightning flashed again, sending tree-shadows through the room. The strangeness reminded Jack of his first nights in a foster home, listening to unfamiliar noises in a room that wasn't his. A neon sign at a convenience store down the street had burned through his thin curtains, disturbing him with memories of the outlets where his father had bought booze.

Troubled, he exited the bedroom with the growl of thunder following him like a threat. Since becoming an adult, Jack had refused to be intimidated, so he threw on a jacket and went onto the front porch.

Drifts of rain undulated in the wind, parting at the porch roof and sheeting around him as if he stood beneath a waterfall. Trees swayed and bent, their leaves sending up a swishing noise.

Abruptly, the storm split the dark sky with renewed fury and brilliance. From a fork high up in the heavens, lightning cascaded to earth, followed moments later by a boom that shuddered through the porch.

Uphill, in the direction of Enid's house, an eerie flush caught his eye. For a moment, as he turned, he wasn't sure what he was seeing through the trees and rain, and then he made sense of the flickering red-and-yellow glare. Judging by the height above ground, he guessed a tree had caught fire.

Jack had no idea how much threat a lightning strike posed amid heavy rain. But the blaze appeared dangerously close to the cabin.

He ran into the house and dialed 911, using the kitchen phone so the dispatcher could fix his location. Did a town this small even have a 24-hour dispatcher? he wondered, and was relieved when a brisk female voice answered.

Jack described what he'd witnessed. "You've got a volunteer fire department in Richfield Crossing," she told him. "I'll notify them at once."

"How long till they get here?" he asked.

"About half an hour."

Curiosity prompted him to ask, "Aren't you in Richfield Crossing?"

She explained that she worked from a regional headquarters that relayed emergencies to seven counties. Jack thanked her and hung up.

He dressed quickly and went to wake Casey. It took a long time to pull her from sleep, and even longer to make her understand that the lightning had ignited a blaze. "I need Enid's phone number," he said. "I want to make sure she's awake."

It only took minutes for lethal levels of smoke to fill a house, not to mention waves of heat scorching enough to kill. The half hour before the fire truck arrived could be an eternity if she failed to awaken or became trapped.

Casey sat up sluggishly. "You think the fire's at Enid's cabin?"

"I'm not sure. It might be a tree, but it looks awfully close." Jack didn't dare linger a moment longer. "I'll tell you what. You call her and warn her to get out. I'm going up there to make sure she's okay."

Alert at last, Casey grabbed her robe from a nearby chair. "I'll come too."

That was all she needed, to go tromping around in the pouring rain. "For once in your life, listen to reason!" he snapped. "Stay in the house!" In a milder tone, he added, "Get some coffee going for the firefighters. And for Enid, in case she has to come here."

"Okay." She swung her feet to the floor with a trace of awkwardness. "Jack, I promise not to do anything stupid. Just keep me posted, all right?"

"You bet. I'll take my phone." He went out, throwing on a jacket and adding an umbrella and flashlight he found in the house.

The storm engulfed him the moment he stepped off the porch. Despite the umbrella, rain slashed against his face. Overhead, lightning swelled. Heaps of newly fallen leaves and twigs crunched on the driveway beneath his shoes.

Jack listened instinctively for the wail of sirens, but there was no sign of a fire truck yet. Considering that the volunteers had to dress and assemble before they could head this way, he hoped the estimate of half an hour wasn't overly optimistic.

Ahead, flames wavered in midair, distorted by the rising ground and torrents of water. At times they seemed to subside, then flash back quickly. A wooden house such as Enid's would provide ready fuel unless it had been treated to make it fire-resistant.

At last he came around a bend and got a clearer view. The fire had almost engulfed a craggy tree, one limb of which overhung the roof. So far, the blaze hadn't spread but it might at any moment.

He hurried along a bark-strewn pathway. At the door, he pounded hard. "Miss Purdue! It's Jack Arnett!"

When no one answered, he tried the knob. Locked tight. From the interior came the sound of the phone ringing, probably Casey trying to rouse the occupant. She failed to respond.

Maybe Enid had gone away for a few days, although she'd made no mention of planning a trip. Jack stepped back, and saw her car still in the carport.

Any number of factors could prevent an elderly woman

from responding. She might have taken a sleeping pill or fallen while trying to flee.

Descending from the porch, he circled to the back, where he tried to peer inside. In the uneven glare from the flames, he couldn't make out much.

The tree blazed and crackled. Jack kept a wary eye on the jutting branch and the sparks showering onto the wet ground.

The rear door held fast. A faint light, apparently from the bathroom, provided enough illumination to show that everything appeared normal and undisturbed.

When he reached the bedroom window, a spurt of lightning showed him a form lying motionless on the bed. She was there, all right. What had happened to her?

Furiously, he banged on the window, and hoped he wouldn't have to break it. Finally, the figure stirred and groped around as if dazed.

Jack rapped again. "Miss Purdue!" he called. "The tree's on fire! You need to get out!"

She sat up stiffly and swung her feet over the edge of the bed. After giving him a nod, she grabbed her bathrobe and shuffled out of the bedroom.

"The window!" he yelled. "Come through the window!"

She ignored him.

Darn it, why didn't she let him help her out by the shortest route? As a police officer, he'd learned that fire victims often died trying to reach a door when they could easily have escaped through a window.

But he could do nothing about that now. Dodging a falling cluster of burning leaves, he pushed his way toward the rear exit.

The elderly woman emerged seconds later, pulling an overcoat around her. Anxious eyes peered at him from beneath an umbrella. "What's happening?"

"Lightning hit your tree." As he assisted her away from the cabin, Jack informed her he'd called the fire department. "Casey tried to reach you. Why didn't you hear the phone?"

"I put in earplugs so the thunder wouldn't keep me awake," Enid said over the patter of rain. "It didn't occur to me it might be dangerous. I never expected anything like this."

They took refuge inside a small gazebo in the yard. Rain slanted in from the sides but at least they were clear of the downpour.

Through the gloom, Jack spotted someone moving toward them. Surely Casey hadn't disregarded his instructions! With relief, he noted as the figure approached that it was too tall and thin.

The arrival turned out to be an old dark-skinned man in a cape and broad-brimmed rain hat. "Miss Purdue? Are you all right?"

"Yes, thank you." She introduced him as Matt Dorning, the one tenant Jack hadn't met.

They shook hands. Despite his advanced age, Matt had a firm grip.

"Let's get a hose and see if we can't put this thing out before the house goes up," Jack suggested.

"Right you are."

They hurried through the storm to the back of the house. Matt uncoiled the hose and fed it to Jack, who aimed the hand sprayer into the tree.

By playing the force of the water against the fire, he began pushing it away from the overhanging branch. Slowly, with the help of the deluge, the virulent flames subsided into embers.

Enid cheered.

"Somebody needs to make sure that thing doesn't reignite," the elderly man said as he came to stand beside Jack. "I'm a mite old to be climbing up there, but if you're willing, I believe we can find a ladder in the carport."

"You don't happen to be a retired firefighter, do you?" Jack asked, impressed by the fellow's thoroughness.

Matt shook his head. "Just a handyman. Used to be, anyways."

From a distance came the wail of a fire truck. "The cavalry at last," he said.

"Late as usual," Matt added. "They do their best, but folks have to rely on themselves around here."

"Unfortunately, that appears to apply to some police business as well," Jack murmured, remembering his wife's complaints about Larry Malloy.

"That's right," the tenant replied. "I was glad to hear you're checking into that trouble we've had."

"I'm making a few inquiries." Jack preferred not to exaggerate his own importance. "Do you have any suspicions as to who's behind it?"

"I don't know that it means anything, but just the other day I remembered something that didn't seem important at the time. It happened 'bout three weeks ago."

The comment caught Jack's full attention. He never underestimated the value of a witness's offhand remarks. "What's that?"

"Real early in the morning when I was out collecting wood for whittling, I saw a man skulking around the playground," he explained. "I guess he spotted me, 'cause he headed off the other way. Later, I heard a car scrape our mailbox. At the time, it didn't occur to me there might be a connection, and maybe there isn't. Still, I thought I'd mention it."

The siren drew closer. In the unfamiliar terrain, Jack found it hard to gauge the distance remaining. "Did you recognize him?"

"No, sir. Didn't get a good look," he said regretfully. "I couldn't tell much of anything."

"Height? Weight? Age? Clothing?"

"Average height and weight. He kind of shambled when he ran, so he's no athlete, I can tell you that. He wore the kind of plaid jacket and jeans you see a lot of. Sorry I can't be more specific."

"Every detail helps." The playground lay behind Casey's

house, a fact that troubled Jack because it indicated further risk to her.

Also, although Matt's information didn't point to anyone specific, it strengthened the possibility that the mailbox incident indicated intentional vandalism. Come to think of it, what made him so sure this fire was an accident?

True, he'd seen lightning, and the thunder might have covered the sound of it striking the tree. All the same, he'd learned to question coincidences. And, coming on the heels of so many other problems, this blaze deserved to be regarded with skepticism.

He definitely wanted to take a closer look at that tree when circumstances permitted. But the firefighters should arrive any minute.

Remembering Casey's request to keep her informed, he moved to the porch and called her. To his relief, his phone finally worked.

"I've got coffee ready," she said after he finished recounting the events so far. "I could bring some down."

"You stay put. I'll send someone for it. All right?" He knew if he tried to boss her, she might simply disobey.

Over the phone, he heard his wife sigh. "I hate sitting around doing nothing, but I guess you're right."

"It won't be long."

Jack had just hung up when the fire truck arrived. At the wheel, he identified Sandra's father, not exactly the person he most wanted to see right now.

When Al got out and started giving orders, it became apparent that he headed the fire brigade. However, as he listened to Jack's account, the weathered theater owner gave no sign of the animosity he'd shown at church. Neither did he display any great concern once he learned no one had been harmed.

The small group of men and women set to work with ladders and axes, searching for embers and removing limbs to make sure the tree posed no further threat. He admired their dedication, coming out here in the middle of a stormy night for zero pay. They appeared well prepared, a sign that they'd probably undergone the same training as professional firefighters.

Even out here in the hinterlands, public safety had achieved a high level of sophistication, Jack reflected. He supposed that, as a Los Angeles native, he'd been a bit arrogant or at least ignorant.

Matt, who'd volunteered to fetch the coffee, returned with a large thermos and a stack of disposable cups. "Casey told me to make sure this doesn't go to waste," he said as, sheltered by the gazebo, he poured the steaming liquid for the volunteers.

"Yeah, she's a real saint," Al muttered, blowing steam off his cup.

Jack tried to keep his tone neutral, although the man's comment set his teeth on edge. Based on what Bo had told him earlier, he needed to question the fellow, and this presented a low-key opportunity. "When the weather clears up, I was thinking of going fishing," he remarked. "You recommend any particular spots around here?"

"Why ask me?" Al said.

"You come up here 'bout once a week," Matt put in, saving Jack the need to answer. "I see you when I'm out collecting wood."

The fire chief scowled into his coffee. "They're building new houses down where we live, making so much noise they've scared the fish away. It's more peaceful up here." Casting a dour look at Jack, he added, "At least it used to be peaceful."

At the implied insult, his temper frayed. "Was that before or after somebody attacked my wife?"

Matt's eyebrows lifted but he refrained from comment. Al shrugged. "If you knew anything about fishing, you'd know I'm not about to reveal the best spots. But I don't think that's what you're doing. I think you're snooping."

"My wife does own this land," Jack pointed out. "I have a right to know who comes and goes."

"She doesn't own the other side of the creek," Al told him. "That's Owen Godwin's land." He moved away.

The rain had dwindled. Jack took advantage of the lull to walk over and examine the tree. Although arson investigation wasn't his field, he could at least scout around for anything obviously out of place.

The firefighters had piled the cut branches to one side where, he presumed, they'd serve either as firewood or as material for Matt's carvings. Since they'd left one of the ladders braced against the house, he climbed up and shone his flashlight across the roof. He kept an eye out for stray embers or indications of storm damage that needed repair; however, that wasn't really his focus.

He played the flashlight at varied angles. Down below, someone approached the ladder.

"Anything wrong up there?" came Al's voice. "Maybe I'd better take a look."

Something shiny caught the beam. Jack leaned forward, half-expecting to find an old Christmas bulb or a wind-borne scrap of foil.

Reaching out, he scooped up the object. With a twist of dismay, he guessed what he'd found even before he brought it close enough to examine.

It was the sparkly casing of a cigarette lighter.

AFTER THE FIREFIGHTERS LEFT and the property had fallen quiet in the wake of the storm, Casey sat up with Jack trying to make sense of what he'd discovered. She found the implication distressing, yet she trusted his judgment and the evidence was hard to ignore.

Al had dismissed the lighter as irrelevant. He'd pointed out that the fire had begun in the tree, not on the roof, although that didn't preclude the possibility that the lighter had passed through the branches. Most likely, he'd said, some smoker had had trouble getting it to work and given it the heave-ho weeks or even months ago.

But no one around here smoked as far as Casey knew. Her mother hadn't rented to smokers because the smell could permeate carpets and drapes. And the lighter didn't appear weathered.

Jack had borrowed a plastic bag from Enid and collected the object on the chance that they might find fingerprints. Given the heavy rain, however, he admitted the odds were against them.

"I'll take it to the police tomorrow." He stretched his feet from an easy chair toward the fire he'd built in the hearth. "I can drop you off for your doctor's appointment."

"Thanks." Casey still struggled to understand. "Do you really think someone tried to set Enid's house on fire? I mean, if they meant to burn it, why do so in a rainstorm when the rain was likely to put it out?"

"Maybe the point wasn't to burn her house down but cause some damage. It would be the third time someone's tried to cover up an attack as an accident around here." In the firelight, Jack's green eyes took on emerald depths. He'd already explained what he'd learned from Matt about the mailbox. "Besides, the lightning offered a perfect way to deflect blame."

"But it's so sneaky!" Casey hugged herself, despite the warmth from the hearth. "And if you hadn't spotted it, it could have killed Enid."

"People who hold grudges seldom stop to think that they're blowing things out of proportion," Jack said.

"You mean Larry?" Casey asked. "Flunking a student in class isn't a good enough reason to try to kill her, especially not after all these years!"

"I don't necessarily think it's him. The incidents with the mailbox and my car wouldn't fit that scenario."

"Then who could be doing this?" She spoke more to vent her frustration than because she expected an answer.

"Al's shown hostility toward you. He might be trying to frighten your tenants into moving. Plus, don't forget that firebugs are sometimes drawn to jobs in fire departments," Jack added.

"I think we're getting carried away," Casey said. "Maybe lightning *did* cause the blaze. That tree was overgrown. I should have had it trimmed long ago."

"We still have to account for the lighter."

"People hunt and fish around here without permission." Travelers and transients sometimes slept in the woods. "They leave trash around and don't always bother to extinguish their campfires. I wouldn't put it past one of them to have thrown it up there as a stupid joke."

"Let's hope you're right." He leaned his head back in his chair.

Casey's eyelids felt heavy, but her body hummed with tension. She might have won the argument, at least on the surface, but she hadn't dispelled all doubts from either of their minds.

The thunderstorm, now grumbling its way south, raised primal fears. What if the next house targeted turned out to be hers?

"I'll never get to sleep," she complained. "I hate that someone has the power to mess up my peace of mind! I wish I had Enid's attitude." The former teacher had insisted on staying home rather than going to Casey's tonight, saying she was too old to worry about things that might never happen.

"Why don't you sleep out here?" Jack indicated the open couch, made into a queen-size bed. "You might feel safer. I'll be comfortable right here."

"You can't sleep in a chair!" The only alternative, she realized, was either for her to leave this cozy room or for him to sleep next to her. Well, it wasn't as if they were strangers. "There's room for both of us."

"Not if it makes you uncomfortable," he replied.

"It won't." Now that she'd suggested it, she found she wanted to feel the warmth of his body next to hers. "I wasn't exactly shy around you earlier, was I?"

"Are you suggesting a rematch?" Jack teased.

If she hadn't felt so weary, she'd have been tempted. As it was, Casey shook her head. "I'm afraid I'm not up for it."

"Fortunately, neither am I." His grin made it clear he was playing on her choice of words.

"Jack!"

"You're the one making the Freudian slips," he teased.

"I'm too tired to debate the point," she said. "Good night."

"Sleep well. Don't have any naughty dreams or, if you do, at least promise to tell me about them."

"I'll keep them all to myself," she teased back. "Unless you hold me and keep me warm."

"It's a deal."

When Casey crawled beneath the covers, she meant to stay awake until Jack finished changing and got into bed with her. A heavy swirl of dreams overtook her best intentions, however, and her head sank sleepily onto the pillow.

WHY DID PEOPLE GET nostalgic about small towns as if they were havens against the cruelty of the world? Jack mused as he pulled on his pajama bottoms. So far, his investigation had convinced him this town stewed with petty resentments, and the evidence indicated it held at least one person with a criminal bent.

He wasn't ready to sleep so, after finding Casey dead to the world, he slipped into the office. On the computer, he checked out Enid Purdue, in case she'd omitted any circumstances that might lead someone to want her dead, but she didn't have a figurative hair out of place.

For good measure, he put in Matt Dorning's data after finding a file in the drawer that provided the necessary details. He had a clean record, too.

Jack returned to the living room. When he turned off the lamp, the undiluted firelight made him nostalgic for the fairy tales his mother had read him long ago. The soft crackling and the tang of smoke brought home the simple truth that what could ravage in one context could soothe and preserve in another.

Attachments were like that too, Jack thought as he eased into bed. Love could illuminate your world or break your heart. Sometimes both at the same time.

Despite his promise to keep her warm, he knew he ought to stay as far from Casey as possible in the confined space, but when she shifted toward him, he let her nestle against his chest. Silky hair tumbled over his torso, sensuous and soothing.

Something rubbed Jack's rib cage. He thought at first it must be one of her arms, but they were both accounted for.

The undulation came again, followed by a distinct nudge. Startled, he realized it had to be the baby. He wondered what she thought of the obstacle she'd encountered, or whether babies formed conscious thoughts at this stage.

He hadn't expected Diane to be awake while her mother slept. Although he knew the baby had a separate existence, it hadn't occurred to him that she kept her own schedule while still in the womb.

The squirming resumed. Apparently the excitement of the evening had been transmitted to her. If she kept this up, she'd rouse her mother.

How did a person soothe a baby, especially one still inside the mother? Jack wondered. Obviously, he couldn't rock her. If she could hear his voice, a soft lullaby seemed the only option.

He arched beneath the covers, trying not to disturb Casey as he brought his face close to her bulge. A sense of absurdity nearly sent him scrambling for a more dignified position until a little fist—or something else—thrust lightly into his cheek.

"Settle down in there," he murmured, and could have sworn the baby reacted with a start. Okay, he might be reading things into the situation, but now that he apparently had Diane's attention, he'd better deliver the goods. She didn't need a father who let her down.

Jack struggled to remember a lullaby. Nothing came. He tried for any song; however, his mind went blank.

A wiggle hinted that his audience might be losing patience. Maybe she didn't care whether he sang or spoke as long as he made reassuring noises.

Jack searched his memory for a poem, perhaps a sonnet from Shakespeare, but right now he couldn't even recall the words to the Gettysburg Address. At last his mind dredged up the one speech he'd repeated an uncounted number of times.

It began, "You have the right to remain silent…"

He couldn't use that, or could he? To someone who didn't understand the words, what difference could it make?

Jack began to recite. Whether mesmerized or simply bored, Diane lay quiet while he delivered the Miranda warning. By the time he finished advising her of her right to an attorney, she'd apparently fallen asleep.

Mission accomplished. He might not be much of a father, Jack reflected as he rested his head on the pillow, but at least he knew how to work with what he had.

Chapter Ten

On Monday morning, before driving Casey into town, Jack took a walk around her property. A creek bordered the Lone Pine on the east. With its overgrown shady spots and rocky pools, he could understand its appeal to anglers.

To the north, no fence indicated exactly where the property line lay. Amid the thick woods blanketing the rising hills, he saw plenty of fallen branches, some old and half-rotted, others newly blown down with still-fresh leaves. A few deer moved lazily off as he approached, and here and there squirrels peeked at him curiously before darting out of sight.

The air carried a ripe scent brightened by the sweetness of spring blossoms. Jack couldn't remember why he'd felt so uneasy yesterday about all these open spaces, when they abounded with growing things.

To the west, he noted an uneven sprawl of trees and outcroppings. From a vantage point atop a stump, he made out a narrow, unpaved road that apparently lay beyond Casey's land, although he didn't make out any cars or signs of habitation.

On the way back, he swung by Enid's house. He found her inspecting the tree, which, although heavily pruned and charred in spots, appeared to have survived the fire.

After greeting him, she gestured at the tree. "It looks tame enough this morning, doesn't it?"

"I hope there've been no flare-ups," he said. "Or prowlers, either."

"Fortunately, not." She collected a few cut-up branches into a basket, probably for use in the hearth. "I'm thinking of getting a dog. Casey's mother wouldn't allow pets. However, I'm hoping she'll think differently. It might have warned me something was wrong."

"They make great companions, too." As a child, Jack had longed for a dog, but now that he was an adult, his frequent absences made pet ownership impossible. "Why don't you ask her? Maybe she'll want one for herself." It struck him as a helpful suggestion.

"I'll do that." Enid cocked her head at him. "You're good for her, you know."

"For Casey?"

The elderly woman added a couple more sticks to her small load. "I may never have married, but I know a couple who belong together when I see them."

Jack didn't know how to answer, so he didn't try. "Need any help carrying that?" he asked.

Enid hefted her basket. "No, thank you. It's not heavy."

"Then if you don't mind, I'm going to check around to see if there's anything else amiss." Having other people discuss his private life never sat right with Jack, and he felt an urge to move on.

"I understand. I'm sorry if I spoke out of turn," Enid said. "And thank you again for last night. You may have saved my life."

"Glad I could help."

Relieved to escape the discussion, Jack circled her house looking for footprints or any rubbish a transient might have left. The rain, however, had washed the place fairly clean. Besides storm debris, he found only a few stray bits of paper and Styrofoam that might have blown out of trash cans.

When he got back, he found Casey on the front porch

wearing a loose sweater and flowing skirt. With her hair billowing in the breeze and the old-fashioned house as a backdrop, she made a classic picture of feminine welcome.

"Any luck?" she asked.

He shook his head. "No. But Enid seems fine."

"I'm glad to hear it." She glanced at her watch. "We'd better go. Do you think we should take my car?"

"Let's use mine. I need to have it looked at." Although he didn't really plan to have the repairs done in Richfield Crossing, Jack wanted to make the acquaintance of the town mechanic, whose name appeared prominently on his list of suspects.

"I'll get my stuff." Casey retrieved her purse from the house. At the last minute, she remembered to lock up.

On the way into town, Jack noted other storm damage, including loosened shingles, tilted fence rails and considerable debris. He saw no other signs of lightning strikes, however.

The doctor's office to which Casey directed him lay on the town's main street, Lake Avenue, next to a one-story clinic that bore that grandiose name Richfield Medical Center. "Is that the only hospital around here?" he asked as he parked.

"It's the only one in town," Casey confirmed.

"Not exactly impressive." He didn't mean to give offense, but his wife planned to trust her life to this place.

"They refer major illnesses like cancer to Nashville, but they deliver babies and perform routine operations," she explained. "They just bought new childbirth monitoring equipment a few months ago."

"How many beds?"

"Half a dozen, I think." Honesty made her add, "I know it's not what you'd find in a city. Still, we're lucky to have it."

All the more reason for her to move back to Los Angeles. This wasn't the time to bring it up, though. "How long do you think you'll be?"

"It usually takes about an hour," Casey said. "Would you like to come in with me?"

The memory of communing with Diane last night popped into Jack's mind. He would enjoy learning more about the little person he'd Mirandized. But he had work to do.

"I've got to see a man about a car, and another man about a lighter," he said. "I'll pick you up as soon as I'm done."

"Okay." If he'd disappointed her, she gave no sign.

Jack watched as Casey strolled into the small office building. From the sign, it appeared two doctors worked there. Only two? His wife and daughter deserved a major teaching facility with the world's best professionals on staff!

He knew he was being unreasonable. Maybe he simply didn't trust small towns.

Once Casey disappeared from view, Jack put the car in gear and headed down the street to where she'd indicated he would find the Ledbetter Garage. Standing alone on a blacktop with its wide door lifted to reveal triple work bays, it appeared well kept despite the inevitable splashes of grease and the pervasive smell of motor oil.

In front lounged a mechanic in a blue coverall, taking a cigarette break. He was the only person in view.

As Jack pulled up, he noted that the man, who wore his long brown hair tied back, had the name Royce embroidered on his pocket. Even had he not known the man was an ex-high-school football player, he'd have guessed it from his beefy build.

Jack parked and exited the car. After extinguishing his cigarette, Royce ambled over to inspect the broken window.

"Storm damage?" he asked in a friendly tone. It got much less friendly when he caught a clearer look at Jack across the hood. "Oh, it's you."

"You recognize me?" Jack refrained from offering to shake hands. He had no desire to do so, even assuming Royce's wasn't covered with oil. "I didn't realize I was famous."

"I saw you at church." The mechanic grimaced at the window, which Jack had taped into place. "You want an estimate for that?"

"That's the general idea." *And to take your measure.* "Can you handle glass and paint work?"

"People around here expect me to fix whatever needs to be fixed." Royce fingered the scratches on the roof. "You'd have to leave it for at least a few days. It's a rental, right? If I were you, I'd let the rental company take care of it. I doubt they'd approve an estimate without taking a look for themselves."

Jack suspected the same thing. At least Royce had passed one test: he appeared to be honest. "You're probably right."

"You didn't really come here to get this fixed." The mechanic scowled at him. "You want to let me know you're staking out your claim to Casey. Well, that's up to her, isn't it?"

Jack decided not to answer directly. Instead, to learn what kind of reaction he'd get, he threw out a question. "Did you hear somebody tried to burn down Enid Purdue's cabin last night?"

The mechanic answered without missing a beat. "According to Sandra, it was lightning."

Jack hadn't counted on the efficiency of a small-town grapevine. That made it hard to surprise information from a suspect. "What did she do, call you with the news?"

Royce jerked his head toward an aging sedan inside the garage. "She brought her parents' car in this morning for a tune-up."

"What else did she say?" Although he didn't like the fact that two people he mistrusted had been conferring, Jack at least wanted to gather as many details about the conversation as possible.

"That you found a lighter on the roof." The mechanic paused.

"That's right." Jack paused, too.

Silence lengthened between them as they tried to wait each other out. The tension must have bothered Royce more, because he was the first to break it. "Could have been some bird dropped it there. They like bright objects."

Jack hadn't considered that possibility. Although feasible, it was unlikely. "This damage to my car wasn't an accident. Someone tried to make it look like one, though."

Again, he failed to startle a telling reaction from Royce. "I guess you're not too popular around here," the man drawled. "I don't believe in vandalism, but I can understand the sentiment."

Jack hid his annoyance. "I didn't realize I'd entered a popularity contest. As far as I'm concerned, the only person whose opinion of me matters is Casey."

The man's face flushed. "People around here believe a man ought to stand by his wife."

So that was his issue. Or, at least, the excuse he used to justify his enmity.

"Not that it's any of your business, but Casey's the one who chose to leave," Jack said. "She's welcome back any time."

"Then she must not like you too much," Royce retorted. "Or else you did something to drive her away."

The man's needling hit close to home. He *had* driven her away by refusing her a child, and now she was having one anyway.

She'd wanted the baby more than she'd wanted Jack. And she apparently loved her home more than she loved him, as well. Lots of things other than her husband seemed to come first with Casey.

All the same, his marriage was none of this jealous mechanic's business. "What matters is that I'm the one she called when she needed help. If you've got some idea of driving me away, forget about it."

Royce snorted in disbelief. "You think I'm still carrying a torch? No way. There's plenty of other pretty girls around here."

"Glad to hear it," Jack said. "So I can assume that if you find something suspicious in one of your customer's cars, you'll let the police know?"

"Like what?" Royce demanded.

Since the attacker tended to use whatever weapon fell to

hand, Jack didn't have an easy answer. He'd have loved an excuse to go through the Rawlinses' car, sitting right there in front of him, but he didn't have that either. "You'll know it if you see it," he replied.

"If I found evidence somebody was trying to hurt Casey, you bet I'd turn it in," the mechanic said. "Some of us stick by our friends." Wiping his hands on his coveralls, he marched into the garage.

That hadn't gone well, Jack thought as he got back in the car. It bothered him that Royce and possibly other people assumed he must have mistreated Casey.

By his standards, he didn't believe he'd been a bad husband, but he had no idea how most marriages functioned. It wasn't as if his parents had set a shining example.

The interview hadn't made up his mind about Royce, either. He still considered the man a suspect, but no more so than before.

To reach his next destination, the Civic Center, he backtracked up Lake Avenue. As soon as he swung left into the parking lot, he spotted a banner draped across the front of the library.

"Spring Fling on Wednesday Night," it read. Underneath: "Community Center, 7 p.m." The banner bore a number of streaks and smudges from the storm, but either it had held fast or someone had reattached it.

The police station, a one-story brick building, occupied the site next to the library. He entered directly into a large room furnished with a bench and bisected by a counter. Behind it, instead of a desk sergeant, a dark-haired young woman in civilian clothes sat typing at a computer.

"You were at Casey's party, weren't you?" he said.

She quit typing and swept an appreciative gaze over him. "Sure was. I'm Angie Margolis." Standing up, she shook hands vigorously. "You met my older sister Bonnie, too—sometimes people mix us up. She works here as well."

Jack wasn't accustomed to people providing so much unsolicited information, but he appreciated the fact that this woman, at least, didn't consider him an unwelcome intruder. "I wondered if I might speak with the chief."

"He isn't feeling too well. It's his arthritis," she confided. "I bet he'll want to meet you, though. Just a sec." With a wink, she disappeared through a door.

Since there was nothing to look at on the walls other than photographs of former police chiefs, Jack glanced at the log-in sheet on the counter, which displayed a couple of recent entries. Under "reason for visit," one person had written, "Lost dog." Another said, "Fender bender." Not much of a crime wave, he thought, amused.

When the door opened, a white-haired man emerged. Although he appeared well beyond the usual age of retirement, he had a commanding presence that made Jack respect him immediately. "Mr. Arnett? I'm Horace Roundtree," he said. "I'd shake hands, but I'm afraid my arthritis is acting up."

"I understand." Jack produced the plastic bag containing the cigarette lighter, along with the one holding the rock that might have broken his side window. "I wanted to turn these in and talk to you about the incidents on my wife's property."

"I figured you'd be stopping by. I heard about the fire last night. Glad to see you brought the evidence." After accepting the bags, the chief waved him into the building's interior. "It's always a pleasure to welcome a fellow professional. I understand you used to be an officer. LAPD?"

Jack knew he shouldn't be surprised that everyone around here appeared fully informed about him, but, all the same, he hadn't expected it. "That's right. I worked there for six years. Now I'm a partner in a private security agency."

"So I heard. Men At Arms, isn't it?"

"That's right." Figuring the chief had probably researched it on the Internet already, he didn't bother to add any details.

They entered a short hallway with several rooms opening

off each side. The place seemed unusually quiet for a police station, but then, Jack remembered, Richfield Crossing didn't employ its own dispatchers and had only two officers.

"Care for a tour?" the chief asked.

"Sure, if it wouldn't be too much trouble."

"No trouble at all."

Despite its modest size, the station came equipped with rooms for property and evidence, booking, briefing and interviews, along with a couple of holding cells. The only person they encountered was Bonnie, a slightly older version of her sister, who took the lighter and rock to test for fingerprints.

"There's no watch commander or patrol supervisor other than me," the chief explained as he ushered Jack into his comfortable office. "I've got one part-time officer who works at another job to make ends meet. Not exactly what you're used to."

Jack accepted his offer of a worn upholstered chair. "Running a small security company has taught me how to be flexible. Besides, I don't suppose you need a lot of manpower in a town this size."

"Folks get rowdy sometimes at the Whiskey Flats." The chief sank into a seat behind his desk. "That's the bar down near the Benson Glassworks. And we have our share of domestic quarrels and traffic accidents. Plus you never know what's going to happen."

"People can be unpredictable," Jack agreed. A smart officer never let himself become complacent.

"Well, you didn't come here to listen to the trials and tribulations of small-town police work," the chief said. "Other than the items you brought in, what else have you uncovered?"

Jack took out his notebook. "I've talked to a few people."

"I'd expect nothing less. I was planning to do it myself, but I don't mind having a little extra help."

Glad that the chief didn't resent his encroachment, Jack shared his notes and observations. Despite some concerns, he decided to include Enid's remarks about Larry Malloy.

"Larry's no saint and he might have pulled some pranks when he was younger, but he's not your prowler," the chief said. "On Friday night, he went right to the Pine Woods from his second job over at the glassworks. He was scheduled on duty there last night as well. He may not be the brightest bulb on the Christmas tree, but this doesn't sound like him."

Jack nodded, willing to accept Roundtree's assessment and Larry's alibi for the moment, and moved on. "The only motive that might tie these incidents together would be someone wanting to harass Casey. Al Rawlins has expressed some negative feelings about her."

"There's another kettle of fish." The chief sighed. "Al's had a hard time in life and he's not dealing with it too well."

He explained that, eight years earlier, Sandra's older brother, Al Junior, had died after driving his car into a tree. "He was drunk, and it wasn't the first time he'd had an accident, but his parents always paid the damages," Roundtree added. "Al and Mary sure do love their kids, maybe a little too much."

"Overindulgent?" Jack asked.

"And quick to blame their problems on others," the chief confirmed. "After Junior died, his father threatened to sue the town over a pothole, as if that was what killed his son. He saw reason eventually. When Sandra got messed up, I think he wanted someone to get mad at other than his daughter."

"So he picked Casey," Jack said.

"Who else? She'd been Sandra's best buddy and they'd moved away together," Roundtree said. "She made an easy target."

"Do you have any reason to believe he might put that resentment into action?"

The chief considered for a moment before answering. "He did a lot of grumbling after your wife moved back, but I never saw any real danger in it."

"Does he have a clean record?"

"Officially, yes."

"How about unofficially?

Roundtree drummed his fingers on the desk. "A few years ago some out-of-towner opened a rival video store out on the highway. With his big discounts and a stock of those video games the kids love, he took a lot of business away from Al. A month after it opened, the place burned down."

Jack whistled. "Arson?"

"The inspector we sent out there said it looked to be wiring problems." The chief kept his tone noncommittal.

"How convenient for the Rawlinses."

"Al didn't try to pretend he was sorry about it. Still, I don't see how he could have made it look like an accident if it wasn't. Arson's usually pretty obvious, as I'm sure you know." Roundtree broke off when Bonnie Margolis poked her head into the office.

"Hi, there," she said. "I'm sorry, but I couldn't find any prints on that lighter or the rock, either. I really did try hard, Jack."

He'd never before heard a tech apologize for not finding anything. "I'm sure you did. Thanks, Miss Margolis."

She vanished with a little wave. "Those girls like you," the chief said. "I guess an old guy like me isn't too good for morale."

"You obviously know your business and that's what counts," Jack answered.

The white-haired man shook his leonine head. "It takes more than that to run a department, even a small one such as this. I used to think I'd never get old, up to about a year ago. That's when I hurt my back chopping wood—durn fool thing for man in his seventies to do, but if you knew my wife, you'd understand why I don't like to say no to Gladys. Since then it seems as if my aches and pains have started ganging up on me."

"Sorry to hear it." Jack knew the man wasn't looking for sympathy. He didn't seem the type to complain without good reason.

"I'm glad you're around. Not planning to stay in town by any chance, are you?" the chief asked.

"Afraid not. I've got a business to run."

After encouraging him to report any further findings, Roundtree escorted him out. The young woman at the front desk—that would be Angie, Jack remembered—sang out, "Y'all come back now," as he left.

Despite the chief's positive reception, he felt a deep foreboding. The news that Al Rawlins might have burned out a competitor had frightening implications.

The possibility that the head of the local fire brigade might resort to arson would be disturbing under any circumstances. The fact that he openly resented Casey, coupled with last night's blaze on her property, produced a sense of urgency.

If Jack waited too long for the guy to give himself away, it could prove too late. But he didn't know how to hurry things up.

He'd have to find a way. And if it required more than conventional police work, his position as a private security agent might come in handy.

Chapter Eleven

Realizing it had been nearly an hour since he dropped off Casey, Jack returned to the doctor's office. He forced himself to go inside to find her, although he hated anything concerning doctors.

For himself, he avoided checkups whenever possible. He might get stuck with a needle, and the antiseptic smell brought back memories of his mother's illness.

In the waiting room apparently shared by both doctors, a few people sat on the couches, but his wife wasn't among them. "She's with Dr. Smithson," the receptionist said when he inquired. "You're her husband, right? Go right in. It's Room C."

Although he considered begging off, Jack wanted to size up the man responsible for delivering his child. With a nod, he followed her directions.

At the door to Room C, he knocked lightly. A white-coated man in his late forties opened it. "Yes?"

"Jack!" Beyond the doctor, he saw Casey sitting on an examining table, wearing a short white robe that strained to cover her expanded belly. "I'm glad you came in." She made introductions.

"Your wife's doing very well." The doctor picked up a file from the side counter. "She's slightly dilated, one or two centimeters, which is normal at this stage of pregnancy, and the baby's setting lower in the pelvis."

Jack had no idea what that meant. "Is she in labor?"

Dr. Smithson maintained an earnest expression, although a slight wrinkling at the corners of his eyes indicated amusement. "No, Dad, although these are indicators that she's getting ready. Delivery could still be a few weeks off or it could happen any day."

Jack had never heard himself referred to as Dad before. He felt as if the doctor had mistaken him for someone else, a mature, slightly stodgy character from a television show who always knew the right thing to say.

"Your daughter's got a strong heartbeat," he went on. "Dad, would you like to hear it?"

Curious though he was, having such intimate contact with his daughter in front of the doctor didn't seem right. However, the hopeful expression on Casey's face gave Jack pause.

What could it hurt to listen for a minute? "Sure."

The way his wife beamed dispelled his last doubt.

Dr. Smithson turned on a small machine and ran a device, apparently some kind of microphone, across Casey's stomach. He flipped a switch and a rapid rhythm pulsed through the room.

In it, Jack heard the baby's eagerness to be born and her yearning to open her eyes to a vast unexplored world. A million possibilities danced in that series of galloping heartbeats.

The doctor clicked off the instrument. "Well?" Casey asked.

"It sounds a little fast." On a lighter note, Jack added, "That wouldn't be because she gets nervous during doctor visits, would it?"

"An infant's heart beats faster, about 120 times a minute, because it's so small." Dr. Smithson removed the device from Casey's stomach. "The rate for a child at rest is roughly 90 times per minute. For an adult, it's about 70 times."

"Parents need to learn a lot about biology, I suppose. Otherwise they're likely to screw up." Although Jack had met far too many people who raised their children with careless disregard, he believed in doing a job right.

"Fortunately, nature takes care of things most of the time, but information can help you avoid unnecessary worry," the doctor said. "I've recommended a couple of books on baby care and child development to your wife."

"I've been studying them," Casey assured him.

A tap at the door preceded Gail's entrance. "Sorry to disturb you, but we're running behind schedule, Doctor."

"I wanted to make sure I answered all of Dad's questions. Have I?" Smithson inquired.

"I can't think of any more," Jack admitted. "Thanks."

After Smithson left, Gail lingered to make sure Casey had enough vitamins and to ask whether she'd been practicing her breathing. "I can come over after work to help you," she added.

"That would be great." Casey glanced wistfully at Jack, perhaps hoping he'd volunteer to coach her.

Part of him wanted to stay, to live up to the name Dad and to see Diane open her eyes on the world for the first time. But he felt a profound restlessness and longed to return to L.A., where he felt capable and in charge.

All this kindness and good fellowship, this cozy universe that Casey inhabited, appeared to Jack as a bubble that might burst if he said or did the wrong thing. Maybe for a while he could pretend to fit in, but sooner or later the darkness inside him would spill over. He wasn't really Dad, no matter what anyone called him.

"If you're worried about Casey, you needn't be," Gail assured him. "Dr. Smithson is the best obstetrician I've worked for, and you can trust me to keep a close eye on your wife. She and this baby are precious to all of us."

"I can see that." He clung to the reassurance, because it allowed him to do exactly what he wanted: to escape.

"You're doing it again," Casey said.

"Doing what?"

"Disappearing in front of my eyes. Drawing back from Diane and me." Grumpily, she swung her legs over the edge of the examining table. Jack stepped forward to help her, but the nurse beat him to it. "I thought maybe when you heard her heart... oh, never mind."

He wanted to assure her that the experience had been stirring. It hadn't, however, transformed him into someone who fit neatly into a story-book family.

"By the way," Gail asked, "did you ever find out who that lighter belongs to? Enid told me about it."

"The police couldn't find any prints," Jack replied, glad for the change in subject. "Chief Roundtree's as puzzled as I am."

"I certainly hope it isn't Dean, but I wouldn't put it past him." She drew a curtain that covered half the examining room, giving Casey the privacy to dress.

He explained about what he'd learned about her ex-husband. "Unless someone spots him or you hear anything directly, I think we can rule him out."

"That's a relief. I'd hate to think this was happening because of me," Gail confessed. "Maybe it's a transient, then, someone with mental problems."

"Seen anyone like that around? I'd sure like to catch this guy before I have to leave."

She shook her head. "I wish I could be more helpful. Now I've got to go help the other patients, but I'll see you both later."

"Thanks," he said.

After she left, Jack searched for a topic of conversation while Casey finished putting on her clothes behind the screen. Finally, he said, "What's this Spring Fling business? I saw a banner at the Civic Center."

"It's a fund-raiser for the library." Her voice came through the curtain slightly muffled. "There's a potluck dinner, a bake sale and a raffle. It gives people a chance to socialize and do good at the same time."

"Sounds like fun," he replied automatically, although he'd never been anywhere near a bake sale or a potluck dinner and had no desire to experience either one. "Why don't they hold it on the weekend?"

"Local superstition." She gave a rueful chuckle. "They used to schedule it on a Saturday and every time, it rained. Somebody suggested we try holding it midweek, and it worked like a charm."

"The timing doesn't hurt attendance?"

"In a town this size, no one wants to miss a big event." Pushing aside the curtain, Casey emerged. "Although this year, I should probably skip it. I'm reluctant to leave the Pine Woods just when the prowler will be expecting it. With most of my tenants gone, too, heaven knows what he'll do."

A light went on in Jack' s mind. He'd been seeking a way to become proactive, and here it was.

The man had taken advantage of the storm and, on other occasions, of the cover of darkness. He also seemed well-informed about activities at the Pine Woods, since he'd attacked Jack's car the first night.

"Good," he said.

"What's good?" Casey asked.

"We should spread the word that Pine Woods is going to be empty on Wednesday night. I'll fill you in later."

He ushered her out of the room. Casey paused at the front desk to make another appointment.

They were on the way out when they ran into Mimi in the waiting room. "I took a few hours off work to bring Mom and Dad over here," she explained. "Mom asked me to come along for moral support, although Dad doesn't want me in the examining room with them."

"What's the matter with him?" Casey inquired.

Mimi glanced at the other people on the couches. It seemed to Jack some of them had stopped paying attention to their reading and were listening surreptitiously, and obviously Mimi gathered the same thing. "I'll tell you outside."

They stepped into the mild April sunshine. "He's not seriously ill, I hope," Casey said.

"Not in the physical sense." Her friend folded her arms protectively. "He's showing signs of senility."

"But he's only in his sixties!"

"My grandfather died of Alzheimer's in his early seventies," Mimi explained. "It might have started this early."

Jack had dealt with mentally disordered patients during his police years and he knew such cases could be complex. "Other factors can cause similar symptoms. I presume they're checking for that."

Mimi nodded. "Dr. Engle's going to run some tests. If he can't find anything, he'll refer Dad to one of the doctors at Vanderbilt University in Nashville."

"What are the symptoms?" Casey asked.

"He's become forgetful and irritable. He argues with Mom all the time and with other people, too."

"Anyone in particular?" Jack prompted, and hoped his interest wouldn't be interpreted as rudeness. But he hadn't forgotten about Owen Godwin owning the land next to Casey's—the same land Al Rawlins apparently crossed to go fishing.

It wasn't Al with whom Jack had a quarrel, however. "He and Mayor Lanihan got into a fight over some issue they disagreed about years ago—Mom doesn't even remember how it started—and now the families are barely speaking," Mimi said. "It's not only affecting him, it's isolating my mother, too. She won't take him to the Spring Fling because she's afraid he'll disrupt it."

"That's too bad," Casey said.

Deciding they should start spreading their cover story, Jack added, "My wife and I are looking forward to the party. I hope you'll be able to make it."

"I don't know. It would do my mother good to get out," Mimi replied. "Maybe I can persuade her to come for a few minutes."

Casey patted her friend's arm. "I hope your Dad's condition turns out to be treatable."

"So do I." The young woman blinked away tears. "I'd better go back in. Mom might need me."

After she left, Jack helped Casey into the car. "Now tell me why you want us to announce that we're going to the Spring Fling," she demanded after he slid behind the wheel. "You've got a plan, don't you?"

He should have known she'd figure it out. "I realized it might be a good thing if this perp decides to take advantage of our absence. The more people we tell, the faster word will spread."

Jack backed out carefully. He'd noticed that the drivers of the town's unusually large complement of aged pickup trucks and old clunkers didn't pay much attention to where they were going.

"You want him to come by," she reflected. "That must mean you're going to set a trap."

"In this kind of case, the guy will set his own trap," Jack said. "We just have to keep our eyes open."

"You mean we aren't really going to the party?" She added quickly. "That's okay, just so we catch him."

"You bet we're going." Jack wanted his wife as far from any action as possible, although he itched to be the one who sprang the trap shut. "We're going to be the prime distraction. The more visible we are, the better."

"Like bait?"

"Not exactly, since we'll be safely away from the property. That is, assuming I can work out someone reliable to cover for us." Jack didn't like improvising, but with luck Chief Roundtree would cooperate.

"Well?" Casey demanded. "Don't keep me in suspense! What's the plan?"

"I'm still working out the details," he admitted. "Right now, all I've come up with is the general principle that we coax the guy into the open. Taking him down won't be easy, given our limited resources and the fact that everyone knows I'm here to investigate."

"We can do it," Casey said. "I hate having this guy push me and my tenants around." Her chin came up stubbornly.

Jack remembered how she'd plunged into the darkness with no weapon other than a camera. "Don't try shooting from the hip. You wanted an expert, so you need to follow my lead on this."

For a moment, he feared she might squawk. Instead, she nodded reluctantly. "But I don't want this guy getting free rein to smash up my place. We'd better come up with a strategy that works!"

"Don't worry. We will."

THAT AFTERNOON when Casey arose after her nap, she moved quietly through the house, not wanting to disturb Jack. She spotted him in her office, intent on the computer, and stopped to enjoy the stolen pleasure of watching him.

She loved the way his hair, which always seemed to be slightly overgrown, hugged the back of his neck, one lock sticking out in a tiny gesture of defiance against his otherwise spruce appearance. Despite the informal surroundings, he wore a sports jacket, button-down shirt and creased slacks, evidence of a mind-set focused on business.

He was doing exactly what she'd asked when she phoned him—using his skills to catch their troublemaker. Maybe she didn't have the right to ask for anything more. But the past few days had shown her that their marriage wasn't over unless they allowed it to be. Why couldn't he see how much she and their baby needed him?

In the doctor's office, she'd had to fight the urge to jump off the table and give Jack a shake when he refused to show his excitement at hearing Diane's heartbeat. The fact that he was falling in love with their daughter had been obvious to her and to Dr. Smithson, yet he kept drawing back.

There must be some way to reach him, but it didn't seem likely that it would happen spontaneously. Maybe the answer was to formulate her own plan. While Jack arranged to catch a crook, she intended to catch him.

Nabbing the prowler, even though he might be an arsonist and a vandal, seemed less important than winning back her husband. Or, more accurately, than truly winning him in the first place, because she now saw the fundamental flaw that had doomed their relationship from the beginning.

Jack had never fully committed himself. Between them lay a barricade of emotions as thick and high as a castle wall. Maybe, over the next day or so, he'd drop a clue to the inner thought processes he guarded so closely. She hoped so, because if she couldn't figure out a way around his defenses in the next few days, she never would.

Noticing her, he closed his file. "Good, you're awake. I've been going over some ideas for Wednesday night. Before I contact the chief, I'd like to get your opinion."

"Sure." Casey took a seat beside him. His excitement and pride in his work inspired her confidence, and she appreciated the invitation to review the plan. "So you're going to involve the police?"

"I'll have to. It's a good idea to anyway, on general principles. Despite what you see on TV about private eyes butting heads with the cops, real-life investigators have to coordinate with the authorities," he explained.

Casey wasn't convinced Horace with all his infirmities or slapdash Larry could handle even a relatively simple operation. She hoped Jack would be running the show. But first she needed to know what it was.

"Okay, so we're assuming this guy's going to act while he knows we're at the Spring Fling," she said. "What do we do? Have somebody hide and watch the property?"

"Basically, yes, but one person can't handle this alone. To begin with, you can't see the whole place from a stationary post."

"You need a whole bunch of people?" she guessed.

"If I had unlimited manpower, I'd suggest we tail our suspects, but that isn't feasible here," Jack answered patiently. "What I'm going for is a combination of several observation posts plus roving patrols."

Casey blinked. This sounded way beyond complicated. "How will that work?"

"I'll ask the chief to take up a station in full view outside the community center," Jack said. "People won't be surprised to see him there in case of a security problem, plus that should help convince our perp that he can safely sneak out here."

"That sounds like you're sidelining him." Despite Horace's infirmities, Casey doubted he'd take to the idea. "Won't he want to be center stage?"

"He will be, as the incident commander," Jack explained. "Plus if he notices someone suspicious leaving the Civic Center, he'll have the option of tailing him or notifying the onsite supervisor."

"Then you'll be out here on guard?" she asked.

"I'll need to be at the party with you. Most likely the perp will want to make sure the coast is clear before he acts," he said. "And since everyone knows about me around here, I'm going to have to stay visible." His rueful tone made it clear he didn't relish the prospect.

"Then who's going to be at the Pine Woods?" Casey braced herself. She had a feeling she wasn't going to like the answer.

"Larry Malloy," he replied.

She shook her head. "You heard what Enid said—he might be the guy we're looking for. Even if he isn't, he's inexperienced and not very thorough."

Jack shrugged. "I don't like it either, but I prefer someone who's authorized to carry a weapon and physically strong enough to bring a guy down if necessary. He's the only one available."

"You might be giving him exactly the opening he wants!"

"According to Chief Roundtree, he has alibis for the last

couple of incidents, so I think we're safe in assuming he's not our perp." Jack's assumption reassured Casey. "Also, if the chief agrees, I'll provide special training to help him become more professional. That's going to include an attitude adjustment."

"You think he can do this by himself?" Casey persisted. "You just pointed out that one person can't see the whole property."

From her husband's hesitation, she gathered he didn't expect her to approve of the rest of the plan. "That's where the patrol comes in. We're going to need help from your tenants."

"You're kidding!" She couldn't picture any of them playing a law-enforcement role. "Nobody in their right mind would consider them combat ready!"

"How diplomatically spoken," Jack teased. "I assure you, I'm in my right mind. I'm not exactly sending them into battle here."

"You might as well be!" Casey couldn't stop herself from working up a head of steam. "I can just see Enid stumbling through the bushes in the middle of the night, ready to stab some evildoer with her knitting needles!"

"That wasn't exactly what I had in mind."

"Or Gail—she'd do a great job if the perpetrator happens to be a pregnant woman who goes into labor!" she went on. "Now Matt at least has his carving knives. If the prowler turns out to be about ninety, he might even be able to outrun him."

Jack reached over and cupped her chin with his hand. "If they all had your spirit, this guy wouldn't stand a chance."

She held her ground. "I won't agree to put them at risk."

"I plan to use them as observers, not daredevils. I don't want anyone to get hurt, either."

"Then please leave them out of this," she said. "I know they'll agree if you ask them, but that doesn't make it right."

His expression sobered. "The pattern of attacks has been escalating. Whoever's doing this has progressed from trespassing to arson. There's no telling what might happen next or who's going to be affected. I think your tenants have the right to decide for themselves whether they want to participate."

Casey had to concede the point. This plan offered their best chance of catching the prowler while Jack was still here. Once he left, they'd probably have to organize their own patrols, and they'd run a far greater risk that way.

"How many people will you need?" she asked warily.

"You're agreeing?" he probed.

"Reluctantly. Don't rub it in!"

"I won't," Jack promised. "I'd like two backup teams, one on the property and one at the potluck."

"At the potluck? Why?"

"First, because there's no guarantee whoever's doing this won't try to harm you or Enid or whoever his target is when you're least expecting it. Also, I want a record of any questionable behavior, such as someone trying to sneak out who changes his mind when he sees the chief."

"Gail or Enid could do that. It doesn't sound dangerous," Casey admitted.

"I'd like them to work together. In a situation like this, you really need two people," Jack said. "One might have to stay and observe something while the other makes a phone call. Also, they can help each other keep the mission on target even if someone tries to distract them."

The mission. The term put her in mind of commandos operating in a jungle. Kind of a far cry from a small-town potluck, Casey thought.

"All right," she said. "What about patrolling the property? That could be a tough job, especially at night. I don't think any of my guys are up to it."

"Don't forget the team concept. I want Bo Rogers and Matt Dorning to work together."

"Bo and Matt? Now there's an odd couple!" The two men formed about as unlikely a pair as Casey could imagine, the one young and robust but of limited intellect, the other physically frail but mentally sharp. "You really think so?"

"Together they have all the attributes we need. Sometimes you need to get creative," Jack advised.

Matt would relish the challenge, Casey supposed, and Bo often sought ways to be helpful. "It wouldn't hurt to ask them, I guess."

"I appreciate your cooperation. I know this whole situation makes you uneasy." Reaching over, Jack began massaging her shoulder lightly.

"'Uneasy' is too mild a word," Casey confessed. "Plus I hate the idea of us prancing around at the town social while other people are running risks."

"Once we get a bead on things, I don't intend to stay on the sidelines." Jack eased his chair away from the desk and positioned himself so he could apply both hands. "Feel good?"

"It's fabulous." Casey closed her eyes and gave in to the soothing sensations. The tightness in her back yielded rapidly to his pressure.

She wished she didn't have to think about anything else, just her husband's touch. As her mind began to drift, she realized that spending time together at the Spring Fling wasn't such a bad idea after all.

Seeing Jack in a different context might provide the insight she needed for her plan to win him back. She smiled at the name she thought of: Operation Rescue Jack.

"What's so funny?" he asked.

She could hardly tell him the truth. "I was picturing Matt and Bo on patrol. That ought to be a lively sight!" Reluctantly, she returned to the subject of the attacker. "You mentioned you'd eliminated Larry as a suspect. Who's on your list now?"

"At the top, Al Rawlins." Jack probed down to the small of her back, where he dissolved taut rubber bands of anxiety. "He's got a grudge and he's been seen around the property in several capacities. However, I haven't completely written off Royce Ledbetter."

"Royce wouldn't do this!" Her old high-school buddy wasn't capable of knocking Casey down with a hose and torching Enid's roof. At least, she didn't think so.

"Friends of the accused are often shocked, even when the evidence proves overwhelming." Jack finished the back rub, leaving her skin and muscles tingling pleasantly. "I can't ignore his motive or his possessiveness toward you."

"He acted possessive?" When Jack recounted their conversation, he hadn't mentioned anything about that.

"He lit into me for not standing by my wife. I'd call that possessive."

"Or moralistic, which doesn't sound like him either," she conceded. "How did you respond?"

"I don't remember." He reached for the phone. "If you don't mind, I'll call Chief Roundtree and get his approval. It's going to take time to set this up."

He was dodging her again! "Don't do that!"

"You don't want him involved? I explained..."

"I meant, don't dodge me when I try to find out what happened between you and Royce. This isn't about him, it's about you and your feelings. Tell me what you said to him!"

"I honestly don't remember." His eyes took on a hooded appearance.

"Yes, you do!"

"I don't recall the exact words. I stalled him. I was trying to figure out if he's a criminal. I don't care what he thinks of me personally." The clipped way Jack spoke revealed that that wasn't entirely true.

Royce's accusation must have rankled. If only Jack would admit how much he cared, maybe she could persuade him to trust his feelings.

Casey wished she knew a way to force him to open up. *Talk to me! Let me inside!* But she feared she'd only send him scurrying further into his shell. "Oh, go ahead. Call the chief."

"Thanks." He picked up the phone.

As she went into the kitchen to start dinner, though, her thoughts remained back in the office with Jack. The man had the power to frustrate her almost beyond endurance!

She had to be content with the observation that at least he was getting to know the world where she'd grown up and the people she shared it with. He already understood her tenants' strengths and how to keep Chief Roundtree happy. He might even whip Larry into shape, if anyone could.

Jack had a lot to offer to a place like Richfield Crossing. If he would only stick around until Diane was born, he might see that there were other, more meaningful ways to live than rushing across the globe risking his neck for strangers.

She didn't know how they'd work out the logistics of his running a security agency. That could come later.

In the meantime, convincing her husband to move here wouldn't be easy, Casey mused as she took down her spaghetti pot. But she must find a way. She simply had to.

Chapter Twelve

To Jack's relief, the chief agreed with his plan after asking a few questions. Not only didn't he object to the idea of giving Larry some extra training, he approved completely.

"He graduated from the police academy in Nashville, but his attitude needs some adjustment and I lose patience," Roundtree admitted on the phone. "He's on duty tomorrow afternoon, if you want to meet with him then, and I'll make sure he's available to help out Wednesday night even if I have to hire a substitute guard for the glass factory."

As for the tenants, Matt's creased face lit up when Jack asked him whether he'd be interested in patrolling. "I hate sitting here knowing some fellow's sneaking around, doing nasty things to my neighbors. A man never gets too old to want to protect his friends."

Bo was, if anything, even more enthusiastic. "I'll be a good guard. I'll take care of Matt, too, if he falls down."

"Hopefully, he won't." Jack suggested that Rita ride to the potluck with him and Casey. However when she heard about the plans, she said some friends from their square dance group would pick her up.

"I won't tell them anything," she added. "We know how to keep a secret."

When Gail came over Monday night to coach Casey, she made an alternate suggestion to teaming with Enid. "You're going to have to run back here at some point, Jack," she said. "I can stay with Casey at the Spring Fling to make sure she's all right. Enid should be able to snoop around the community center by herself."

Although Jack didn't object, Casey nixed the idea. "This is my property. Gail, you're a real trooper, but nobody's keeping me away from here. If Jack heads home, so will I."

Reluctantly, the nurse agreed to the original plan. However, Jack made a mental note to entrust Casey to her care if things got rough. A woman who might go into labor at any moment needed someone watching over her.

Still, he had to admit that even her large girth and occasional sleepiness failed to dampen his wife's spirit. To make sure everyone in town knew she'd be partying, she volunteered to remind a long list of people about the event. The organizers—the wives of the pastor and the department store owner—were more than happy to let her make the calls.

On Tuesday, while she went into town to run errands, Jack spent several hours patrolling with Larry Malloy around the property. He found that the young man had slacked off from his training to the point of becoming slipshod.

He overlooked several suspicious objects planted earlier because he wasn't paying attention. When Jack pointed them out, Larry argued that their conversation had distracted him.

"If somebody shoots you, what good are excuses?" Jack asked. "Think of this as a game, even though it's in deadly earnest. You've got to stay on your toes if you expect to win."

As time went on, the fellow began to shape up. He needed a firm hand but responded well to encouragement, and after a while even made a few suggestions of his own. Among them was to spread word that he'd be working at the glass company that night although he actually had the evening off.

It pleased Jack to see him showing initiative. By the time they took a coffee break at Casey's house, he no longer had any doubts about the young man's ability to handle his part of the assignment.

"Nothing against the chief, but he's kind of stuck in his ways," Larry confided while eating a snack. "I'd rather work for a real leader, somebody I could learn from. Like you."

"I'm sure there's a lot he could teach you." Jack didn't want to detract from Roundtree in any way.

"Maybe so, but he's too impatient," Larry mumbled between bites of a sticky bun. "You explain things so I understand them."

Never having served as a training officer, Jack had been relying on his instincts. He was glad to hear they'd paid off. "Thanks."

The young cop paused between bites. "I'd offer to come work for that security agency of yours, except I like it around these parts. I just wish I could hire on full-time at the PD."

"Isn't there enough money in the budget?" It seemed to Jack the town needed at least two full-time officers.

"There could be. Some of the farmers outside town asked the council if they could contract with us to patrol their areas. The chief turned 'em down. He said he didn't need any more administrative burdens."

"Too bad." Jack finished his coffee and carried the cup to the sink. "Whenever you're ready, let's give it another go."

He arranged for the two of them to go over to Matt's cabin so the men could meet. The elderly tenant took a keen interest in the preparations and seemed impressed by Larry, who basked in the admiration. The three of them arranged to meet again after dinner when Bo could join them.

After seeing the younger man off at the parking lot, Jack listened for a moment to distant sounds, automatically screening out the birdcalls and the noise of homebuilding down near Old Richfield Road. With satisfaction, he recognized the hum of Casey's motor as she turned onto Pine Woods Avenue.

Having lived his whole life in Southern California, he hadn't realized he could adjust to a new place so quickly. Already, his brain was sorting out familiar from unfamiliar sounds and smells.

In his pocket, the cell phone rang. While keeping watch for Casey's car, Jack answered.

"Good news." It was Mike. "I met with Paul Mendez this morning and he's exactly what we need. Plus, he's leaving the Denver PD earlier than expected because he's accumulated so much vacation time. If it's okay with you, he can begin familiarizing himself with our projects right away."

"That's great." As they discussed Mendez and the qualities he could bring to the firm, Jack imagined himself back at the Men At Arms office.

Located in an old building in the Hollywood area, it lacked charm. Since they did all their work on-site and their clients never visited, however, the ritzy-sounding address was all that mattered. Despite the faded exterior paint and clouded windows, Jack loved the leather smell of his secondhand desk chair and the nearby buzz of traffic. But his satisfaction went way beyond mere pride of ownership.

When he and Mike had signed the lease, he'd felt a high rivaled only by his wedding day. Having his own company meant no one could fire him or order him around. Although Mike served as elder partner and tended to take the lead, they owned everything together.

Perhaps bringing in another partner ought to faze him, but Jack had never been a control freak. The new arrangement should strengthen the firm and help it expand.

"As it turns out, we can use him this weekend," Mike was saying. "That meeting in Athens is coming together. Nicos has done the legwork. However, we need a partner on hand to supervise. I'd like to send Paul."

"You think he's ready to handle this on his own?" Jack asked.

"I'd rather one of us joined him," Mike admitted. "I've got

the Hong Kong trade meeting to set up. I was hoping you could make it."

Having flown to Athens a couple of times previously, Jack understood the complexities involved. He wished he'd been able to arrive well in advance to make sure of the arrangements himself, but he trusted Nicos. "Sure. I should have things wrapped up here by Thursday."

"You'll need to leave that afternoon at the latest." Mike promised to arrange for their assistant to check with the travel agent to see if Jack and Paul could catch the same flight from New York. That would give them a chance to get acquainted before their arrival.

Jack took down more phone numbers. He needed to call Paul and Nicos and step into the traces as head of the operation. Already, he could feel himself mentally pulling away from Richfield Crossing.

As he dialed Paul, Casey came in. Seeing him on the phone, she waved as she carted in an armload of groceries.

He tried to hurry it up so he could help her. But by the time he finished touching bases with both men, she'd hauled in and stowed her purchases. Already feeling as if he'd let her down, Jack decided to postpone mentioning he had to leave on Thursday. She already knew he'd have to head out soon, so it wasn't as if he were keeping her in the dark.

Besides, he wanted to enjoy what little time they had left. It felt too precious to waste on recriminations.

AFTER DINNER, while Jack went to confer with Larry and the two male tenants about the following night, Casey prepared a bag to take to the hospital when the time came. She wouldn't need much, just some toiletries and a bathrobe, but Gail had advised her not to wait until the last minute.

She finished tucking items into the case and went to the kitchen, where she took a roll of cookie dough out of the refrigerator. Although she certainly didn't need the extra calories, she remembered Jack telling her long ago that the smell of cookies baking reminded him of his mother. It was one of the few things he'd confided about his early life.

If she planned to get him to open up, this seemed a good place to start. Sneaky, but, Casey hoped, effective.

A few minutes later, he returned. The crisp night air had reddened his cheeks and he wore a distracted air.

He halted in the living room, his expression lightening. "That smells great. Are you baking?"

"I thought you might need something to warm you up." Pleased by the timing, Casey retrieved the tray from the oven. The cookies had started to brown but remained slightly chewy in the middle, the way she preferred them. "They're chocolate chip."

"Is there any other kind worth mentioning?" Shedding his outer garments, Jack came to stand behind her. "Hand me one, would you?"

"They'll burn your mouth!" When Casey turned, he stood so close he overwhelmed her senses. "And we wouldn't want that to happen. There are too many other good uses for it." Lifting her arms impulsively, she drew his mouth down to hers.

Despite the awkwardness of the bulge, Jack kissed her for a long time. She gave herself over to enjoying his solid strength and answering tenderness.

Although Casey's blood pulsed faster, it wasn't only physical longing she felt. The child they shared united them at a level she'd never experienced before, as if the two of them had melted together.

He seemed to burrow into her, not only his tongue but also the way his tall frame arched over her and into her. She wanted him inside her, truly inside, but they couldn't do that.

Not yet. But maybe in a few weeks. If only he'd stay.

When Jack lifted his head, his gaze lingered on hers. "I want to give you the same pleasure you gave me the other day."

She knew what he meant, and she wanted it too. With a

wrench, Casey remembered her plan to get him to reveal more about his past so she could win him over. Lovemaking between them had always been passionate and intensely satisfying, but although they had no trouble expressing themselves physically, it wasn't enough to save her marriage.

"We should eat the cookies first," she said. "Before they get cold."

"You're a wicked woman," Jack murmured. "Tempting me and then stringing me along."

"What could be more tempting than chocolate chip cookies?" she answered, and reluctantly slipped from his arms.

At the table, he took his first bite. She wondered what images flooded through him but realized that if she asked too bluntly, he was likely to brush it off.

"You know," Jack said, "I think things will go well tomorrow night."

"You do?" Although she would have preferred not to talk about their plan, Casey decided to follow his lead. "I hope we catch this guy."

"That's hard to predict. Still, it's amazing how this thing is bringing people together," he said. "Larry and I stopped by to talk to Enid. The two of them seemed a bit awkward at first, but soon they were actually joking with each other."

"Enid didn't treat Larry like a kid?" Casey asked.

"No. After a while, she picked up on his confident attitude and I could tell she respected him. And he knew it."

"Maybe she won't flunk him this time," she joked.

"He's going to pass muster." Jack's confidence dispelled the last of her doubts about the young officer.

"So you're not worried about something going wrong tomorrow?" Casey pressed.

"There's always some risk, even with trained personnel," Jack replied. "On the other hand, our group is highly motivated and willing to follow directions. And I trust their innate good sense."

"What if this guy does an end run? Since we don't know what his motive is, he might surprise us. Strike at one of our cars at the Community Center, for instance."

"That's why I want the chief outside and Gail and Enid on the inside." Jack downed another cookie. "The point is to plan for as many eventualities as possible and to build in enough flexibility to go with the flow. After that, if all hell breaks loose, we just have to accept it and move on."

"I'm not sure I'd be good at accepting whatever happens." Casey plopped her feet on an empty chair. "Still, I'd love to be the one who captures this jerk. I still resent the way he hosed me."

"It's hard to figure you out sometimes," Jack said.

"What do you mean?"

"Sometimes you're a mass of anxieties, and then you can be a real fireball." Going to the fridge, he poured them each a glass of milk. "I can't predict how you'll respond to a situation."

"Is there some virtue in being predictable?" Casey realized she needed to give him a more complete answer. If she expected her husband to reveal his vulnerabilities, she'd better be willing to start with herself. "I tend to be assertive by nature but I worry about the people I love. When I rely on my impulses, I go for broke, but when I picture all the bad things that could happen, I turn into a worrier."

"What do you fear most?" Jack asked.

On the verge of saying she feared losing someone she loved, Casey realized that wasn't the whole truth. "It's hard to explain."

"Death? Dismemberment?"

"Ouch!" She made a face. "I don't think in those terms. Let me tell you an anecdote instead. Mom and I used to drive to Nashville to visit my grandmother in an assisted living home. She had her friends and her favorite TV programs, but what lit up her face was seeing us."

"Because she loved you."

"Mom explained it to me once," she said. "Lots of people at the home had activities and casual friends but no family. There was no one who shared their memories, no one tied to them in a way that could never dissolve no matter what happened. Isn't that what everybody fears most, losing that intimate connection, being really and truly alone?"

She felt as if she'd laid herself bare in front of him. Surely now he'd understand why their marriage had to take priority over everything else, because they had the capacity to mean that much to each other.

"That's not exactly what I fear most, although I guess it used to be," Jack replied.

"What do you mean?"

"The worst thing I could imagine actually happened when I was eleven." He turned his glass around and around on the table, scarcely registering his repetitive action. "Pop bailed out while Mom was sick, and there were just the two of us. Even though I knew she had cancer, I never imagined she might die. Even at the funeral, it didn't seem real. Then a neighbor took me home and told me to pack. She'd called Child Welfare and someone was coming to get me."

"How awful." Casey could feel the lost little boy aching inside the man.

"While I was packing, I kept listening for Mom's footsteps or her voice. The silence was so deep it nearly swallowed me," he said. "I remember thinking it would be a relief to go outside into the sunshine. But when the social worker took me to her car, the street looked empty, too, because none of the faces belonged to my mother. Every place felt empty after that. At least, until I got used to it."

Casey didn't see how a child could survive such a loss. "So you adapted?"

"It took a long time. I'd start to make friends and get attached to someone, then I'd get transferred to another place."

"Why?" she asked.

"All sorts of reasons. My first foster family didn't like me." His matter-of-fact tone couldn't mask the devastation he must have felt. "One family decided to leave the area. I wasn't really their kid, so I got left behind. Another family couldn't handle the way I kept getting into fights at school."

"That's awful." Now Casey understood his mistrust of closeness, despite his obvious longing for it.

"For a while, I got seriously depressed, then my survival instinct kicked in," Jack went on. "I realized that if you tear yourself apart over things you can't help, it will destroy you. From then on, I accepted that nothing was permanent."

"But it doesn't have to be that way," Casey said.

"When we're grown up, it's true we can take more control of our lives." He sat back in his chair. "That's why I left the LAPD and went into business with Mike. I know companies can fail, but I'd found something that belonged to me, that I could put my guts into and depend on."

"You didn't feel that way when we got married?" she asked.

A startled look came into his eyes. "I never thought of it in those terms."

Now she understood what she'd only guessed at before. "You didn't really expect our marriage to last, did you?"

He frowned. "I wouldn't say that."

For once, Casey borrowed a leaf from Jack's book and kept silent. *Give him room to think out loud.*

"To me, personal relationships are like shifting sand," he said. "My business won't run out on me. It's solid. I understand it. There are rules I can depend on."

"But if you don't have someone to love you, someday you'll end up with nothing."

"I could end up with nothing anyway," Jack told her. "The worst thing is to keep on hoping, to keep on needing people and letting it devastate you when they leave. That would eat me alive, Casey. And I won't let it."

She hadn't expected this. She'd thought that when she finally saw inside him, the last barriers would fall and he'd admit his need for her. Instead, she realized, the more he allowed himself to love her and become part of her world, the more he stood to lose.

Still, she couldn't give up that easily. "Sometimes you have to take a chance," she said.

"It took me a long time to know myself," Jack answered. "I'm sorry if I let you down. I wish I could have been the man you wanted and deserve, a guy who fits the bill as Father Knows Best, but I'm not him, Casey."

"You could be."

Sadness and anguish mingled in his gaze. "I'm afraid you see things in me that aren't there."

She wanted to pummel him with arguments. How could he fail to understand his own depths and his own needs? But the self-protection he'd built to survive as a teenager had hardened into a wall that kept other people out, even her. Perhaps especially her.

And the baby. Opening up to that special, all-encompassing love a parent felt toward a helpless infant must be the most threatening thing in the world. No wonder he hadn't wanted children. You could divorce a spouse, but once you gave your heart to your kid, you could never raise those defenses again.

At last, she'd begun to understand her husband—only to realize that perhaps she'd really and truly lost him.

Chapter Thirteen

By Wednesday morning, Casey had regained some of her normal optimism. Deep inside, Jack obviously missed the closeness and connection of having a family. He also possessed strengths that he didn't fully appreciate, including the ability to take a chance on what he feared most.

She still didn't know how she was going to help him see that the risks were worth taking. She'd just have to play it by ear.

He spent much of the day on the phone, apparently organizing something related to his company. Since Gail had the afternoon off, the women scheduled a childbirth class at two o'clock.

At Gail's suggestion, they met at her cabin to avoid disturbing Jack. A virtual twin to Enid's in terms of layout, it had a rustic front room, a single bedroom and a cheery kitchen.

Her taste in decorating varied dramatically from the teacher's, however. Instead of overstuffed coziness, the place had a simple, spare look. Aside from a couple of souvenir plates on the wall, a framed collage of babies she'd helped deliver constituted the only decoration.

Casey noticed right away that the nurse had installed folding child gates at the doors and a playpen in one corner. "What's that for?" she asked in surprise.

"You're going to need a baby-sitter," the nurse pointed out. "A client was giving these away because her kids are too old, so I figured I'd put them to good use. This way, Diane can sleep here whenever you're gone."

"You're fantastic," Casey said. "I can't believe you're being so considerate. I don't know what I'd do without you."

"It's no problem. I love kids even though I never had any." On the floor, Gail spread a practice mat for prenatal exercises. "It's too bad your husband won't be here to help. Has he told you when he's leaving?"

"Not exactly." Although tempted to confide what she'd observed about him last night, Casey held back out of a sense of loyalty to Jack. If he kept his emotions and memories private, what right did he have to share them with others? "Let's work on that breathing. I've been practicing."

"Excellent!" Gail propped open the front door. "Now we'll have plenty of fresh air."

They were halfway through the session when Casey heard a sound from the doorway. It was Sandra, peering inside.

"Sorry to interrupt," she said. "I went by your house and Jack mentioned you were here. He was just leaving—going into town, I think."

"Oh, right." He'd scheduled a three o'clock meeting with the police chief but obviously hadn't wanted to mention that in front of a visitor. "Sandra, have you met Gail?"

"I don't think so."

Eyeing each other warily, the two women shook hands as Casey introduced them. "I'm a nurse and childbirth instructor," Gail said. "Do you have children?"

Sandra shook her head quickly. "You two go ahead and finish. I'll wait outside." When she turned away and the sunlight hit her face, Casey saw tears in her eyes.

After she left, Gail lifted a questioning eyebrow. "She lost a baby," Casey explained quietly. "I don't think it was very long ago."

"I'm sorry to hear that. We can wrap this up quickly so we don't keep her waiting. You're making terrific progress."

"Thanks." They worked for a little while longer, but both remained aware of the visitor outside. As Casey lumbered to her feet at last, she said, "I really appreciate the time you're spending with me. It's way above and beyond anything I have any right to expect."

"That's what friends are for." The hoarse note in Gail's voice hinted at the emotion she hid behind her no-nonsense manner.

Even had the bassinet and child gates not made it obvious, Casey knew how deeply Gail cared about her and Diane. In a way, she supposed, this connection might substitute for the family she didn't have.

Impulsively, she caught Gail's hand. "We're more than friends," she confided. "You're like a favorite aunt."

"I feel that way too." The nurse squeezed her back. "Now you go and see what Sandra's here about. Still, be careful. From what I've heard, she's not the most trustworthy person in the world."

"That's what Jack says, too," Casey noted. "But I know her. She can't have changed that much."

Outside, Sandra waited with her hands jammed into her coat pockets. The daylight emphasized the hollowness of her cheeks, but at least she'd regained some healthy color since Sunday.

By unspoken accord, they took the footpath toward Casey's house instead of the paved drive. "What's up?" she asked her visitor.

"I came to warn you to be careful."

It didn't exactly sound like a threat. It was hardly reassuring, either. "What do you mean?"

"Everybody in town knows you and Jack are going to the Spring Fling tonight," Sandra said. "Why did you broadcast the news? I mean, with the trouble you've had, I think you should be more discreet."

Although her critical tone of voice put Casey's back up, she tried not to respond in kind. "People keep asking if we're going. I could hardly pretend we weren't."

"You could stay home."

"I want Jack to get to know this town. It means a lot to me."

Ahead of them, a couple of squirrels whisked past each other as if playing a game. Sandra gave no notice. "Don't be an idiot! Surely you're at least leaving someone to watch the property."

"Maybe I don't think there's a serious problem." Abruptly, Casey remembered her friend's previous questions about the prowler. "You were asking about this the other day. Why are you so interested?"

"I was just making conversation. For heaven's sake, don't make a federal case out of it!" The blond woman kicked a rock out of her way. "I'm trying to do you a favor. You ought to listen once in a while instead of thinking you know everything!"

When she scowled, she didn't look like the Sandra who'd grown up here. The little girl who'd livened up their school days with her joking had turned into an adult filled with anger.

Casey became sharply aware of how isolated they were. Sheltered by a canopy of trees, they'd passed out of sight of Gail's cabin, and, since Jack had gone into town, there was no one to watch or hear them from below.

She shook off her fears. This was Sandra, her best friend. She certainly couldn't be the prowler, anyway, since she hadn't returned until this past weekend.

"I'm not going to let some trespasser run my life," Casey announced. "Why should I miss a chance to enjoy myself with my husband?"

In the old days, she would have explained how much tonight meant, how she hoped against hope that Jack would begin to put down roots in Richfield Crossing. But she didn't really know the woman beside her any more, certainly not enough to confide in her.

"That's all you talk about! Jack this, Jack that," Sandra

lashed out. "Things must really be going well. Well, if he's so wonderful, why isn't he doing those baby exercises with you? I guess things aren't as perfect as you pretend!"

Heedless of their remote surroundings or of anything except her annoyance at Sandra's attack, Casey stopped to face her. "Nobody's pretending anything. Why don't you get over yourself? You're so eaten up with envy you can't see straight, but the only person responsible for what's happened to you is yourself!"

"I never said it wasn't!"

"Did you listen to what you just said? My relationship with my husband is none of your business. Once upon a time, I would have told you everything, but you chose to push me away," Casey shot back.

"You're the one who left!" Sandra snapped. "You dumped me with those druggies."

"I dumped you?" She couldn't believe this self-serving version of the truth. "You made it clear I'd better shape up or ship out, so I shipped out. And now you're mad because you're suffering and I'm not down there in the pit with you! What would make you happy, Sandra? If my life was a miserable as yours?"

"My life isn't miserable!" Tears spilled over. "Oh, yes, it is. You've got everything I wanted."

"No, I don't."

"Yes, you do, and the worst part is, you deserve it," Sandra admitted. "And I hate the fact that you deserve it! And I hate the fact that I hate you!"

"You hate me?"

"Sort of," her friend said. "I hate the idea of you. And I hate being away from you. I hate seeing that nurse helping you when your best friend ought to be there. I hate that you had a baby shower and you didn't even know I was in town so you could invite me."

Casey couldn't figure out whether to laugh or get mad. "You don't sound like you know what you want."

"I want us to be exactly like we used to be, and we can't. It's awful. I miss you."

She threw her arms around Casey and ran smack into the bulge. They both started to giggle.

"I got fat," Casey joked.

"It's a good kind of fat." Sandra sniffled. "I'm sorry. I've been running you down to my parents, and I wish I hadn't. I'm a coward. I couldn't bear having my father look at me as a failure, so I tried to pin the blame on you."

"We can start over," she offered. "That's why you came home, isn't it? To make a new beginning?"

"I guess so."

The two of them stood for a while talking. Casey saw her old friend regaining a little of her old animation, and hoped Sandra had turned a corner today.

Remembering her friend's concern about leaving the property unguarded, she nearly blurted out that they had plans. What restrained her was the fact that Sandra's father remained one of Jack's primary suspects.

She'd admitted making Casey out to be the villain of her story. No wonder Al held a grudge. And Sandra knew it.

Maybe she was so interested in the prowler because she feared it might be her father. Obviously she didn't want any harm to come to Casey, or she wouldn't have bothered warning her to be careful.

But when push came to shove, as Jack had pointed out, families closed ranks. Surely Sandra would do her best to protect her father, which meant she'd warn him if she learned a trap was being set at the Pine Woods.

Even if Al stayed away tonight, that didn't mean the attacks would stop. And next time, there'd be no Jack around to protect her. Although she hated holding such suspicions about Sandra's father, she didn't dare trust her.

"It's turning chilly," Casey said. "We'd better get going." The forecast called for another storm to move in tomorrow.

Sandra accompanied her down the lower stretch of path. "I'm thrilled about your baby. Envious, but happy for you. It's not as if I can't have another child someday."

"I hope you will." Noting the time, Casey added, "I'd like to swing down and pick up my mail." The post generally arrived between two and three.

"I can use the exercise." Sandra stumped alongside her. "Besides, you shouldn't be wandering around unaccompanied."

"I'm not a china doll!"

"You're a pigheaded pregnant woman who doesn't know when to take it easy," her friend replied with a grin.

They connected with the driveway and followed it toward the street. Rita, returning with a small package, greeted them enthusiastically.

"Our new video!" She waved it happily. "We'll watch it tonight. No, not tonight. We're going to be busy, aren't we?"

Apprehension dimmed Casey's mood. If Rita said the wrong thing, Sandra would pick up on it at once. "I'll see you at the Community Center, then." She quickened her pace toward the mailboxes.

Her tenant didn't take the hint. "Bo's very excited. He always wanted to be a policeman and now he is, kind of."

Casey knew her face must be reddening. Sandra's mouth tightened into a straight line.

"See you!" With a little skip, Rita moved up the path. Grimly, Casey continued on to collect her post, which consisted of the usual bills plus a baby magazine.

As soon as Rita had passed out of earshot, Sandra's voice rang with reproach. "You weren't going to tell me. You think it's my dad, don't you? And you're not leaving the place empty. You're planning to catch him."

Since there was no avoiding the confrontation, Casey didn't try. "No, I wasn't going to tell you. As for who it is, we don't know. Jack has a list of possibilities, but we aren't even sure it includes the real culprit."

"You say that, but you don't mean it!" No sign of warmth lingered now. "You're sure it's Dad."

"Whether it is or not, we have to act," Casey snapped. "I can't afford to pay someone to patrol this place twenty-four hours a day, and we need to catch this guy before somebody gets seriously hurt."

"So while I was all emotional about how much I missed you, you were figuring out how to keep me in the dark." Anger drove the healthy bloom from Sandra's coloring, leaving her white with rage.

Casey knew she ought to guard her tongue, but she couldn't. "Why are you getting paranoid again? This isn't about you! It's about protecting me and my tenants from whoever's stalking us! I hope it isn't your dad, but if you warn him and nobody shows up tonight, that's going to make him look even guiltier, isn't it?"

"What's the difference? As far as you and your husband are concerned, Dad's already tried and convicted!" Without waiting for a response, Sandra strode up the drive toward the parking lot. By the time Casey puffed her way there, the Rawlins' car passed her heading for the road.

What a mess, she reflected wearily. Just when their friendship might have had a second chance, circumstances and Sandra's temper had blown it away.

If Al was the man who'd been targeting her property, his daughter was going to help him escape. Which meant that, indirectly, she'd be making it possible for him to strike again.

"DON'T DWELL ON IT," Jack said that evening as he tucked Casey into her car. He'd arrived home from town to find her so upset about Sandra's visit that she'd messed up a section of her crocheting. "There's nothing you could have done differently."

"You and everyone else have put so much work into this." Her lower lip quivered. "I feel like I let you down."

He got behind the wheel. They'd decided to leave the rental

car behind as bait. It had already inspired one attack, and they'd parked it in a place that would be easy for Larry to keep in his sights. "Has it occurred to you that maybe Al Rawlins isn't the perpetrator?"

"Even if not, he might tell everyone he knows out of spite." On the seat beside her, she adjusted the salad she'd fixed for the potluck.

Jack cupped his hand over hers. Although he too wished Sandra hadn't learned of their intentions, it was water under the bridge. "Let's not worry. Even if the guy we're seeking hears what's going on, he might try to pull a stunt just to thumb his nose at us."

"Great," Casey muttered. "Something else for me to worry about."

"Are you going to be like this all evening? Lighten up! We're supposed to enjoy ourselves."

"You always hate parties," she reminded him.

"That's because I feel out of place," he said. "Tonight, it's easier because we have a job to do."

"What, exactly?"

"Sparkle and look happy," he told her. "Like we haven't got a care in the world."

It wasn't going to be as difficult as Jack might have expected. Running an operation like this filled him with confidence, not the cockiness of a fool who believes nothing can go wrong but the keenness and quick reflexes of a man preparing to play a game at which he excels. Why shouldn't he enjoy himself?

In fact, he'd had a double dose of adrenaline today, coordinating with Nicos and Paul on the phone about the Greek conference and meeting with Roundtree in town. The chief had seemed eager to see action and rueful that he was no longer physically able to take on any rough stuff. He'd also been complimentary about Jack's work with Larry.

"The guy's got a whole new attitude," Roundtree had said

as the two of them inspected the entrances and exits at the community center. "I always liked him but I didn't see his full potential until now. Maybe I should have agreed to expand our service area when I had the chance."

Jack hadn't commented. He'd focused on familiarizing himself with the layout for tonight's event, reminding himself that the operation of the town's police department was none of his business.

However, he suspected that if the chief really wanted to, he'd find a way to put the young officer on full-time duty. That would not only be good for him, it would benefit the community.

The place was growing, he noted now as he and Casey passed the housing development under construction. The chief had also mentioned a shopping center planned south of town.

Noticing how long his wife had been silent, he said, "Are you okay?"

"I just had another Braxton Hicks contraction," she admitted.

"You're sure that's all it is?"

"I absolutely refuse to go into labor tonight and spoil everything!" she shot back.

"It's not the sort of thing you can control."

"I am not in labor." She folded her arms.

If anybody could rule the forces of nature, it would be his wife, Jack thought in amusement. Whatever happened, he planned to take it in stride. New mothers didn't deliver instantaneously, Casey had informed him earlier, so even if labor was starting, they'd still have a few hours to catch their guy.

And he had a good feeling about the operation, no matter how Al Rawlins reacted to his daughter's news.

DESPITE HER MISGIVINGS, Casey's spirits rose when they entered the community center. The organizers had festooned it with silk blossoms and paper greenery, and the scents of home-cooked food from the buffet table stirred her appetite.

But what excited her most was seeing so many old friends,

including farmers who didn't often come into town. Chatter filled the air as people greeted each other, showed off their fast-growing children and swapped news. Affairs like this reminded her that, even though TV and the Internet tempted people to stay home for their entertainment, there was no substitute for a community gathering.

Plus, it was for a good cause. In addition to the inexpensive admission tickets, a silent auction and crafts sale would likely net hundreds of dollars for the library. Casey had donated an autographed copy of a Munch Mancini mystery by Barbara Seranella that she'd bought in L.A.

As they walked through the large activities room, she enjoyed the way others came over to be introduced to Jack or greeted him with genuine liking. His calm assurance made people respect him immediately, she could tell. Even those who'd had reservations about her absentee husband seemed eager to talk to him tonight.

She didn't know exactly what had changed in the past few days. Maybe it was the by-now well-known story of how he'd saved Enid from the fire. More likely, it was the natural charisma that Jack didn't seem to realize he possessed.

She loved him so much. She knew this feeling must show in her face, and didn't care.

He, too, seemed different. Although she realized he might simply be playing a role as they'd arranged, his self-assured smile made him almost irresistible.

With an inward sigh, Casey forced her attention away from her husband. If she hung on too tightly, everyone would speculate later about the reason. Instead, she surveyed the room until she spotted Gail and Enid.

They must have arrived early. Although the two women didn't normally socialize together, they were doing their best to stay close, she could see.

The pairing seemed to work well. Former students and their parents made a beeline for Enid, leaving Gail free to

watch the crowd. Between them, they should be able to iden-
tify who was present and who was missing.

She'd already spotted Royce, who would probably be calling square dances later on. If he decided to slip out, they'd
have no problem detecting his absence.

She'd never believed her old boyfriend wanted to harm
anyone. Furthermore, the prowling had started before Jack returned, at a time when Royce might still have hoped to win
Casey back if he'd really felt possessive.

Nevertheless, her opinion wavered as she caught a less-
than-friendly glance he slanted toward Jack. When he noticed Casey staring, Royce shrugged and turned away,
nearly colliding with Mimi Godwin. His lips formed a silent
whistle as he took in her appearance in a new, figure-hug-
ging dress.

"I'm glad she came." Casey spotted Mimi's mother, Jean,
talking with the mayor's wife, but didn't see Owen. "I wonder where her dad is."

"He's the one that's suffering memory problems, isn't he?"
Jack said. "Let's find out. I want everyone accounted for."

Casey almost broke off their approach when she saw how
animatedly Mimi was talking to Royce. She hated to spoil a
possible budding friendship, but at this point it would look odd
if she suddenly changed direction.

As she'd feared, Royce skittered away. Despite a regretful
glance at his retreating back, Mimi didn't seem perturbed. In
answer to Jack's question, she said, "Dad fell asleep early. We
didn't think it would do any harm to slip out."

"Will he be all right by himself?" Casey asked.

"Our neighbor offered to peek in on him," Mimi said. "Besides, we won't stay long."

"I hope you don't have to hurry too much. Royce seems
interested in you," she said.

"How could he help it?" Jack added diplomatically. "You
look great tonight, Mimi."

She gave them both a broad smile. Casey, who'd never seen her husband act so sociable, nearly fell over.

"He's a good guy." Mimi's gaze shifted to Royce, who was checking the sound system. "I'm hoping it's finally sunk in that you're not interested. Once he gets it through his head, maybe he'll be looking for someone who's available."

"He couldn't find a better partner than you," Casey said.

"Hold that thought!" Mimi broke off. "Uh-oh. Look who just showed up in a bad mood."

Across the large room, Casey caught sight of Sandra with her parents. Al wore a scowl dark enough to dim the lights, and his daughter avoided Casey's gaze.

Neither she nor Jack could say anything with Mimi standing right there. But she suspected they shared the same thought.

Al obviously knew what they were planning tonight. If he was the guy they sought, their efforts had been in vain.

Chapter Fourteen

Although Jack could see Casey's spirits plummeting, he didn't share her pessimism. Even if the prowler stayed away tonight, his conspicuous absence would cast extra suspicion on Al Rawlins, potentially narrowing the field for Chief Roundtree in the future.

Besides, the evening wasn't over until it was over. And that point lay hours ahead.

As soon as he could arrange a private moment, he called the chief and Larry to find out what they'd observed so far. Roundtree said that, as far as he could tell, most of the town had crammed itself into the community center, since parked cars were spilling into adjacent lots. "I don't think there's anyone left to keep an eye on," he joked.

Larry had a different story to tell. "On my way over, I saw an old pickup with out-of-state plates and a camper shell heading west on Pine Woods. Kind of unusual, since there aren't any homes past Casey's place. Then a few minutes ago, I observed some lights in the woods just beyond her property. Might be a transient living in his truck."

Jack remembered noticing a road on that land a few days ago, although he hadn't seen any signs of habitation. "I don't see what you can do as long as he stays off Casey's land."

"I might go talk to him," Larry persisted. "If it makes him nervous, well, that'll tell me something."

"It'll tell you he's scared of cops, but not why. He could just be an oddball." Although Jack admired the rookie's enthusiasm, he wasn't eager to leave the Pine Woods unguarded. "It's nearly dark, which means our guy's likely to show up any time. I'd advise sticking around."

"Okay," the officer said. "But I'll have Matt and Bo keep an eye on that side of the property."

"Sounds good to me." As he clicked off, Jack wondered whether a transient would be aware of the festivities.

If the guy had a proclivity for spying on people, he might have noticed the signs around town. If not, well, they'd have to hope he chose tonight to act stupid, assuming he *was* the interloper. But he hoped Larry wasn't making that assumption.

Laziness and bad police work could lead to focusing on the wrong guy just because he was an outsider. Jack's teenage run-ins with school authorities had taught him the unfairness of that approach.

After filling Casey in on the developments, he accompanied her to the line of people waiting their turn at the buffet. The variety and abundance of food amazed him. "I guess I've missed out by not going to potlucks before," he told her.

"You sure have." When asked, she identified some unfamiliar dishes, including black-eyed peas, grits and chicken-fried steaks.

Jack tried not to load his plate too high, since overeating could make him groggy. Even so, by the time he added a second, smaller dessert plate, he'd amassed a respectable amount of food.

They ate with Mimi and her mother. Even as the conversation flowed, Jack remained aware of the Rawlinses shooting the occasional glare his way from a nearby table. He could tell Casey and Mimi noticed them too.

"They're consumed by resentment," he observed as he finished his dessert. "Not a fun way to live."

Mimi swallowed a mouthful of lemonade. "I don't see how Sandra's going to get better with that attitude."

For once, Casey didn't stick up for her former pal. "She can get better if she wants to. She's been telling her parents I caused her problems. If she ever 'fesses up that she made this mess all by herself, it ought to clear the air."

"I hope she does soon," Mimi said. "She's being a real pain."

The sound system issued a preparatory squawk. "Are they starting the dancing already?" Jean asked. "Mimi, if you're interested in Royce, you should get moving."

"No one dances with the caller!" her daughter protested.

"I mean, you should show him there's other fellas interested in you." Her mother pointed out an unaccompanied young farmer. "Leland Jackson's a nice man."

"I hardly know him," Mimi objected.

"He's still nice."

"It looks like Bonnie and Angie have partners," Casey said. "You can tell Leland we need him to make up a square."

"Three couples isn't a square, it's a triangle!" her friend teased.

"You think I'm sitting this one out? No way!" she said. "Come on, Jack." She hoisted herself to her feet.

"Whoa." He raised his hands. "First, I have no idea how to square dance. Second…"

His wife's expression brooked no argument. "The first one's always for beginners. Royce will explain everything. Besides, I thought we wanted to…" To his relief, she stopped short of admitting they were trying to call attention to themselves. "…to make a good impression," she finished.

Jack's instincts urged him to head for the corridor and make another round of calls. But Roundtree was the incident commander, not him. And joining the square dance *would* make them highly visible.

Besides, if he didn't accompany his wife, she might grab the first guy she saw. Someone responsible needed to make sure she didn't trip on the dance floor and injure herself.

"I'm game." He rose and took her arm.

After greeting them cheerily, the Margolis sisters introduced their partners. By the time Mimi strolled over with Leland, Royce had seized a microphone and introduced himself, receiving scattered applause.

"Some of y'all practice with me a couple of times a week, and we'll have advanced patterns for you later, but right now I want to explain some basics for the beginners in our crowd." He glanced at Mimi. "I could use a little help to demonstrate the moves."

"Oh!" With an apologetic glance at her partner, she scooted forward. "I volunteer!"

"Don't worry, Leland, I'll have her back to you in a minute," Royce said, and proceeded to demonstrate steps with names like do-si-do, promenade and swing-your-partner. As Jack tried to absorb the information, he regretted having to remove his attention from the comings and goings around the room, but at least Enid and Gail were on guard.

At last Royce finished demonstrating. A flushed Mimi rejoined her friends and the four couples took their places. Jack, who'd never danced as part of a group before, wasn't sure what to expect, but Casey bubbled with anticipation.

When the dancers launched into their first maneuver, they set off so quickly he nearly got left behind. It took a while for him to catch the rhythm, to grow accustomed to Royce's singsong voice and to feel comfortable shuffling between the ladies. He enjoyed a challenge, though.

Despite the fact that Jack fluffed half the moves, nobody seemed to mind. Before the dance ended, almost all the couples had made at least one mistake, resulting in mass confusion and a lot of laughter.

The experience proved headier than Jack had expected. This might not be bad if you knew what you were doing.

"Well, now, that was interesting," Royce said as the music ended. "Some of you picked that up quicker than others, but we're all having fun. Let's try another one."

The second time around, Jack got the hang of it sooner and, despite a few mix-ups, ended beside Casey as he was supposed to. With everyone in the square laughing and cooperating, he felt as if they'd all become friends.

He also noted the way the caller had smoothly choreographed their movements. It showed a sophisticated side of Royce that surprised Jack.

Gazing at Casey's lively face, he understood what she meant about belonging to a community. Sure, he and his police buddies had shared a kind of fellowship, but it had been tempered by the pressures of the job and the knowledge that anyone could be transferred with little notice to another division in L.A. It was a temporary comradeship at best.

Mimi's voice broke into his thoughts. "If y'all will excuse me, I've got to call my neighbor and make sure Dad's okay. Leland, that sure was fun." With a wave, she slipped away.

The farmer wasted no time finding another partner. Noting how hard Casey was breathing, Jack drew her aside. "You've had enough."

"I'm afraid you're right." She accompanied him to their table and sank down beside Jean Godwin.

The overhead clock indicated they'd been occupied for over a quarter of an hour. A scan of the room showed Enid at the crafts table examining a blanket and Gail talking to a pregnant woman who must be one of her clients. Neither appeared to be paying attention to the rest of the scene.

Unease crept through Jack. He should have kept a closer watch on things. His discomfort intensified when he discovered that the Rawlinses had abandoned their table and were nowhere in sight.

Heading for the corridor, he took out his phone. Before he could dial, however, Sandra emerged from the ladies' room. Catching sight of him, she stopped short.

"What's up?" he asked.

She pressed her lips together and, for a moment, he thought

she might walk off. Finally, she said, "My dad just went out. I have no idea where."

"How about your mother?"

"She's visiting with some friends." Sandra thrust out her chin pugnaciously. "I know what you're thinking, but you can tell Casey I didn't rat on her, although maybe I should have. If Dad gets hurt out there, I'm holding you two responsible."

Jack had had enough of her selfishness. "We'll do our best to see that nobody comes to harm. If he does, it's no use trying to pin this on Casey or me. You want to know who's at fault? Take a good hard look in the mirror."

Her face tight with anger, she stalked away. Jack rapid-dialed the number he'd programmed earlier and explained the situation to Roundtree.

"I see him now, getting into his car," the chief said. "In fact, I was debating whether to follow him."

It seemed more productive to tail their primary suspect than to keep the chief on guard duty. "Go for it."

"Let's hope I remember how to conduct surveillance," came the response. "Stay tuned."

After clicking off, Jack strode back into the main room. On the floor, square dancers swirled in a complicated maneuver. Mimi had rejoined her mother and Casey and the three sat talking earnestly.

In his pocket, the phone rang. "Arnett," he answered, watching the area around him to make sure no one approached close enough to overhear.

It was Larry. "Matt and Bo found a rabbit trap on the edge of Pine Woods land. About a quarter of a mile away, they observed a parked camper truck with a guy sitting out front bold as you please, roasting something over a bonfire. I'm on my way to talk to him now."

Jack explained about Roundtree following Al. "Maybe you should stick around. They could be headed that way."

"No, the chief just called. They're eastbound."

"East?" That was the opposite direction from Casey's. "What's out there?"

"You got me," Larry said. "I'll call you back when I know anything."

"Thanks." Jack signed off.

He didn't like the fact that no one was watching Casey's house. However, it did make sense to check on the transient. As for the chief, he himself would have to decide whether to continue his surveillance or break it off.

Jack's earlier edgy feeling returned in full force. He didn't exactly believe his men were being manipulated away from the Pine Woods, but things seemed to be working out that way. He had a strong urge to drive back there himself, if only Casey would agree to remain here, out of danger.

Wondering how to phrase this so he neither alarmed her nor aroused her innate stubbornness, he returned to the table. Three anxious faces tilted toward him. Something else was going on, he saw.

"Mimi's neighbor says her father isn't home," Casey informed him. "She went inside with a key and he's gone."

"So is our other car," Jean told him. "I don't like to think about Owen driving alone in the dark, considering how forgetful he's been."

A senile old man out for a drive might merit calling the chief off his surveillance, although Jack hadn't ruled out the possibility of Al's doubling back. But another thought tickled the back of his mind.

Owen had tried to buy the Pine Woods, but Casey's parents had succeeded where he'd failed. A grudge had seemed unlikely, since it had occurred long ago and hadn't involved her directly.

But Mimi had mentioned her father quarreling with the mayor over a long-ago issue. "Has he mentioned anything lately about the McNaughts?" That was Casey's maiden name.

Jean twisted her hands together. "He's been going on about

all sorts of old grievances, real and imagined. Their names did come up a few times."

"In what context?"

"As Casey knows, the former owner of the Pine Woods discussed selling it to Owen, but he got tired of dickering and sold it to them instead," she explained. "Owen always felt he'd been robbed."

"You didn't tell me that!" Mimi said.

"I didn't think it meant anything. Does it?"

A thin line creased Casey's forehead. "I can't believe he'd do anything to hurt us!"

"Owen's not himself," Jean replied. "Please, Jack, don't let anything bad happen to him. Underneath, he's a good person."

"I'll do my best."

"There's one more thing," she added.

"Yes?" He swung back.

"My husband has a gun. I tried to take it away but he got so upset about the possibility of burglars that I…I just couldn't leave him unarmed."

"Thanks for the warning." Jack dialed Larry's number to alert him to the new developments. However, the call didn't go through. Two additional tries netted the same error message, and he couldn't get through on Bo's phone, either.

Silently, he cursed the poor reception. There was no way to contact them at a distance.

At least he managed to reach the chief. "I'm outside the cemetery," Roundtree said when asked his location. "I'd forgotten it was the night of the Spring Fling eight years ago that Al's boy wrapped his car around a tree. I guess that's what's been eating him. Looks like he's out here visiting the grave."

Jack told him about Owen. "How far away are you?"

Roundtree whistled. "A lot farther than you are."

"I'll meet you there." Jack signed off and closed the phone. "I'm going to the Pine Woods. Casey, you stay here."

"I'm coming, and you can't stop me," she shot back.

"We're all coming," Jean put in. "You might need me to talk sense to my husband."

"You three can drive together. I'm going ahead." This time, Jack refused to compromise. And he had a key advantage over Casey in her current condition: speed.

Without waiting for the eruption he knew would follow, he sprinted out of the room.

IF CASEY'S STRONG WILL HAD been able to move mountains the way her mother used to claim, it would certainly have found a way to loft Mimi's car into flight. Instead, it took ages for them to maneuver out of the jammed lot, while, with his usual finesse, Jack had already vanished.

The distance along Old Richfield Road seemed to stretch forever. She had to force herself not to nag Mimi to drive faster, reminding herself that the Godwins had as much at stake as she did.

Jean had chosen to sit in back, leaving the two younger women side by side. From the rear, she said, "I should have seen this coming. A couple of times Owen disappeared for an hour or so, but I was just glad when he came back safely. It never occurred to me he'd been up to mischief."

Mischief wasn't exactly how Casey would have described what had happened, but she declined to say so. "Did you happen to note the dates? It would help if we could compare them to the prowler's activities."

"No. It didn't seem important at the time," Jean replied.

"We don't know for sure that Dad's headed to the Pine Woods," Mimi reminded them. "This might be a false alarm. And it just occurred to me, I don't think he went anywhere Sunday night, when Enid's place caught fire."

"He did go out," her mother put in. "While you were at the movies with Bonnie."

"You never mentioned that!"

"We'd turned in early. The thunder woke me and he wasn't

in bed," Jean said. "I found him sitting in the kitchen, all wet. He said he'd been looking for our little girl, as if you were still a child. I completely forgot about it until now."

Outside, lights shone in some of the scattered houses they passed. Mimi pressed their speed to well over the limit. At least there weren't any cops around to give them a ticket.

"Can't you go faster?" Jean asked.

"I'm trying," her daughter replied. "You're always the one who tells me to slow down."

"This is different."

Casey understood completely. "If it is Owen, I'm sure Jack will do his best not to hurt him."

"Your husband's great," Mimi said. "I hope you two can make it work."

"So do I." Casey hesitated, not wanting to share too much, and yet she needed to talk. Before she could stop herself, the words spilled out. "He had a terrible early life. He got hurt so often that he built up a protective wall. I think he's afraid to care too much about anyone, including me."

"Are you and I talking about the same man?" Mimi asked. "You have got to be kidding! That man's love shines like a searchlight every time he looks at you."

"I'll vouch for that," Jean added. "It makes my heart feel young just watching the two of you."

Earlier, sharing the community event with Jack, Casey had imagined she saw tenderness in him. Maybe it hadn't been wishful thinking, after all.

"He may not be in touch with what he feels," she admitted. "Hardly anything scares Jack except facing what's inside."

"If that man wasn't crazy for you, why would he risk his life?" Mimi said. "And then there's your baby. I know you told me he didn't want kids, but that was theoretical. I've never seen a guy more suited to being a family man."

"Amen to that." The change of subject appeared to have

calmed Jean. It made Casey feel better about bringing up such a personal topic.

"I'm still not sure he's going to stay," she confided.

"All you have to do is make him see what's already there." Mimi turned onto Pine Woods Avenue. Only a few miles to go. "Which is exactly what I intend to do with Royce. There's another fellow ripe for the taking, although he isn't in love with me yet."

Casey provided appropriate encouragement as she listened, but her mind raced ahead to Jack. Was it possible he'd decide to stay? Did he love her enough to accept her way of life and become a real father to Diane?

Her fists tightened with determination. She didn't care what it took, she was going to help him see the truth. If she had to stay up all night and ravage that man right down to his socks, she was going to change his mind.

Maybe she'd get lucky. Maybe his mind no longer needed changing.

"What is that?" Mimi said.

Yanked from her reverie, Casey stared ahead. Above the trees, she saw a bright and deadly corona gleaming through the darkness.

Just like before. Just like at Enid's.

"Oh, dear heaven," Jean said from behind her. "It looks like your house is on fire."

Chapter Fifteen

As she listened to Jean on the phone calling the dispatcher about the fire, Casey's greatest fear wasn't for the house. It was for Jack.

She'd always known his work involved physical risk, but his expertise and apparent lack of fear had reassured her. Even on Sunday night when fire threatened Enid's cabin, her worry about him had been tempered by the belief that he could control the circumstances.

Tonight, the fact that their entire futures hung in the balance gave her a greater sense of vulnerability. What if Owen had brought his gun?

When they turned into the driveway, she noticed how high above the ground the flames leaped. Her thoughts flew to the nursery she'd spent so much time decorating and the baby items that Diane would need. And her precious books.

She pushed those concerns aside. "Do you see Jack?' she asked.

"Not yet," Mimi said. "Hang on."

As they zoomed past a stand of trees, the scene spread before them. Sparks showered her roof from a blaze in nearby branches. This time, there was no storm to put it out, only whatever protection remained from the fireproofing Casey's parents had applied.

Jack had left her car across the driveway and a safe distance from the house, although he was nowhere in sight. A few yards ahead of it, at a skewed angle, sat the Godwins' other car.

"Oh, my gosh." Jean's hand flew to her cheek. "It *is* him."

"Where are they?" She barely restrained her impatience as Mimi pulled into the parking bay. "I've got to find Jack."

"We ought to think this through," her friend advised. "You won't do him any good if you get yourself hurt."

Although Casey's instincts urged her to race into action, she could see the point. "Let's circle the house to see if we can locate him. He might need help."

"Owen, too!" Mrs. Godwin said. "Whatever he's done, he isn't in his right mind."

"I'll wet down the roof," Mimi volunteered.

Moving as fast as she could with the extra weight of the baby, Casey led the way along the connecting path toward the house. At first, she saw nothing except flickering light and showers of sparks, and then she made out movements beyond the structure, in the playground.

Hurrying forward, she spotted two male figures locked into a struggle on the ground. She hesitated, aware that if she distracted Jack by calling to him, she might unwittingly aid his opponent.

Jean caught up. Shakily, she called. "Owen, it's me, dear! You have to stop this and come home!"

The struggle on the ground intensified. From underneath, an arm waved wildly. Then a shot rang out.

Mrs. Godwin screamed, and Mimi came running. "Mom! Are you hurt?"

"No. Who got shot?"

Was it Jack? Casey's heart thundered so hard she could barely breathe.

Mimi tried to soothe her mother. "Maybe it went wild."

On the playground, one of the men rolled astride the other and pinned his arms behind him. Firelight wavered across the pair, bringing out Jack's grim determination as he wrenched the gun from his fallen foe's hand.

Casey's spirits soared. He was all right. Dirty and sweaty and streaked with soot, but in one piece.

At last she noticed the sirens wailing toward them from town. From closer at hand came the crunch of tires in the parking bay.

On the far side of the playground, two figures emerged—Matt and Bo. A moment later, Larry ran up, apparently having driven over from the neighboring land.

"What's going on?" He noticed the men on the playground. "Never mind. I see them." He sprinted over and knelt beside Jack. "I got here as soon as the chief reached me. Is it Owen?"

"I'm afraid so." Jack yielded his captive, whom the officer handcuffed. "He set the tree on fire and tried to shoot me."

Tears ran down Jean's cheeks as her daughter hugged her. Casey wished she could soften their pain.

After that, events happened quickly. The chief arrived, followed a short time later by a fire crew that made short work of the blaze. Owen himself remained well enough to snap at his wife to stop fussing over him.

The transient, Larry reported, had produced gas and grocery receipts showing he'd been driving cross-country during the earlier attacks. Disgruntled at being questioned, the man had vowed to depart in the morning.

"Good work," Jack told him. "I'm glad you thought to ask for the receipts."

"I wish I'd stuck around," Larry said. "I should have been the one to bring him down."

"It was a team effort," Jack replied. "Everybody shares the credit."

"That includes our civilian patrol," Larry added with an uncharacteristic touch of generosity. Perhaps Jack's approach was rubbing off. "I knew I could rely on them."

Matt ducked his head modestly. Bo drew himself up straighter.

The chief shook Jack's hand. "You're my kind of guy, Mr. Arnett."

Mimi indicated the handcuffed Owen, who sat sullenly in the rear seat of the police cruiser. "Do you have to take him to jail?" she asked. "You can see my dad's not well."

"I'm afraid he'll have to face charges," Roundtree said. "I'd suggest you hire the best lawyer you can find."

"Dad says he doesn't want one."

"I know. He told me that when I read him his rights," said the chief. "But he's going to need one. If this is handled properly, he might end up in a treatment facility rather than a prison, although I don't suppose that's for me to say."

"I hope so." Mimi blinked back tears. "My mom wants him at home, but we obviously can't handle him."

"I'm so sorry," Casey said.

"I'm just glad everyone's all right." Her friend retreated to relay the response to her mother.

Jack went to the cruiser, where he crouched near Owen and began questioning him. Casey wished he'd hurry.

Police work took a lot longer in real life than it did on television, she reflected. Although she longed to throw her arms around her husband, it appeared she'd have to wait quite a while for that.

At last he returned to consult with Roundtree and Larry. Since no one objected to Casey's presence, she listened in. Not that she'd have let them chase her off her own property.

"Godwin admits to damaging the mailbox a few weeks ago and to squirting my wife with a hose, but he says he had nothing to do with vandalizing my car or setting the fire at Enid's," Jack reported. "He contends that's what gave him the idea to try arson tonight."

"Do you believe him?" Larry inquired.

"The guy's not exactly in full possession of his faculties," Jack replied. "For one thing, he kept referring to my wife as Denise, which was her mother's name. If he's confusing the two of them, I don't see how he can distinguish exactly between what he has and hasn't done."

The chief seemed satisfied. "We'll step up patrols around here in case there's another prowler. Still, I'd be surprised if we find one."

A short time later, Enid and Gail returned. The retired teacher did her best to comfort Jean and reassure her that she held no grudges about the fire at her place.

Gail glared at Owen through the open door of the cruiser. "How could he?" she demanded of no one in particular. "That awful, evil man. Someone ought to string him up."

Casey had never seen the nurse so angry. "He's senile, not evil."

"There's always an excuse, isn't there?" Gail said. "He resents the baby. That's what's behind this."

"He resented my parents," she corrected. "He's got me confused with them. He thinks he should have been the one to buy the Pine Woods."

The nurse shook her head as if waking from a daze. "Do you know who he reminded me of a moment ago? With that mean expression on his face, he looked like Dean."

"I'm sorry this whole business brings back such awful memories for you," Casey said. "Thank goodness it's over."

"You shouldn't be standing out here in the cold," Gail added. "You go on inside and take the weight off your feet."

"I guess you're right." Although she hated to leave the scene, there was no chance to talk with Jack, anyway.

It was at least another hour before the last official vehicle departed. In the house with her feet up, Casey had plenty of time to think about what she wanted to say to Jack, assuming he wasn't too exhausted to talk.

So much hung in the balance. With her attacker captured, his reason for coming here had vanished. But despite his protective mechanisms, she hoped he'd begun to realize tonight that home wasn't a single household but a community where people pulled together.

He not only belonged in Richfield Crossing, he had the potential to become a real leader. Sure, it might take a while to re-establish himself, but surely that came second to being with his wife and daughter and many new friends.

When Jack walked inside, however, she forgot everything except how much she wanted to hold him. Hauling herself off the couch, Casey said, "Thank you."

"For what?" He seemed puzzled.

"For saving me from Owen Godwin, for one thing." She wound her arms around him and drank in the heady male scent of a man who's been in a knockdown, drag-out fight. "You're my knight in shining armor."

She could feel his grin against the top of her head. "More of a sore knight in dusty armor."

Casey wasn't sure she could fulfill her earlier intention of seducing him. Still, she longed for physical closeness. "How about if I give my hero a massage?"

"That sounds like a plan." Tipping up her chin, he studied her tenderly. "I'm glad you called me to catch this guy. I get the chills thinking about you and Diane out here alone with that maniac running around."

Stay and be my protector for always. Casey swallowed the words. She wasn't going to pressure Jack.

"Before I get my massage, I'd better hit the shower," he added.

"I like the way you smell right now."

He stroked her hair. "Do you like my muddy clothes, too? I could dress this way all the time and save a lot on laundry bills."

"Actually, I'd prefer you naked," she told him.

He shook his head in amazement. "Under other circumstances, I'd take you up on that remark, so be careful what you say."

She planted her hands on her hips. "Go ahead. Strip."

"Excuse me?" The disbelief in those green eyes nearly undid her. How could a man look so cute and so totally male at the same time?

"Laundry," she told him. "I'll throw that stuff in the wash before any stains can set." As he hesitated, she went to the window and drew the curtains. "Now even the squirrels can't see you."

"Right here in the living room?" He chuckled. "Well, okay. I appreciate the offer."

Not waiting for him to take action, Casey unzipped his corduroy jacket. After he shrugged it off, she could feel his heart thrumming beneath her hands as she unworked his shirt buttons.

"I didn't know you were going to help," he murmured.

"You've worked hard enough for one night." Casey liked handling Jack. It thrilled her to feel him relaxing in her hands, letting her touch him anywhere she pleased—his chest, his belt, his hips...

His breathing accelerated. She circled behind him and drew off his shirt, relishing the sight of his muscular back.

Lamplight played across a scar on his shoulder blade. "What's that from?" she asked, fingering it. She'd always assumed he'd incurred it during his police work but now she wanted to know everything about him.

"My dad had a bad temper." He kept his face averted.

"He beat you?" Leaning forward, Casey kissed the mark. "That must have been horrible."

"I never think about it any more." He turned so unexpectedly that she found herself kissing his chest, which was fine with her.

"Any more scars you want me to exorcise?" She peeked up at him.

"One right here." He tapped the corner of his jaw.

Casey noted a faint mark she'd scarcely registered before. "Also from your dad?"

"No, that happened at school. A bully threw his book bag at me."

She kissed his jaw. "All better. Anything else?"

"I've had a tough life," Jack murmured. "I've been bruised almost everywhere."

Casey, who'd already undone his belt buckle, unzipped his pants. "Down here?"

"Honey, I'm not asking you to…"

She ran her hands over him and enjoyed the way his breathing quickened. "Why don't we make that a shower for two?"

"You'll need to undress too." His palm cupped her full breast, heating her right through the fabric of her dress.

The idea of removing Jack's clothes in the front room hadn't bothered her, but Casey felt awkward about her own oversized appearance. "Why don't you go get the water started and I'll join you?"

"Don't tell me you're embarrassed!" Jack ran his hands down her derriere and drew up her skirt hem.

"No such thing!" He'd already seen her in the tub, she reminded herself. Besides, his stroking brought a delicious flush to her intimate places.

Encircling her, Jack unzipped the dress. Within a few minutes, they'd shed the last of their garments.

Bare skin brushed bare skin as he commanded a long kiss. She meant to take this slowly and enjoy arousing him until his last reserve fell away, but the heat and scent of him thrilled Casey's senses.

She was the one who couldn't get enough of being fondled, the one aglow with sensations as he drew her onto the folded-out couch. Jack used his lips and palms with just the right amount of command, pausing to let her catch her breath and then heightening his motions.

Casey gave up attempting to apply the brakes as a wave of sheer exuberance swept over her. Just as she thought the ecstasy would drive her crazy, it peaked in a rainbow fountain that shot up to the sun.

Even though her own passion ebbed, she felt the tension in

Jack's body beside her. He remained marvelously erect, she found when her hand strayed downward, and acutely sensitive.

Despite the clumsiness of her bulge, she shifted position. "I promised to heal all the wounded parts of you," she reminded him. "How's this?"

Jack gazed at her with excited anticipation. They'd never done this before, because they'd always been able to make love the conventional way.

As her mouth closed over him, Casey felt him vibrate in response. She teased him along carefully, drawing out the process for maximum pleasure until shudders wrenched Jack and he yielded helplessly.

Casey had never felt so close to her husband. With this form of lovemaking, it seemed as if they'd surrendered to each other.

Dimly, she noticed that he went to throw their clothes in the washer and then to take a shower. She meant to join him, but sleepiness overwhelmed her.

A deep sense of peace flowed through her. After what they'd just experienced, how could Jack do anything but stay?

A MENTAL AND PHYSICAL HIGH kept him awake for a time after he returned to bed. He loved lying here beside Casey, basking in her warmth and alive to the sensual flow of her hair across the sheets.

He'd felt a new kind of passion with her tonight. In a way, this didn't surprise him, because he'd already been flying on all cylinders after helping run the security operation.

Jack had discovered from his first days at the police academy that he entered a higher plane of awareness each time he went on alert, the way he imagined an actor must feel when he stepped on stage. It started the adrenaline pumping and honed his senses.

Casey had known exactly what he needed afterwards. The result had been a complete connection that engulfed them both.

If only he could have both worlds. If only she'd come back to L.A. with him. He knew better than to count on it, though.

Maybe, despite her earlier refusal, she'd be willing to reconsider the idea of a long-distance marriage. At least they'd get to spend some time together and, while he was overseas, she could stay here with the friends who meant so much to her. And Jack had to admit he wouldn't mind visiting Richfield Crossing frequently.

It seemed a reasonable compromise to him.

IN THE MORNING, Casey awoke with a languorous sense of peace, despite the grayish storm-tinged light seeping through the translucent curtains. The threat that had hung over her had vanished, and her body still tingled from the passion she'd experienced last night. Who cared if the forecast called for rain?

She heard Jack moving around in her office and wondered why he'd arisen so early. But perhaps it wasn't quite as early as she imagined.

Pushing herself into a sitting position, she found her wristwatch on an end table. Eleven o'clock. She really had slept late.

"Jack?" Receiving no answer, she swung her feet over the edge of the bed, then realized she had no clothes to put on. She went into the bedroom for her robe before checking on her husband.

Standing in the doorway to the office, Casey stared in dismay. His back to her, Jack was tucking one neatly folded item after another into his suitcase.

She didn't need to ask what it meant. The answer was obvious.

He'd decided to leave.

Chapter Sixteen

"What're you doing?" she asked in shock.

He glanced up. "Hey, I'm sorry. I realize I should have told you sooner, but I've got a plane to catch." To Casey, his casual pose didn't ring quite true. He was ducking out on her and he knew it.

"How long have you been planning to leave today?" she demanded.

"Since Tuesday." Jack went on packing.

She couldn't believe it. "And you never bothered to mention it?"

"You were aware I'd be done here once we caught the prowler." He kept his gaze focused downward, away from her.

"I didn't realize you'd be hitting the road the first chance you got!" The whole time she'd been trying to win her husband back, he'd already set the date of his departure! "What a rotten thing to do!"

Was that guilt fleeting across his handsome face? "I didn't know we were going to make love last night," he said. "I wasn't trying to string you along. Casey, I have a commitment in Athens."

Although she understood that sarcasm wouldn't help, she was too upset to weigh her words. "Couldn't you have picked somewhere even further? How about Indonesia? Or maybe Siberia?"

Jack stuffed socks around the edges of the suitcase.

"Maybe next time. After all, I've got to rack up those frequent flier miles or they might rescind my card." His attempt at humor fell flat.

Casey's anger yielded to hurt. "Why can't you see that those miles are taking you away from home?"

"This isn't my home," he said sadly. "I wish it were, but it's not."

Furious at her own weakness, she ignored a prickly sensation beneath her eyelids. "It could be."

"This isn't the only place we can live. You promised once to move back to L.A. if I agreed to have kids." Jack glanced around in case he'd forgotten anything. *How about your family?* Casey wanted to shout.

"That was before I realized how lonely I'd been," she said instead. "What am I going to do in L.A. when you aren't around? Mothers need support, people they can turn to, people who care about them. And a husband who isn't halfway around the world. If I have to be a single mom, at least I want to live where I won't be alone all the time!"

"I told you before, we could have a long-distance marriage." Finally, Jack met her eyes. "You stay here and I'll visit as often as I can."

"And I get to spend the rest of my life waiting around for you?" she blurted. "Our daughter deserves a real father. And I need a man to hold in my arms, not some stranger who drops by when he has nothing better to do."

He returned to his packing. The meaning couldn't be clearer: she'd lost.

"I want to be your husband and Diane's father, but I won't give up my work," Jack said. "Not even for you."

Tears burned trails along her cheeks. "You make it sound like I'm your enemy."

He made no move toward her. But when he lifted his face, she saw conflict on it. "Do you have any idea how long it took to find my place in the world, or how hard I worked to get there? I can't give that up," Jack said. "What am I supposed to do, become a farmer? Or maybe a motel keeper? That isn't who I am."

"I know who you are! You're my husband!"

"That will never be enough." After snapping shut the latches on his suitcase, he carted it out of the office.

Casey stood rooted to the spot, a painful knot clenching in her chest. Oh, the heck with self-pity and pride. She had to change his mind.

She stormed into the living room. "That's it? You're not going to fight for our marriage?"

Jack zipped up his jacket. "We can discuss this when I finish my job in Greece."

"Discuss it when?" she demanded. "There'll always be some other job or some reason why you have to go to L.A."

"You're right. My home base is in California, not Tennessee." Except for the ragged edge to his voice, he'd withdrawn behind a mask. "It's up to you, Casey. We can stay married but you can't expect me to follow you around like a lapdog."

"You mean we can stay married in name only!" She couldn't bear it. "Go ahead, sign the divorce papers. What's the point of dragging this out?"

"If that's the way you want it." Hefting his case, he indicated the rumpled sheets. "Sorry about the mess."

"That isn't the mess you should be apologizing for!" She wanted to slap his face. And she wanted to grab him and never let go. She felt as if she might shatter into a thousand pieces.

"Take care of yourself and Diane." He opened the door, caught a blast of wind in the face, and stepped outside.

Why had she told him to sign the divorce papers? But try as she might, Casey couldn't bring herself to run after him. Like so many of their arguments, it had gone around in circles, leaving her exhausted and almost as angry with herself as with her husband.

Hurrying to the window, she watched him stride toward the parking lot. Leaves and branches whipped by, and drops of rain splatted against the glass.

The storm outside had nothing on the one raging inside her.

HE HADN'T SHOUTED. He hadn't lost his temper the way his father would have.

Jack supposed it was a victory of sorts. Much as he loved Casey, he resented the way she'd dismissed his hard-won career and the business he'd worked so long to establish.

Yet as he steered through the intensifying rain on the way out of town, he admitted how much he would miss this place. He'd never felt much connection with any particular neighborhood in L.A. The chain stores remained the same no matter where you moved, while your friends moved away or forgot about you.

She'd been wrong about one thing. He *had* expected their marriage to work. He simply didn't have a clue what that would take. He wasn't sure she did, either.

A woman like Casey could drive a man crazy. The funny part was that, no matter how often she reversed herself and no matter how inconsistent she might seem to an outsider, Jack understood exactly what she meant.

She loved him. He loved her, too, and he didn't mean to abuse her trust or let her down. He simply didn't have it in him to be the sort of man she needed.

By the time he reached Nashville International Airport, rain lashed the parking structure and streamed along the pavement. Overhead, lightning split the sky, which had grown as dark as if it were late evening rather than afternoon.

At the rental return, a clerk gave him papers to fill out about the damage to his car. It took a while for a staff member to inspect the vehicle, but he'd allowed for that.

As Jack signed the checklist, he remembered asking Owen why he'd attacked a car he must have known didn't belong to Casey. With a dismissive snort, the old man had replied, "I had nothing to do with your car. You probably messed it up yourself to make me look bad."

Jack would have preferred to tie up all the loose ends. A police officer couldn't close a case unless he'd solved it definitively and, without a confession or some other means of pinning the incidents on Owen, some of them remained technically open.

Like the damage to this car. Well, he could live with that.

"You're all set," the clerk told him. "With the extra insurance your credit card provides, everything should be covered."

Jack thanked him and left. Inside the main terminal, an uncomfortable hubbub warned even before he checked the monitors that something was amiss. Sure enough, he found that some flights had been delayed and others cancelled. Apparently this weather system included a late-season snowstorm sweeping the Northeast.

So far, however, his flight to New York appeared on track. After passing through security with his bag and laptop, Jack headed for the gate.

Too restless to work, he stood staring through the window at the rain lashing the tarmac. At last, he shifted his attention to an overhead TV showing weather news.

Pine trees swayed behind a correspondent in a rain slicker, who had to shout into his handheld mike. "We're getting reports of tornadoes here in northern Tennessee around Clarksville. So far, no damage or injuries, but the Weather Service urges everyone to take precautions."

Tornadoes! The man hadn't mentioned Richfield Crossing, which lay between Nashville and Clarksville, but it was such a small town that maybe he wouldn't bother.

Such a small town. The phrase echoed ironically in Jack's thoughts. Just one more cluster of houses in the middle of nowhere, like countless others. Except that Casey lived there, along with her unborn baby and many other people who'd become friends in a remarkably short time.

He didn't suppose Casey ran much risk of being hit by a tornado. Nevertheless, his anxiety persisted. With labor imminent, the current storm could leave her even more isolated than usual.

The image of Casey alone in the wooded area brought back memories of last night, along with a nagging doubt that Jack had pushed aside earlier. Owen had admitted to some acts and denied others. At the time, it had seemed obvious that his senility accounted for the discrepancy.

Jack admitted the possibility that someone else, intentionally or not, might have used Owen as a fall guy. If so, the perp now had a clear field.

He remembered the recurring nightmare in which he ran through a devastated landscape seeking a woman in a white nightgown. He'd suffered it ever since his mother's death and had accepted it as a symbol of loss.

Jack didn't believe in a sixth sense. Yet at this moment, with the wind gusting so hard airplanes shivered out on the tarmac, he began to wonder if his subconscious hadn't been sending a warning.

The intensity of his concern came as a surprise. He'd never understood why people agonized over events that might not happen. In the security business, you took reasonable precautions but you did your client no favors if you obsessed about the outcome.

He didn't care. Flipping open his phone, he called Casey's number and listened to ring after ring. On the verge of hanging up and calling the police, he heard an answering click.

With a sleepy rasp, she said, "Hello?"

"It's me." Jack angled himself so the conversation wouldn't disturb other waiting passengers. "I'm at the airport. How're you doing?"

"I was taking a nap," Casey muttered, evidently not yet awake enough to be gracious or else still annoyed from their earlier argument.

"I'm sorry." He didn't waste time on further apologies. "Listen, it occurs to me that I may have jumped the gun in assuming that Owen's the only one responsible for what's been going on. Keep the doors locked and your guard up."

Across the miles, he could feel her coming fully awake. "You think there's still danger?"

"I hope I'm wrong, but the more I think, the more it strikes me that Owen wasn't being cagey last night. He confessed to several of the offenses and denied others. At the time, I attributed it to forgetfulness, but we can't count on that."

"What are the odds of having two prowlers at the same time?" Casey inquired skeptically.

"Greater than you might think." In matters of security, Jack never relied on odds anyway. "If you see or hear anything suspicious, call the police at once."

"Okay." She hesitated. Given her usual forthrightness, he sensed she was holding something back.

He made a guess. "What about the labor pains?"

"I've had a couple," she admitted. "Three in the past hour."

"You need a doctor. Get someone to drive you into town."

"Hold on," Casey said. "For one thing, the pains could stop again. Even if this is for real, it'll probably be hours before labor really sets in. And furthermore, the roads are covered with debris. If I wait, the storm may end before I have to set out."

Jack paced away from the gate and along the corridor. "How do you know the roads are a mess? Have you been out?" She shouldn't be driving in her condition.

"Matt stopped by earlier," she explained. "He'd gone for a walk and saw a lot of branches in the street."

Great. She had tenants giving her weather reports. What she needed was professional care. "Casey, if you wait too long, your doctor will go home for the day. It'll take that much longer to get ahold of him."

"I am *not* going to run around like a chicken with its head cut off. Even if this is labor, I probably won't deliver until tomorrow. Jack, what's wrong with you?"

"Call the doctor's office," he said. "At least alert him to the possibility that you might need him."

She heaved an impatient sigh. "I'll tell you what. If the pains start to come fifteen minutes apart, I'll phone Gail. Okay?"

"Remember not to drive if you're in labor."

"Matt's home and I think Enid is too. I'm sure one of them will take me."

He ought to be with her. Oh, for heaven's sake, Paul was waiting for him in New York and he had a duty to fulfill halfway around the world.

Reluctantly, Jack backed off. "Call me if there's a problem."

"You bet."

He wanted to add that he loved her, but what good would it do? At last, he said goodbye. After they rang off, frustration swept over him. He scarcely noticed the foot traffic that swirled past him.

A man in a raincoat sidestepped him irritably and yanked a little boy out of the way. Jack guessed he was about three or four.

The child held up his free arm. "Pick me up, Daddy."

Ignoring the request, the man hauled him down the corridor. The small figure nearly disappeared among the crowd, but his voice drifted back. "Daddy, I want a horsey ride!"

"Just shut up," the man snapped.

The rebuke sparked harsh memories of Jack's own father. How often had he heard that same rejecting tone?

"Daddy, I'm scared," the little fellow persisted. "Pick me up!"

A young woman hauling a large suitcase caught up with them. As she went by Jack, he noted her drawn expression.

She must be anticipating the explosion that would come next. He, too, cringed instinctively.

"Daddy…"

The man in the raincoat swung around in a temper. "You

little pest! Can't you see I'm busy? Sometimes you're more trouble than you're worth!" He grabbed the child's shoulders and began to shake him while his wife uttered ineffectual squeaks of protest.

A surge of disgust propelled Jack forward. He had to stop the abuse, since no one else seemed about to intervene.

Sharply, he reminded himself to control his temper. If he sought revenge for his own past instead of focusing on the present, he'd be worse than useless.

He stopped in front of the man and took a firm but not pugnacious stance. "Excuse me, sir. I need to speak with you." Jack kept his tone professional to match the words.

The whole tableau froze. "You some kind of cop?" the guy demanded.

"I used to be." At close range, he caught a whiff of alcohol on the man's breath. "Shaking a child can cause severe brain damage."

"I got a right to discipline my kid," the man shot back. "I don't see that it's any of your business."

"I'm still mandated to report child abuse to the authorities." That might not be true, but it sounded good. "And morally, I can't stand by because I'm a survivor of this kind of treatment myself."

He hadn't realized he was going to reveal anything so personal. As a cop, he'd never have done it. But he saw from the man's indecision that perhaps he'd gained a small opening.

"I know you love your family," Jack went on. "But if you don't stop drinking and get control of your anger, you'll ruin your life and maybe theirs, too. I can't make you listen but I hope you will."

The man's jaw worked. Building up further rage, most likely.

"You have no idea how much harm you're doing." Now that he'd started, Jack couldn't stop pouring out the things he wished he could have told his father long ago. "You're at a crossroads right now. You've still got your family and you're still young."

"Just what I needed, some damn do-gooder," the man snarled.

He ignored the interruption. "No one can force you to make the right choice. But one of these days you will run out of second chances. That's what happened to my dad. He died from alcohol poisoning and I didn't even attend his funeral."

He braced himself, half expecting the man to punch him. Or, worse, to take out his fury on his wife and son. From the woman's apprehensive look, he gathered that she expected something of the sort.

"I hope I haven't made things worse, but I had to try," Jack added. "I wish someone had done this for me."

The man still didn't answer. His lip curling into a sneer, he turned sharply away, leaving his wife to take the little boy's hand.

Abruptly, he swung back. Jack prepared for a blow.

The man met his eyes. Instead of out-of-control fury, he saw grudging respect. "I don't hold with people pushing into my business, but I guess that wasn't easy for you to say."

"No, it wasn't."

The man gave a tight nod, as if they'd reached some kind of understanding, and moved off. Jack stood rooted there as emotions seared through him.

He felt as if he'd stared down his father and won. It could never have happened, of course. This fellow wasn't blind drunk yet, and he'd been challenged not by his child but by another adult. Most of all, he retained enough judgment to recognize when somebody talked sense.

Jack didn't kid himself that the exchange had reformed the man. At best, he'd halted one incident of abuse.

Staring down the corridor, he caught sight of the family again. It was a swooping movement that drew his attention, and for a moment he feared it signified a blow.

Then he saw the man lift the child and plant him atop his

shoulders, little legs straddling his neck. After a pause for adjustment, the trio moved on.

Instead of venting his anger on the child, the father had reached out to him. It was a first step. Not a guarantee of anything, but a hopeful sign all the same.

Filled with an odd mixture of elation and disbelief, Jack took an empty seat. He sat there trying to puzzle out why he felt as if the Berlin Wall had just crumbled inside him.

He'd learned even before his mother's death to hide his vulnerability. Over the years, the barriers had hardened into a protective shield that kept him safe. Now, without warning, he'd spilled his guts to a stranger in the middle of an airport.

He'd torn open old wounds because that seemed the only way to help that little boy. Miraculously, his intervention appeared to have made a difference.

It had made a difference to Jack, too. He'd always feared that his innate darkness, once unleashed, might overwhelm him. But now he experienced only a vast wave of relief.

Even if he and Casey never resolved their differences, maybe he did have what it took to be a father. One of these days he'd like to hoist Diane on his shoulders and play horsey with her. He might even figure out how to sing a children's song or tell a story rather than reciting the Miranda warning.

He was actually looking forward to it.

Chapter Seventeen

Casey was debating whether she dared eat a snack in case she went into labor in earnest, when she heard a knock on the back door. It was Matt Dorning, his wizened features almost cartoonlike.

He'd come to check on her, since she'd experienced a contraction during his earlier visit. "I'm not believing that man of yours went off at a time like this," he told her, carefully removing his windbreaker in the kitchen. Underneath, he had on a jacket for extra warmth. "You sure he's not coming back?"

"He called from the airport a little while ago. He made me promise to call Gail if the pains come any closer together." She decided to permit herself a cup of tea. "Would you like something to drink?"

"Thank you, no. But you shouldn't be alone here. I can stay until you reach Gail."

"Don't worry, nothing's imminent." She began running water into the kettle. "You shouldn't have come out in this storm. I realize you're in great shape, but at your age, you're vulnerable, too."

"Never mind that. I brought you a gift. Been working on it for a while." From an inside pocket, he produced a carving of a squirrel. "This here's Hopalong. You've probably seen the real one hopping around—he has a limp. I know Diane won't be old enough to play with him for a while. Still, he can keep her company."

"It's adorable!" As she took the squirrel, she caught a flash of metal from inside his jacket. "What's that?"

Matt glanced down. "My knife. I always carry it. You never know when you'll need a blade or a length of good strong twine." He patted one of his pockets. "Whatever happens, I mean to be prepared."

Jack's warning played through Casey's mind. It was ridiculous, of course. Matt wouldn't hurt a fly. On the other hand, that had been a naked blade she'd seen, not a folded-up pocketknife.

The pain started on both sides at once, gripping her so fiercely she barely had time to set the squirrel on the table and grab the rim for support. Casey tried to fight it off, but it gripped her like a giant vise.

"You're in labor for sure," the old man continued. "Don't worry. I'll stay with you."

She wished, desperately, that Jack were here. As the pang abated, she took a couple of deep breaths. "You know, you're right," she said. "I'm going to do what I promised my husband. I'm going to put in a call to Gail."

She reached for the phone. Before she could lift the receiver, his hand closed over hers.

"I'm not so sure that's a good idea," Matt said.

JACK STARED AT THE MONITOR in dismay. His flight had been cancelled. He had a long journey ahead and now it would take even longer.

He dialed Paul's number on his cell. "Mendez," came the response.

"Arnett." He explained the situation.

"I'm not sure we'll be getting out of New York tonight, anyway," his new partner responded. "I flew in early—figured I'd catch up on computer work in the VIP lounge. So here I sit, nursing a Scotch and watching snow stick to the runways."

"If you do take off, you'll have to go without me." Although Jack had allowed layover time in New York, he had no idea when he'd be able to fly out of Nashville. "I'll come to Athens as soon as I can."

"Understood," Paul said.

"I'll call Nicos right away." Thank goodness their European associate could be relied on in a pinch. "Sorry this is all so last-minute."

"I gather it's the client who set it up that way," Mendez responded. "Hey, I'm used to things blowing wide open at the last minute. Doesn't faze me. In fact, I get an adrenaline rush."

"I'm glad you're enjoying yourself." Jack recalled that his new partner was divorced. Mike had said the prospect of traveling appealed to him.

It used to appeal to me, too.

After putting in a call to Athens and double-checking on the arrangements, Jack realized he'd go crazy if he had to spend the next few hours sitting around the airport hoping his flight would take off. His impression of danger closing in around his wife returned full-force.

He still needed to find a new flight to New York and book another plane to Greece. Jack figured he'd better get started.

With every passing moment, his anxiety mounted. It might be irrational, but he'd never experienced anything so powerful.

Except his love for his wife.

"I DON'T UNDERSTAND." Casey's heart thudded.

Matt withdrew his hand. "You haven't noticed anything odd about Gail?"

"About Gail?" She stalled for time as she wondered how he'd react if she grabbed her cell phone and ran outside.

Lumbered outside was more like it. Even an octogenarian would have no trouble catching her. And besides, she had no guarantee the darn phone would work.

"I don't know the lady very well," he said. "The last few

months, a couple times she's lost her temper at me for no reason. You wouldn't believe the bad words that came out of her mouth!"

Casey struggled to make sense of what he was saying. "Gail has kind of a gruff manner, I guess."

Matt shook his head. "One time she lit into me, said I'd been bothering you by dropping by too often. An hour later she started chatting with me as if there was nothing wrong. I call that strange."

Her heartbeat steadied. Maybe his action in preventing the call hadn't been as threatening as it appeared. "So you think Gail's under some kind of pressure?"

"Might be," he agreed. "This prowler business has everybody on edge. I wouldn't rely on Gail. You should let me drive you in to see the doctor."

Although he no longer frightened her as much, Casey didn't intend to get into a car with Matt at the wheel. "It's pretty nasty out there. The way those trees are doubling over, the wind could blow a car right off the road."

He clicked his tongue. "Maybe so, maybe so."

"I'll call and talk to Dr. Smithson," Casey said. "Let's see what he advises."

The tenant nodded. "I better stay with you."

If he were mentally disturbed or violence-prone, she wanted to avoid riling him. But even if he had no bad intentions, the only way he could prove this was by leaving.

"The truth is, I'd rather not have a man around right now, unless it's my husband. In my condition, I feel kind of…constrained." It was the best excuse she could manage.

Matt hesitated. "Well, I wouldn't want to get in the way. I don't know much what's involved with this sort of business, since my three stepkids were already around when I came into the picture."

"I'd be more comfortable alone," she said. "Really."

"You're sure?"

She nodded, scarcely trusting herself to speak. *Please, please go.*

"Well, then, I best be on my way." Reluctantly, he reached for his overcoat.

"Thanks for everything. I love the squirrel." Casey forced herself to smile.

He fumbled with the snaps on his coat. Finally, with one more farewell, he went out the back door.

She waited a few seconds before locking it after him. Then she sank into a chair and tried to pull herself together.

Matt didn't appear to have meant any harm. On the other hand, if he *was* a second prowler, he might be under the delusion of being her protector.

Casey mulled over what he'd said about Gail. If she'd lost her temper at him, he must have done something to provoke her. Could his behavior have been erratic for some time without her noticing?

Her abdominal muscles tightened. The pressure around her midsection drove out all other thoughts until at last the contraction abated, leaving her weak as a wrung-out rag.

If it hurt this much already, what was it going to be like later?

Fifteen minutes had passed since the last one. Not exactly an emergency, but the course of labor could be unpredictable.

Time to alert the doctor.

RAIN CURTAINED the parking structure as Jack ducked into his newly rented car. He folded his dripping umbrella and thrust it into a plastic sleeve the agency had provided.

For an agonized moment, he asked himself what he was doing. His obligation lay in Greece, not Richfield Crossing. He should be pursuing every possible means to speed his journey, not running back to a woman who might not need him.

He hadn't even called her yet. His instinct to rush to her side pulled him so strongly he didn't want to risk hearing her say no.

She could certainly be unpredictable. This morning, Casey had alternated between insisting he stay and ordering him to leave. When he'd phoned to warn her about the prowler, she'd hardly batted an eye.

What if she hadn't taken his warning seriously? He ought to call her now to make sure. Let her rail at him if she wanted to.

He pressed a preset button and waited. A busy signal throbbed in his ear.

In case of an error, he redialed the number from memory. Again the busy signal.

That was good, right? It meant she was either calling the doctor or felt well enough to chat with one of her friends.

Jack tucked the phone into his pocket. He'd try Casey again later. In the meantime, he had a lot of ground to cover.

He started the engine, backed out of the slot and headed for the exit.

GAIL SPOKE with her usual crispness. "Fifteen minutes? That doesn't sound urgent."

"I didn't think so either but I promised Jack to check with you." Casey, who'd decided to make the call from the bedroom, sank deeper against her stack of pillows.

"He's there now?" the nurse asked.

"No, he left this morning. He phoned because he thinks there might be a second prowler." She decided not to describe the visit from Matt. She didn't want to make trouble between her tenants or point suspicion at a man who'd done nothing wrong. "Should I go to the hospital?"

"You'll be more comfortable resting at home," Gail told her. "I can check with Dr. Smithson if you like."

"I'd appreciate it." When Gail put the call on hold, Casey listened to the din outside. Pine trees swished and the thunder rumbled disturbingly.

She didn't know exactly when Jack's flight was scheduled

to depart but she hoped it had taken off safely. Flying through thunder and lightning had always seemed unnatural, although she knew planes ascended above the clouds.

Casey's belly tightened. She lay back, trying to remember the correct breathing pattern as her abdomen went rock-hard.

She wondered how this felt to Diane. It must be confusing and frightening. It even frightened Casey to be so out of control of her body.

The pain had passed by the time Gail returned. "The doctor says you should wait. It may be hours yet, and the roads are terrible."

Casey didn't like the prospect of waiting alone. "I think I'll ask Enid to join me."

A sharp breath came in response. "That woman has no idea what you need, and she's useless in a crisis. Did you see her Wednesday night? She was so busy chatting with her former students, you'd think that was all she had to do!"

Casey hated to admit she hadn't paid any attention to the two women because she'd been so busy with Jack. "She could help distract me, though."

"You know what?" Gail said. "The waiting room's empty and we've only got a couple of patients left in the examining rooms. As soon as I'm free, I'm going to come home and look after you. There's no point in my…"

Lightning flared through the room so fiercely that the hairs on Casey's arm stood on end. The lights flickered and died. It took a second for her to realize the phone had died, too.

"That's great," she muttered.

She'd known that this type of phone required electricity because of its rapid dial and other special features. Although some people kept old-fashioned models on hand in case of emergency, she'd figured she could rely on her cell.

Finding her way by the gray afternoon light from outside, she shuffled into the other room to get it. On the display, she saw the message she disliked most: No Service.

Walking around the house sometimes enabled her to find an area of reception. Not today.

"Terrific timing." In the kitchen, Casey located candles and a battery-operated radio.

She tried not to worry about how isolated she'd become. She'd have to go out in the rain just to summon Enid, and she had no way to contact the doctor again.

But Gail had promised to come home. Casey tried to calculate how long it would take to handle a few patients and drive here from town. Assuming the roads weren't blocked, she could be here in an hour. Maybe sooner if she got worried about the interrupted phone line.

Another labor pain seized her. At least the pattern of peaking and releasing was becoming familiar.

Maybe a little too familiar. Casey glanced at her watch.

Twelve minutes had passed since the last contraction. They were speeding up.

MERCIFULLY, MOST Tennesseans had the good judgment to stay off the Interstate in such foul weather. Despite the usual glut of trucks, Jack made good time until he transferred onto a state highway.

Branches and sodden clumps of vegetation littered the road. Along with the slashing downpour, the debris forced him to stay below the speed limit. Jack still had a good ways to go when he pulled over at a rest stop to try Casey's number again.

No busy signal this time, he thought in relief, and waited impatiently for her to answer. It kept ringing hollowly.

If she'd gone to the hospital, why didn't her machine pick up? Maybe she'd left it off by mistake. Or maybe the phone merely sounded as if it were ringing when in fact the lines were down.

It took a moment to dredge her cell phone number from his memory. When Jack dialed, he heard an announcement that the customer was not in service at this time.

The fears he'd tried to dismiss roared back to life. She might be cut off out there, alone and unable to send for help.

Of course, she had tenants nearby. But in order to reach them, she'd have to brave not only the storm but also the possibility that the prowler had seized this opportunity, with everyone grounded or distracted by the weather, to launch another assault.

Get a grip, man. There might not be a prowler.

Jack wavered as he considered whether to summon help. The tiny police force must be stretched to the breaking with storm-related accidents, particularly if the electricity had gone out. But a pregnant woman alone and about to give birth constituted a serious enough problem to justify a call.

The dispatcher answered with a hurried, "9-1-1 Emergency." After listening to him, she said, "I'll alert the PD. We're aware the power's down in that area. Do you have reason to believe your wife is likely to deliver in the next few hours?"

"I don't know," Jack admitted.

"I'd suggest you contact her doctor, if you can get through to him," the woman said. "He might have a better idea what's going on."

"Good idea." He wished he'd thought of that before. In fact, the nurse might be an even better contact, since she knew Casey so well. "Please tell Chief Roundtree it may not be an emergency but I'd appreciate it if he swung by as soon as he can, just in case."

"I'll relay the message, sir," she replied.

To Jack's relief, the receptionist picked up immediately at the doctor's office. After identifying himself as Casey's husband, he requested Gail.

"She just pulled out of the lot," the receptionist said. "How's your wife doing?"

"I can't reach her. Has she called?"

"As a matter of fact, she talked to Gail about an hour ago."

"Was she in labor?"

"She didn't mention it, at least not to me. Dr. Smithson's still here. Would you like to speak to him?"

"Yes, please."

Jack drummed his fingers on the steering wheel. When the doctor came to the phone, he explained the situation. "How's my wife doing?"

"I don't know. I haven't heard from her today."

A warning bell rang in Jack's mind. "The receptionist said she called Gail an hour ago."

"She didn't mention anything to me," he said. "It must have been personal."

Casey had promised to alert the doctor that she might be going into labor. Why would Gail have left without passing along the information? "That can't be right," he responded. "She told me earlier the pains had started."

"Let me see if I can reach my nurse," he said, and took down Jack's number. "I'll get right back to you."

Although he kept his word, the news wasn't reassuring. "No one answers at her house and her cell's out of service."

Jack swore under his breath. "I already asked the police to look in on her."

"I'm sure she's fine, and Gail's probably on her way. Listen, I'm going home soon myself, but you can reach me if there's a problem." The doctor provided his private number.

"Thanks." Jack wished he also had a way to contact the other tenants. However, it hadn't occurred to him to get their numbers. Anyway, their phones were probably off, too.

As he hit the road again, he kept replaying his conversation with the doctor and the receptionist, trying to figure out if he'd overreacted. He kept drawing the same conclusion: Casey had obviously called the office to alert the staff to her situation, yet Gail had left without mentioning it.

Why?

His subconscious mind must already have been at work,

because an odd coincidence popped up. He hadn't made the connection before and it might not mean anything, but the attempt to ignite Enid's house had occurred right after she offered to become his wife's labor coach, an offer that Gail had strongly discouraged.

Gail had no children of her own. Casey had mentioned that she'd outfitted her cabin with equipment just for Diane.

Was she fixated on the baby?

Jack pressed hard on the accelerator. He hoped he was wrong. But if not, the person who'd been targeting his wife was heading straight for the Pine Woods with no one to stop her.

Chapter Eighteen

The rain had begun tapering off at last, Casey noted as she gazed out the front window. The distant growl of thunder confirmed that the storm was moving away.

Even so, only a trace of sickly yellow daylight remained. The electricity gave no sign of returning.

When she saw Gail's sturdy figure heading up the walk, Casey hurried to open the door. "Hi!" she greeted the older woman. "I'm really glad you got here. My pains are only five minutes apart. I guess the labor's moving along kind of fast."

"I knew it would happen that way." Instead of greeting her, Gail walked inside with a puzzled frown and continued into the master bedroom. Casey trailed her, puzzled, since the nurse had never shown any interest in that room before. "Women in my family always deliver fast. I knew it would be that way with my baby, too."

"I didn't realize you'd had a child." Her neighbor had never mentioned it, Casey was certain.

Gail stared around the heavily shadowed room. "This doesn't look right."

"The electricity's off." Wasn't that obvious? "Gail, I need you to drive me to the hospital."

The other woman didn't seem to hear. "I set everything up. We have to go to my place."

"For what?" Casey asked.

"For the birth, of course."

"Gail!" She wished the nurse would snap out of whatever this was. "I need to go into town."

"I have to make sure he doesn't find us."

"Who?" Casey demanded. "Owen's in jail."

"We'll be safe there."

The response didn't track. It reminded her of a customer at the restaurant where she'd worked in L.A.

One day he'd wandered in muttering, oblivious to his surroundings. "He gets that way sometimes," the manager had said. "Slips in and out of psychosis. Just give him a coffee and leave him alone."

How could that apply to Gail? She wasn't psychotic.

Case recalled the comment she'd made last night about Owen resenting the baby. There'd been a disconnect, but she'd snapped out of it quickly. With luck, she'd do so again now.

She clapped her hands. "The hospital! That's where we're going, Gail."

"No!" Two powerful hands clamped onto her forearms. "I've kept you safe. We're not going anywhere that he can hurt us!"

Kept her safe? As Casey stared up at the larger woman, the truth dawned. Gail was the other prowler, the one who'd vandalized Jack's car and tried to burn down Enid's house. She'd attacked anyone who got close.

That must be why she'd yelled at Matt for visiting too often. He'd been trying to warn Casey earlier, not threaten her.

"Nobody's going to hurt us." She spoke placatingly. "Dean isn't here, Gail."

"Don't you go making excuses for him!" the woman snarled. "He killed the baby inside me and he'll do it again."

She must have had a miscarriage, Casey realized. No wonder Gail had been traumatized. "Listen!" Casey rapped out the word. "Dean has nothing to do with this. That happened a long time ago. Stop this right now!"

A groan wrenched from the woman, animalistic in its ferocity. Without warning, she slammed Casey into the wall.

Pain throbbed through her head. She could barely react as the nurse yanked her through the hall and into the living room.

Another cramp caught her midsection. *Not now!*

"Stop struggling!" Gail roared, sounding not like a battered wife but like an abuser. If she was identifying with her ex-husband, how far would she go?

Casey jerked away from her captor but, gripped by the contraction, she nearly fell. The next thing she knew, she was being dragged out of the house. Mud sucked at her bedroom slippers and drizzle soaked her top as the enraged woman hauled her along the trail.

Casey yelled for help but the wind whipped away the words. There was no one to hear them, anyway. With darkness falling, Enid and Matt must be tucked inside their homes. Even if Bo and Rita returned from work, they wouldn't be able to see her on the secluded path.

When they staggered into the cabin, the presence of the playpen and child gates struck Casey as grotesque evidence of their owner's delusions. Still recovering from the contraction, she tried in vain to resist as Gail thrust her into the bedroom.

A fetal monitoring device, probably discarded by the hospital, occupied one corner. An alarming array of medications and syringes covered the bedside table. And on either side of the bed, Gail had installed restraint straps.

It was a scene from a nightmare. Knowing it might be the last chance she had, Casey threw back her head and screamed.

JACK PULLED UP behind a car he assumed belonged to Gail. Casey's was still in the carport.

The front door stood ajar. He hurled himself through it, shouting for his wife.

A mad race from room to room turned up nothing except

a bunch of lit candles left unattended. Casey must have been forced to exit unexpectedly.

He tried to call the police. Nothing worked—not his cell phone and not her land line.

Jack would have to handle this on his own. His mind buzzed.

If the nurse had fixated on his wife and her pregnancy, she might not be operating rationally. Just because a person suffered from a mental illness, however, didn't mean he or she lacked cunning.

Did Gail keep a gun at her cabin? What a grim irony that he'd queried her about the other tenants' weapons but he had no idea about hers.

Jack was weighing whether to try Bo's house when he heard the scream. There was no time to lose.

He ran to the car and put it in gear.

KNOWING SHE WAS FIGHTING for her baby, Casey attacked her abductor frantically. Biting and kicking, she startled the older woman long enough to twist free.

Gail still blocked the exit. Seeking weapons, Casey snatched a scalpel and a syringe from the bedside table. "You take one step closer and I'll make you sorry!"

The nurse's eyes fixed on the implements as if they mesmerized her. "Put those down. You'll hurt yourself."

"Back up," Casey said. "Get away from me."

The nurse blinked and a shudder ran through her. "He beat me," she half whispered. "I lost my little boy. I never even got to hold him in my arms."

"That was a long time ago. It has nothing to do with me." Casey kept the sharp tools aimed, unable to spare any sympathy while she remained in danger.

"He plea-bargained in court. They gave him three months." Gail's voice broke. "Three months! He cried and said he was sorry, that he'd stop drinking. When he got out, he seemed so different. I thought no other man would love me, especially when they told me I couldn't have any more children."

Tears rolled down her cheeks. Casey felt sorry for what the woman had endured and for the lack of self-esteem that had kept her in such a horrible relationship. But she wasn't foolish enough to let down her guard.

When her abdomen squeezed again, she nearly panicked. She couldn't become vulnerable, not now.

From behind Gail, a scraping noise marked someone's entry into the house. Then Casey heard the most welcome sound in the world.

It was her husband's voice, calling her name.

JACK WOULD NEVER FORGET the sight of his wife crouched in that bizarre room, defending herself with a couple of small implements. Or the slackness in Gail's expression as she hovered between madness and sanity, unable or unwilling to face what she'd done.

He subdued her without difficulty. Sunk into a deep depression, she hardly spoke a word.

Casey leaned against the wall, arms wrapped around her midsection. "You got here in the nick of time."

"I'll never doubt my instincts again," he told her. "I only wish I'd never left."

She grinned crookedly. "So do I."

Matt showed up a minute later, having also heard the scream, and they secured Gail with a length of twine from his pocket.

Her phone, which didn't require electricity, still worked. While Jack put in calls to the police and the doctor, Casey had another contraction.

"They're about four minutes apart," she said.

"You're keeping track?" He couldn't believe her presence of mind.

"I check my watch automatically."

He encircled her with his arm and wished he could absorb the pain into himself. When she gasped, he told her over and over that everything was going to be all right. It seemed to help.

A police cruiser and the ambulance arrived simultaneously. Relinquishing Gail to the chief's custody, Jack thanked Matt and rode with his wife into town.

"I keep wondering when this craziness started and why I didn't notice it." Sweat beaded her forehead as the vehicle crunched over the littered roadway.

"She must have seized on Owen's activities to cover her attempts to drive people away." Jack brushed a damp strand off his wife's brow. "The important thing now is for you to relax."

"Relax? Oh, no, here comes another one!"

Dr. Smithson met them in the labor room, along with a nurse Jack hadn't seen before. They sent him to scrub up so he could witness the birth.

He was glad he hadn't had to deliver the baby himself out there at the Pine Woods. He felt helpless in the face of the powerful forces controlling his wife's body.

The doctor and nurse, by contrast, knew exactly what to do. So, in a way, did Casey, who had all the right instincts.

And she'd been prepared. Gail had managed to do that right, at least.

Soon—much faster than usual for a first-timer, the nurse informed him—the infant's head descended, followed by her perfect body.

"She's fabulous," Jack told Casey as the nurse wrapped Diane warmly. "I can't believe it. She's wearing a hat. Is that stylish or what?"

"The hospital volunteers make them," the nurse explained. "Come on, Dad. Want to hold her?"

"My wife gets priority."

"Go ahead," Casey said. "I want to see her in your arms."

Jack crooked his elbow and accepted the tiny infant with

trepidation. Wrinkled and waxy, she seemed much smaller than the newborns on TV shows. "Isn't she kind of little?"

"Seven pounds eight ounces," the nurse answered. "That's a healthy size."

A miniature hand closed around Jack's finger. He heard himself saying foolish things about what a strong grip she had and pointing out that her eyes were as blue as her mother's.

"And you'll be a perfect angel. You'll never hog the bathroom and you won't date any boy unless I approve of him, right?" he asked his daughter. "Maybe you'll let your old man escort you to the prom."

"Fat chance," the nurse quipped.

"Hey! Let her answer for herself."

He reveled in the joy of cradling the miracle that was his daughter, until he noticed Casey's eyelids drooping. If he didn't hurry, his wife would go to sleep without holding their child.

"Sorry. I'm being selfish," he said, and lowered Diane gently.

Casey buried her nose in the little girl's temple. With a contented sigh, she curled around their daughter.

A sense of awe claimed Jack. He allowed himself to revel in it a little while longer as the nurse removed the baby to be examined at length. But it didn't last.

The danger was over. So why did he still feel unsettled as he paced into the waiting room?

He had unfinished business in Greece, of course. Then what? He loved Casey and Diane so much he didn't see how he could bear to give them up, yet his wife had made it clear their marriage wasn't her top priority.

If she didn't love him enough to come back to L.A., then she might not love him enough to stay together in the face of whatever life threw at them. Even if he had the good fortune to find work here, he couldn't promise they'd always be able to stay in Richfield Crossing.

If he had to live without her, better to do it now while he

still had a place to go and a job to do. Yet leaving her and the baby felt like cutting off his arm.

His spirits flagging, Jack went to check on Casey. She was asleep in the recovery room, a nurse told him. Reassured that she'd suffered no complications, he decided not to disturb her.

At the nursery window, he studied his daughter in her clear plastic bassinet. Since she was the only newborn there, no one disturbed him as he watched her wave her little hands and blink sleepily.

An amazing panorama spread before him—images of a toddler learning to walk, a little girl laughing as she rode her tricycle, a young girl singing in choir. His girl. His Diane.

He would come back to see her as often as he could, even if Casey didn't like it. He'd provide for her, too, of course. This little girl would grow up knowing she had a daddy.

Jack's throat clenched. Finally he tore himself away.

WHEN CASEY AWOKE, weak morning light seeped through the hospital window. Now that the medications had worn off, her body ached from labor and delivery and from Gail's assault.

Yet at the same time she felt a profound relief. She'd stood up for herself, and Jack had come back when she needed him.

She smiled when she saw him in the doorway. The smile faded as she took in his business suit. "You're leaving?"

"I still have a job to do," he said. "I went by your house and secured everything. I talked to Enid and she promised to drive you home from the hospital when you're ready."

Casey didn't want Enid to drive her home. She wanted her husband. Wasn't there anything she could do to make him stay?

Nothing she hadn't already tried, she thought unhappily.

"Thank you," she told him. "If you hadn't showed up, I don't know what would have happened."

"Matt was on his way," he answered. "And Gail didn't appear to have much fight left in her. You were quite a tiger, sweetheart, defending your cub."

"But nothing's going to be the same without you," Casey blurted. "I'm not Superwoman. I can't do everything myself."

"There's no point in going over the same ground again." Jack thrust his hands into his pockets. "I wish ... well, never mind what I wish. Some things weren't meant to be."

This isn't one of them! Casey felt like shouting, but she didn't want to waste their last few minutes on a quarrel. "You're welcome any time."

He didn't answer. He'd retreated behind that mask again.

A nurse's aide entered with breakfast. Jack gave Casey a quick kiss, mumbled something about catching his flight, and fled.

The world had become much too big a place, she thought glumly as the aide plumped up her pillows. And Richfield Crossing suddenly seemed very small.

CHIEF ROUNDTREE DROPPED BY later that morning. "I thought you and Jack might like to hear the latest." Moving with a trace of a limp, he took a chair.

"He had to leave." Casey adjusted the covers over the robe Enid had brought her. The tenant had arrived earlier, eagerly recounting how the electricity had come on in the middle of the night and awakened her.

"Gone already? Darn shame. Well, Mrs. Fordham's lawyer had her transferred to a mental facility for evaluation."

"I couldn't believe the change in her," Casey admitted. "It's as if I never knew her."

"I don't hold with insanity defenses but that woman's not right upstairs." The chief's wrinkles seemed deeper than usual, and she realized he must have had a long night. "I made a call back to Michigan. The police had to do some digging but it turned out a patient had filed a complaint about her a couple of years ago. Apparently Mrs. Fordham became obsessed with the woman's pregnancy and began calling her at home, saying she wanted to come and get her baby."

Casey had never imagined the troubles went back that far. "I'm surprised Dr. Smithson hired her."

"They never filed any charges because she left her job voluntarily," Roundtree explained. "It's not the sort of thing one employer relates to another. These days, you can be sued if you give an employee a bad report."

"So he never knew about it?" Casey didn't need an answer. "But she's been here two years. How come this never happened before?"

"I'm no expert in psychology." The chief sighed. "Maybe that incident in Michigan shocked her into behaving. Then you came along, alone and needing a friend."

Casey didn't want to think about what might have happened had she never phoned Jack about the prowler. Yesterday, Gail had become so delusional, she'd have done anything to get the baby.

"What about Owen Godwin?" she asked. "What's going on with him?"

"He may be senile; however, he's not so far gone he can't be held responsible for his actions. At least, that's my opinion, but it'll be up to the jury. Still, if they convict him, he may get to serve his sentence in a special facility."

"I hope Mrs. Godwin and Mimi are bearing up."

Roundtree cleared his throat. "According to my wife, they're getting some help from a very sympathetic young man. That would be Royce Ledbetter, in case you hadn't guessed. He's serving as volunteer chauffeur and shoulder to cry on."

Casey remembered the way he and Mimi had danced at the community center. "That's good news."

The chief arose stiffly. "Your husband is an impressive fellow. I hope we get to see more of him."

"I do, too." She preferred not to burden Roundtree with her problems. Besides, she didn't want to risk him repeating anything to his wife.

After he left, Casey thought about Royce and Mimi. How incredibly lucky they were to fall for someone who lived in the same town. Life would have been so much easier if she'd never gone to L.A.

But then she wouldn't have met Jack. And no matter how much it hurt to lose him, she would never wish that.

Chapter Nineteen

On the next afternoon, Casey's milk came in. Despite some initial awkwardness, she managed with the nurse's guidance to provide Diane's first feeding. It gave her immense satisfaction.

Only after she'd laid the baby in the bedside bassinet did Casey realize that, under other circumstances, Gail might have been the one to instruct her on infant care. Or that, at least, she'd have been a steady and welcome visitor.

It saddened her that the older woman had cut herself off. Of course, she hadn't done so intentionally. Casey supposed she could find a way to forgive. Still, she'd never trust Gail again or allow her near Diane.

She couldn't be allowed to return to the cabin, even if she got out of jail. Casey would have to arrange a formal eviction—which shouldn't be difficult, since it violated the lease to engage in illegal activities—and locate a new tenant. Perhaps she ought to put in a call to the local real estate office. Instead, she closed her eyes and pictured Jack.

Instantly, his vibrant green eyes and wry masculine smile came to her. He must have arrived in Athens by now. What was he doing? How long would he need to stay?

She missed him intensely. At the same time, he appeared to her so vividly that she couldn't imagine he was more than a few steps away.

Her spirit lulled by the reassuring image, Casey dozed off.

The sound of footsteps woke her a short time later. She looked up to see Sandra standing near the bed, tears brimming as she regarded Diane.

She'd lost a baby too, Casey remembered. But there was nothing predatory or resentful in her friend's face, only longing.

"I can have the staff take her to the nursery," Casey offered.

Sandra shook her head. "You don't have to hide her from me. She's a precious little girl and I'm happy for you." She perched on the edge of the mattress. "When I heard what happened, I couldn't stand it. That awful woman might have killed you, and I'd never have had a chance to apologize."

"For what?"

"For poisoning my parents against you." She cleared her throat. "I really did think Dad might be the guy you were looking for. Even though he wasn't, there's no excuse for the way I treated you. Yesterday, I confessed that you'd tried to help and I drove you away."

"How did he take it?" Casey asked.

Sandra picked at a loose thread on the sheet. "He told me that when he went to visit my brother's grave, he finally realized that it was his fault Little Al and I got so wild. When we made trouble, he always bought our excuses instead of holding us accountable. He said he's glad I'm facing up to my problems."

"He's not mad at me anymore?"

Her friend smiled. "He said you've got two free passes to the movies and ten free DVD rentals. I couldn't convince him to make it unlimited."

Casey laughed. "I wouldn't expect that!"

By the time Sandra left, they were exchanging jokes and planning to get together for lunch. It would take time to reestablish their friendship, Casey knew, but she was glad they'd made a start.

Other visitors drifted in that afternoon and evening. Tactfully, they refrained from asking about Jack's whereabouts. Apparently word had spread, and for once she was grateful.

When Dr. Smithson arrived to examine Casey, he apologized profusely for hiring Gail. She assured him she didn't hold him at fault.

Through it all, she kept hoping the phone would ring and she'd hear Jack's voice. No such luck.

When it was time to go home, Enid arrived and helped her strap Diane into the car seat. She looked so tiny and helpless that Casey almost expected the nurse to say she couldn't possibly release a newborn to someone so inexperienced. Instead, the nurse gave her a hug and told her she'd do fine.

As they approached her house, a twinge of anxiety ran through Casey. The last time she'd seen it, Gail had been dragging her out the door.

Outside, everything appeared normal. The reddish bricks and sloped roof sparkled as if newly washed—which in a sense they were—and she saw that the azaleas beside the porch were beginning to bloom.

Inside, a vase of fresh flowers sat on the coffee table. Enid, to whom Jack had given a key, had done a thorough job of cleaning away any reminders of Thursday. She'd also stocked the refrigerator with fresh milk and other essentials.

"I'll leave you to settle in," she said after making Casey a cup of tea. "Unless you'd prefer company?"

"I need a nap," she admitted. Also, she wasn't eager for a witness during the still-awkward business of feeding her baby. "You've been wonderful."

"Are you kidding?" The retired teacher gave her a hug. "It's a pleasure to be useful."

When Casey nursed Diane, she treasured having the baby to herself for the first time. "We're going to be great buddies, you and I," she told her daughter. "I might start reading to you. Not tonight, though."

As soon as she lay down, she fell asleep. An uncharted time later, the ringing of the phone dragged her into wakefulness.

Casey fumbled for it. "Hello?"

"It's Mimi!" Her caller didn't waste time on pleasantries. "Turn on your TV!"

"Why?" Puzzled, she groped on the bedside table for the remote control. Although Casey's mother had installed a small set on a shelf facing the bed, she hardly ever used it.

"Turn to Channel Six. My mom swears she saw Jack on an earlier broadcast. I didn't believe her, but they just said something about an American security guard in Greece, so I think they're going to repeat the item."

Casey scarcely noticed when her friend said goodbye and hung up. The images on the screen transfixed her.

In front of a hotel, a group of protesters waved signs written in Greek and several Asian languages as well as English. One read, Don't export our jobs!

A couple of businessmen hurried out the front door, heading for a limousine. She spotted Jack near one of them, his gaze sweeping the crowd.

"This was the scene today in Athens, where representatives of private companies from three nations conferred about a new manufacturing and trade contract," intoned a reporter's voice. "Although they claim they'll be creating jobs, not destroying them, protesters showed up in force."

Abruptly, a man lunged from the throng toward one of the representatives, swinging a heavy picket sign. Leaping forward, Jack tackled him. The pair dropped to the ground and disappeared from view behind surging protesters.

"An American security consultant fended off an attack on the conferees," the reporter's voice continued. On-screen, Casey saw only confusion. "We don't have his name but we understand he's from a Los Angeles company called Men at Arms."

The camera cut to an anchorwoman seated at a desk. "So far, no word on whether the security guard was injured," she said. "Now, this just in from London…"

Casey watched for a while longer in case of a follow-up. At last she clicked off the TV.

The memory of what she'd seen infuriated her. The attacker had endangered her husband! No matter what political point he wanted to make, he had no right to do that.

Call me, Jack. Please let me know you're not lying in a hospital in a foreign country with no one to look after you.

Finally she got up and went to read the mail Enid had left on the coffee table. Much as she loved this house, it seemed empty without Jack. A lingering whiff of his aftershave lotion only made her more keenly aware of his absence.

She finished the mail and had just eaten dinner, with Diane asleep in a portable basket beside the table, when Jack phoned at last. "Somebody told me I made the national news back home," he said. "I didn't want you to worry."

"I was getting ready to hop a plane and go bean that stupid picketer!" Casey declared. "I hope you socked him a good one!"

He uttered a weary chuckle. "Let's just say he got the worst of the bargain. How's our baby?"

From the basket, two bright blue eyes peered back at her. "She says she misses her daddy and wishes he'd called sooner."

"Tell her it's the middle of the night here and this is the first spare minute I've had. Listen, I don't know when I'm going to make it to Tennessee. Something's come up in L.A. It'll be at least a week before I'm free."

That sounded like forever. "Diane'll be ready for preschool by then!"

"She's growing up that fast? It must be that weird weather you get in Tennessee," he joked.

Casey wanted to tell him what she'd learned about Gail and Owen, but someone called his name and he had to go. "I love you," he murmured.

She barely had time to reply in kind before the connection broke.

Although he'd done exactly what she'd hoped for by calling, Casey wanted to fling the phone across the room. Why wouldn't the man listen to reason? Lots of people led happy lives in towns like Richfield Crossing. He could find something to do here if he tried.

But their problem didn't stem from the size of the town, she thought. Maybe it wasn't even a matter of what kind of work Jack performed.

He was pushing her away before she got the chance to hurt him. He'd said so himself a few days ago. He didn't want to risk having his heart torn apart when someone he loved abandoned him.

"He has no reason to doubt my loyalty," she told Diane. "Why should he think I'd leave him?"

Maybe, a little voice whispered inside her, because she already had. She'd packed her bags and filed for divorce.

Casey scowled. They'd broken up because he'd refused to have a child. She would never give up her baby.

But, the voice murmured, Jack didn't expect her to. He loved their daughter. Yet she still refused to return.

Didn't she have a right to be surrounded by people who cared about her? Casey thought angrily.

But military wives spent months and even years alone. Didn't she love her husband just as much?

She glanced out the window toward the west, where the sun was setting behind the pine trees in a blaze of pink and gold. She loved this rugged landscape and this kitchen, with its warm memories of her parents.

She thought about the Spring Fling and the square dance. The church and the eager faces of her Sunday school class. Enid and Matt, Bo and Rita.

In L.A., she'd have to pack Diane into the car and drive to a park if they ever wanted to see a squirrel. No one would notice when she started walking or said her first word.

No one except Jack. Assuming, of course, that he wasn't halfway around the globe.

Casey buried her face in her hands. She had to make a decision. But she couldn't.

If only Jack were here! When he came, they'd talk it over. Seeing him might be all she needed to make up her mind.

Surely he'd arrive in another week. She could wait until then.

APRIL TURNED INTO MAY, the days overflowing with sunshine. Two weeks passed, then three.

In the woods, purple passionflowers and white Queen Anne's lace overshadowed the shy violets. Pushing Diane in her stroller along the curving drive one morning, Casey spotted a fawn at its mother's side and a couple of baby squirrels scampering in a clearing.

Gail's attorney had arranged to remove her possessions. She noticed that the young couple who'd moved in had planted flowers around the porch.

Jack had called every few days, first from Greece, followed by Japan—to which he had to make an unexpected trip—and again from L.A. Catching up on paperwork, he said.

He made a point of talking to Diane through the receiver. From the way she brightened when she heard her father's voice, Casey felt certain their daughter actually recognized it.

Reluctantly, she wheeled the stroller into the carport and removed her daughter. The day seemed so beautiful, she hated to drive into town, but she had a checkup with Dr. Smithson.

As she steered, she wondered if Jack was coming at all. True, he'd promised, and he always kept his promises, but what if it took months?

The longer he stayed away, the more chance of his old demons seizing control. Why risk loving and losing when he could keep tabs on his daughter by phone and reassure himself that Casey had everything she needed?

But she didn't.

After Dr. Smithson finished the exam and declared her in excellent shape, Casey asked if Diane was old enough to travel. "We need to fly to Los Angeles," she told him.

"I'd recommend waiting a while." He leaned against the

counter. Casey found herself still half expecting to see Gail pop into the room, but pushed away the thought. "If it's urgent, a newborn can fly at one week, but it's better to wait until they're four to six weeks old."

"Why?" In the hallway, she heard women's voices in passing. One, with a charming Virginia accent, belonged to the new nurse he'd hired and the other, she presumed, to a patient.

"First, it's a good idea to make sure there aren't any underlying health issues that might cause difficulty, although I don't see anything," the doctor said. "Second, babies catch germs easily because their immune systems haven't matured. Although it helps that you're breast-feeding, don't forget that the air on those planes is recycled, which means you get multiple exposures to whatever bugs the other passengers are shedding."

Casey wrinkled her nose. "Sounds charming."

"I'd advise you to give yourself longer as well. You've been through a lot." The doctor's words carried the weight of experience.

"Would five minutes be long enough?" she asked. "That's longer than I usually wait before making a decision."

He didn't bat an eye. "Yes, I get that impression. But in the past month, you've undergone a traumatic experience at home, followed by childbirth and the challenge of caring for a newborn. And you still haven't recovered your full strength."

"It doesn't matter. I'm going to L.A.," she blurted. When he failed to react, she guessed he was waiting for her to reconsider. Was she really so predictable that *everyone* knew she changed her mind a lot? "Okay, maybe not right away."

"I have confidence that you'll give my advice due consideration," said Dr. Smithson.

"Thanks," she replied. "I will."

On the way home, she bought groceries and borrowed her first free DVD from Al Rawlins, who seemed less gruff than usual. "Cute baby," he said as he finished the checkout process.

Casey thanked him. She wished she could think of something else to add, but all that came to her was, "Say hi to Sandra for me."

"I sure will." He strolled across the store and held the door for her. For him, that bordered on effusiveness.

"We're going to have a big exciting night," she informed the baby while strapping her into the car seat. "We'll be watching *Baby Boom.*"

Diane formed a large bubble of spit that surely indicated unusual control of her lip and tongue muscles. She'd probably learn to talk early, Casey thought, although she suspected she might be guilty of bias.

At the entrance to the Pine Woods Court, she retrieved her mail and sorted through it. Baby coupons, bills, a promotional magazine for new moms. Oddly, she realized that she was dragging her feet about returning home.

It seemed so empty these days. Nothing was the same since Jack left.

Oh, stop moping! She got into the car and drove around the curve toward the house.

In front sat a neutral-colored sedan with plate frames bearing the name of a car-rental agency. Her heart rate quickened.

He was sitting on the porch, his long legs outstretched, his eyes half-closed in the sunlight. When she pulled into the carport, he got up lazily and strolled over, acting as if it had been hours and not weeks since they'd seen each other.

"How's my favorite girl today?" Jack peered into the back seat at Diane.

"You should have told me you were coming," Casey grumbled, although she couldn't have been more pleased.

"As penance, I'll carry the groceries inside and let you take the baby," he offered.

Casey wasn't that cruel. Besides, he looked so splendid that she wished she could haul him inside, strip off his sports jacket and make another baby.

"Never mind," she said. "Let's see you undo those straps on her. It's a test of your fitness as a father."

"Piece of cake." Despite his words, he made several unsuccessful attempts before finally figuring out the latch on the buckle. He also needed another minute to work out how to raise the protective shield without removing part of Diane's nose. "Why do they make these things so complicated?"

"You got me." Hefting a sack, she preceded him along the walkway and unlocked the door.

As soon as she deposited the groceries in the kitchen and he gently laid the baby in her basket, however, they flew into each other's arms. It took a lot of hugs and kisses before they separated.

For the next hour, Jack told funny stories about his adventures overseas and listened with interest to news of Mimi and Royce's budding romance and Sandra's decision to volunteer at a drug-prevention program for teens. But Casey hadn't yet shared her biggest news—her decision to join him on the West Coast.

Her hands got tingly as she tried to figure out how to bring it up. What if he didn't want to resume their marriage after all? What if he'd gone ahead and signed the divorce papers?

Before she could broach the subject, Jack went out to his car and came back with a rectangular package. "I nearly forgot your present," he said, and presented it to her with a flourish.

"It's beautiful." As she admired the shiny red paper and smart black bow, Casey wished he'd brought something smaller—specifically, one of those little jeweler's boxes containing a special locket or a ring to wear when they renewed their vows.

Instead, it must be some knickknack he'd bought overseas. She braced herself to show pleasure, and then found she couldn't open it yet.

"Jack?" she said.

"Hmm?" Perching on the couch beside her, he slipped

one arm around her waist. "You can sit on my lap while you open it."

"Jack!"

"What?" He didn't let go.

"I have something important to tell you."

A trace of uneasiness dimmed his expression, but he didn't loosen his grip. "Go ahead."

"I'm moving to Los Angeles." Seeing his blank reaction, Casey elaborated. "We'll figure out the details as soon as Diane's old enough to travel. I'll arrange to sell the Pine Woods."

"May I ask what inspired this decision?" He gave no sign of his reaction.

Summoning her courage, Casey plunged ahead. "I miss you," she said. "I think a family ought to be together, and we're a family."

"No conditions attached?" he asked.

"Such as?"

"More kids."

She felt a twist of disappointment. "I was hoping…you seem to enjoy the baby. But I'm willing to compromise."

Why didn't he answer? Why didn't he give her a big hug and tell her how thrilled he was?

"Are you sure you won't change your mind?" Jack asked.

"Never!" Casey vowed. "Never never never. Not five minutes from now, not a year from now and not ten years from now." She didn't see how she could make her resolve any clearer.

Jack made a noise she couldn't interpret. "I'm afraid that's going to be a problem."

She refused to accept his answer without a fight. "No, it isn't!"

One eyebrow lifted. "Oh, really?"

"Absolutely not!"

"Casey…" Jack hesitated.

"What?"

"I think you'd better open my present."

"For heaven's sake!" She might as well humor him, she supposed.

So irked that she hoped she didn't end up bashing it over his head, Casey tore off the wrappings.

Chapter Twenty

Inside a burnished oak frame, a black mat surrounded a card that looked too small for its fancy presentation. "What's this?" On closer inspection, Casey saw that it bore the name of an airline.

"My frequent flier card," Jack said.

"What's it doing in a frame?" she inquired.

"Retiring."

His meaning took several seconds to sink in, because she feared she might be deluding herself. "You're moving here?" she asked at last.

"I hope you're not disappointed." Jack seemed to be struggling to keep a straight face. "I could see how much you looked forward to living in California."

"But what are you going to do?" Casey asked. "I don't want you to end up resenting me because I destroyed your career."

He drew her closer. "I came to this decision because it's what will make me happy. And you too, I hope."

She nestled against him, still finding it hard to believe that they could go to bed together every night and wake up side by side every morning, right here in Tennessee. "I'm thrilled. But Jack…"

"If you keep quibbling, I might decide I made a mistake."

"I want you to be happy!" she protested. "You're not the kind of guy who can be happy doing just any old job."

"I phoned Chief Roundtree in advance and stopped to see him on my way in," he said. "I pointed out that he richly deserves retirement and his wife apparently would like that too."

"You mean he's offering you his job?" Casey nearly couldn't breathe. It seemed too perfect.

"It's up to the town council, but he's going to recommend me," Jack told her. "He thinks they'll go for it."

Casey had no doubt of that, but, overjoyed as she felt, she had to make sure her husband wouldn't regret his decision. "You've worked so hard building up your business. Now you'll have nothing to show for it."

"I wouldn't call it nothing," he assured her. "Our new partner bought me out. I started a college fund for Diane and there's enough left over for a second kid. Possibly a third. But I know how hard pregnancy can be. So if you'd rather not, I'll understand."

"Quit teasing me!" She mussed his hair and, for good measure, ruffled it a second time. "Three kids. I could go for that."

"Could you go for me?"

"You bet!" she said and, leaving their baby dozing in her basket, did exactly what she'd wanted to do since she first saw Jack on the porch. She kissed him over and over, then lured him into the bedroom.

Beneath his clothes, she found him hard and ready for her. Taking him inside her exhilarated them both, and they exploded together in sheer ecstasy.

Afterward, as Casey dozed in his arms, her mind wandered over the delicious possibilities that lay ahead. More babies—square dancing together—long walks in the woods. "You know what," she murmured.

"Hmm?"

"You once mentioned that you'd always wanted a dog. We could check the bulletin board at the library. Folks are always giving away puppies in the spring."

"I want a nice scruffy mutt," Jack said. "Just like me."

"You're not a mutt!"

"Yes, I am. I'm the fool who nearly signed those divorce papers."

"Well, I'm the fool who took them out in the first place," she said.

He propped himself on one elbow. "That's right, you are."

She didn't even get mad. "Tear them up."

"My pleasure." Jack's green eyes sparkled. "I'm having my shredder shipped from L.A. along with a few million other items."

"You already arranged it?" Casey pretended to glare. "That was taking a lot for granted."

"Call me impulsive."

"That's my territory!" She grinned. "But you're welcome to the club."

"Would you really have moved to Los Angeles?" he asked.

"I already cleared it with the doctor." She thought she could be forgiven a slight exaggeration. "What changed your mind?"

"I never thought I'd get used to all this scenery, but it grows on you," her husband confessed. "The people aren't bad, either."

Casey laughed. "Yes, and we've got nine free DVD rentals left, courtesy of Al Rawlins. That's his way of making amends."

"I don't think we're going to have much time to watch DVDs." Jack's breath tickled her ear.

"What on earth can you mean?" She blinked in feigned innocence.

He proceeded to demonstrate exactly what he meant. Then he held her in his arms all night.

Except, of course, for the two times they got up to feed the baby. Jack even changed the diaper once.

He'd turned into a father. And she, Casey reflected happily, was going to thoroughly enjoy being the police chief's wife.

*Turn the page for a preview of next month's
American Romance titles!*

*We hope these brief excerpts will whet your appetite
for all four of January's books...*

One Good Man by Charlotte Douglas (#1049) is the second title in this popular author's ongoing series, "A Place to Call Home." Charlotte Douglas creates a wonderful sense of home and community in these stories.

Jeff Davidson eased deeper into the shadows of the gift shop. Thanks to his Special Operations experience, the former Marine shifted his six-foot-two, one-hundred-eighty pounds with undetectable stealth. But his military training offered no tactics to deal with the domestic firefight raging a few feet away.

With a stillness usually reserved for covert insertions into enemy territory, he peered through a narrow slit between the handmade quilts, rustic birdhouses, and woven willow baskets that covered the shop's display shelves.

On the other side of the merchandise in the seating area of the café, a slender teenager with a cascade of straight platinum hair yelled at her mother, her words exploding like a barrage from the muzzle of an M-16. "You are so not with it. Everyone I hang with has her navel pierced."

Jeff grimaced in silent disapproval. The kid should have her butt kicked, using that whiny, know it all tone toward her mom. Not that the girl's behavior was his business. He hadn't intended to eavesdrop. He'd come to Mountain Crafts and Café to talk business with Jodie Nathan, the owner, after her restaurant closed. Lingering until the staff left, he'd browsed the shelves of the gift section until she was alone.

But before he could make his presence known, fourteen-year-old Brittany had clattered down the stairs from their apartment over the store and confronted her mother.

"Your friends' navels are their mothers' concern, not mine." The struggle for calm was evident in Jodie's firm words, and the tired slump of her pretty shoulders suggested she'd waged this battle too many times. "You are my daughter, and as long as you live under my roof, you will follow my rules."

Was the kid blind? Jeff thought with disgust. Couldn't she see the tenderness and caring in her mother's remarkable hazel eyes? An ancient pain gnawed at his heart. He'd have given everything for such maternal love when he'd been a child, a teenager. Even now. Young Brittany Nathan had no idea how lucky she was.

Daddy by Choice by Marin Thomas (#1050). A "Fatherhood" story with a western slant. This exciting new author, who debuted with the delightful The Cowboy and the Bride, writes movingly and well about parent-child relationships...and, of course, romance!

JD wasn't sure if it was the bright sunlight bouncing off the petite blond head or the sparkling clean silver rental car that blinded him as he swung his black Ford truck into a parking space outside Lovie's café. Both the lady and the clean car stood out among the dusty, mud-splattered ranch vehicles lined up and down Main Street in Brandt's Corner.

Because of the oppressive West Texas heat wave blanketing the area, he shifted into Park and left the motor running. Without air-conditioning, the interior temperature would spike to a hundred degrees in sixty seconds flat, and he was in no hurry to get out.

He had some lookin' to do first.

A suit in the middle of July? He shook his head at the blonde's outfit. Pinstripe, no less. She wore her honey-colored hair in a fancy twist at the back of her neck, revealing a clean profile. Evidently, she got her haughty air from the high cheekbones.

All of her, from her wardrobe to her attitude, represented a privileged life. Privileged meant money. Money meant trouble.

His gut twisted. Since yesterday's phone call from this woman, his insides had festered as if he'd swallowed a handful of rusty fence nails.

Fear.

Fear of the unknown…the worst kind. He'd rather sit on the back of a rank rodeo bull than go head to head with her. Too bad he didn't have the option.

Table for Five by Kaitlyn Rice (#1051) is an example of our "In the Family" promotion—stories about the joys (and difficulties) of life with extended families. Kaitlyn Rice is a talented writer whose characters will stay with you long after you've finished this book.

Kyle Harper glanced at his watch and uttered a mild curse. He'd worked well past a decent quitting time again—an old habit that was apparently hard to break. Shoving the third-quarter sales reports into his attaché case, he closed his eyes, claiming a few seconds of peace before switching gears. He pictured a perfect gin martini, a late version of the television news and a bundle of hickory wood, already lit and crackling in the fireplace.

Heaven.

Or home, as he'd once known it.

Life didn't slow down for hard-luck times, and it didn't cater to wealth or power. Kyle could afford only a moment to ponder used-to-be's. He popped open his eyes and grabbed his cell phone, the fumbling sounds at the other end warned him about what to expect. "Grab the guns!" Kyle's father yelled. "There's a gang of shoot-em-up guys headed into town!"

The Forgotten Cowboy by Kara Lennox (#1052). An unusual take on a popular kind of plot. Thanks to the heroine's amnesia, she doesn't recognize the cowboy in her life—which makes for some interesting and lively complications!

Willow Marsden studied the strange woman in her hospital room. She was an attractive female in her twenties, her beauty marred by a black eye and a bandage wound around her head. The woman looked unfamiliar; she was a complete stranger. Unfortunately, the stranger was in Willow's mirror.

She lay the mirror down with a long sigh. Prosopagnosia—that was the clinical name for her condition. She'd suffered a head injury during a car accident, which had damaged a very specific portion of her brain—the part that enabled humans to distinguish one face from another. For Willow, every face she saw was strange and new to her—even those of her closest friends and relatives.

"You're telling me I could be like this forever?"

Dr. Patel, her neurologist, shrugged helplessly. "Every recovery is different. You could snap back to normal in a matter of days, weeks, months, or…yes, the damage could be permanent."

"What about my short-term memory?" She couldn't even remember what she'd had for breakfast that morning.

Again that shrug. Why was it so difficult to get a straight answer out of a doctor?

Willow knew she should feel grateful to be alive, to be walking and talking with no disfiguring scars. Her car accident during last week's tornado had been a serious one, and she easily could have died if not for the speed and skill of her rescuers. Right now, though, she didn't feel grateful at all. Her plans and dreams were in serious jeopardy.

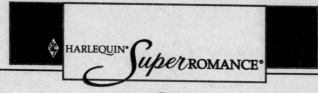

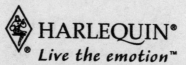

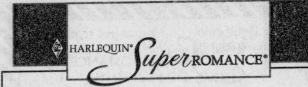

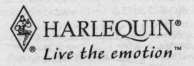

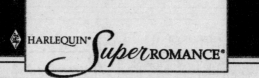

HARLEQUIN *Super*ROMANCE

Mother and Child Reunion

A *ministeries* from
2003 RITA® finalist

Jean Brashear

Coming Home

Cleo Channing's dreams were simple: the stable home and big, loving family she never had as a child. Malcolm Channing walked into her life and swept her off her feet and before long, she thought she had it all—three beautiful children in a charming house she would fill to the rafters with love.

Their firstborn was a troubled girl, though, and the strain on their family grew until finally, there was nothing left to do but for them to all go their separate ways.

Now their daughter has returned, and as the days pass, awareness grows in Cleo and Malcolm that their love never truly died.

Except, the treacherous issues that drove them apart in the first place remain....

Heartwarming stories with a sense of humor, genuine charm and emotion and lots of family!

On sale starting January 2005
Available wherever Harlequin books are sold.

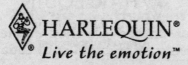

HARLEQUIN®
® *Live the emotion*™

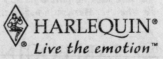